Once Upon A Time In The City Of Criminals

A novel by
Mark Barry

Green Wizard Publishing
Southwell
Nottinghamshire

Once Upon A Time In The City Of Criminals.

A novel. Written by Mark Barry

Edited by Max Thomson Jones, Newmarket

Copyright© 2015 by Green Wizard Publishing

ISBN

This book is sold subject to the condition that it shall not by way of trade or otherwise, be lent, resold, hired out, or otherwise circulated without prior permission and consent in any form of e-transaction, format, binding or cover other than that in which it is published and without a similar condition, including this condition, being imposed on the subsequent purchaser.

This is a work of fiction. Any resemblance of characters to actual persons, living or dead, is purely coincidental.

Second Edition.

Cover design by Dark Dawn Creations

Second printing published in November 2015 by Green Wizard Publishing, Southwell, Nottinghamshire

Dedication

This novel is dedicated to Mrs. Patricia Barry, who lived life to the max, with spirit and with gusto, and who never took much notice of authority in all its forms.
Just like the characters in the book.

RIP 1940 – 2014

"When I travel to meetings throughout the country and engage in informal discussions, it is easy to form the impression that the city I represent is regarded by many of our colleagues in other local authorities as a city full of criminals."

(Anon: Minutes of the Nottingham City Council *Crime and Disorder Steering Group*, P 19, May 2001)

Part I: The Driver

Benediction

We pull up outside Benedictine Court, a regenerated textile factory, like most of the Lace Market. Nottingham lace. The envy of the Victorian world, the pride of the Great Exhibition. It's a magnificent building, two hundred years old if it's a day. Jam packed full of yuppies, the only people able to meet the rent. Even a gaff the size of a hamster cage would be three monkeys a calendar month easy - and no room for the wheel.

The building's agents vet too. If you're working in a contact centre in the inner city and you happen to win a few quid on the horses, (enough for a deposit and six months advance rent), you still wouldn't get in. The agents wouldn't blink twice in telling you where to stick your plebby interest. They credit check you and there is a twenty page application form that your family doctor has to sign when it is finished.

Despite all that, there's a waiting list of three years.

Quite a few of the tenants are from the Tigers and Russia. There is a certain pleasure in hating the people who live here, but a man can't take it out of the building itself. It's a lovingly restored resurrection. I remember what it was like before too – a bombsite, a blast casualty. Every resident of Nottingham can remember what it was like. The whole Lace Market was a shithole and now you have a nirvana.

Pity such a magnificent edifice comes at a price.

My bitterness is not about injustice. I don't want anyone to tell me that. It's about envy.

I admire the people who can afford to live in The Benedictine. When I was a kid, I had the brains to earn the big cash to live in one of these places, but the dogs of stupidity, misfortune and unconscious self-destruction barked every time I tried something. They bit my arse and they never left me alone and even now, when I'm embarking on the last couple of decades of my useful existence before I meet my much deserved end, there they are, snarling and wagging their tails on the next street along. Places like the Benedictine make the resentment taste like acid in my mouth but it isn't the fault of the building.

I've made a complete bollocks of my life.

I couldn't have wanked it up better had I practiced.

I check my watch. It's ten. Dark outside, the glow of the late summer evening sun dissipating as the moon opposite rises to its zenith. It's unseasonably warm and the AC is on full.

I'm on time for the appointment. Early by ten minutes. My ride is sitting behind the empty passenger seat. I close my eyes for a second and sense her. I smell hair gel, perfume, leather, jasmine, bath oil, hand ointments and rose petals infused with lemon juice. Where I've been, smells are essential. Sometimes a smell was the only thing that kept you from insanity. And the smell of a woman is bang up there – fresh cut grass, hot toast, hot mushy peas at the funfair, napalm in the morning.

(Woman. This one).

She smells special and I don't want her to go where she has to go. I look at her in the rear view mirror, but I don't stare too long because it makes me seasick. It makes my stomach separate from the rest of my body. I can't look at her anymore, not since…since…

Do you want me to walk you up? I say.

No, Chloe replies quietly, matter of fact. I'll be fine.

Each vowel of her voice is airbrushed and lacquered, tainted with nicotine and peaches; each consonant stroked, massaged and caressed with a mysterious, nameless balm dripping with solace. I could listen to her recite the Yellow Pages and not interrupt her for one single second.

(That voice…)

She's originally from Lancashire somewhere, Rochdale, Oldham, some shithole like that. Major battlezones in the old days, (Preston away, 1989). Cloth caps and Stanley blades. The middle gaff on some council estate. It may not be Hell, but you can sense the flickering flames somewhere near. I'm not sure exactly where she's from. She told me once, but I've forgotten.

Living down south for several years, at Uni, and now here, mellowed her accent and you only detect the occasional subtle inflection of the dark satanic mills. She's definitely North though; she couldn't be from anywhere else. I've known her for four months and she's employed me for three.

How long will you be? I ask.

Two hours or so if I'm lucky. Probably three. Could be. Depends how it goes. Hope it's not too gross.

Won't be. I'll read my paperback. Alarm on?

Yes. So, what are you reading?

I open the glove compartment and pull out a paperback. *Jack's Return Home*. I tell her that this is the novel that the film Get Carter is based on. I don't know if she had ever heard of the film. Everyone my age knows the film backwards (but not the book).

(God above, she's...)

You should read something modern, she sighs. Old music. Old films. Old books and stuff. Yadda yadda. Get something new. You always read old stuff.

Classics, I reply.

Old classics, then. Come round to see me tomorrow and I'll show you some awesome new stuff. I love reading.

I know you do, I say.

I remember asking her a question over a cup of coffee in Pietros: *If you had to lose books, films or music from your life, which would it be? Lose forever, that is. Not for a week or so, but forever.*

Most people say they would lose the ability to read books, but not Chloe.

(*Films,* she said, straight as an arrow. *Definitely. Films. OMG, losing books? Are you crazy?)*

I'm the same. I'd never watch a film again if it meant I couldn't read a book or listen to music. I think I fell in love with her there and then *(no, it was before that)*. But I'd never tell her that and she'd never ask.

You're one of those Kindle merchants, I say playfully, almost accusatory. She leans over, into the cavernous gap between the passenger seat and mine.

I swing both ways, as you well know, Mr Valentine. When it comes to reading and stuff, I so don't do boundaries. Kindles, old books, new paperbacks, hardbacks. I'll read anything, in any media. I do love an awesome Happy Ever After. I've read, like, loads of those. Have you bought yourself a Kindle yet?

No.

Is that objection, like, *political*, Mr Valentine?

Probably.

I hear her giggle a little, but I might have imagined it. Had she been drinking? Dutch courage? The giggle, if it had happened at all, disappears into the ether.

Two boys, no older than twelve, wearing brightly colored puffa jackets and balloon jeans inlaid with giant patches, cycle past on BMX bikes. They take a gander at the car, which isn't mine, but I wish it were. I have never owned a nice car – not a decent Audi like this one.

You old men, she continues. OMG, you are so ancient.

I like it real, Chloe, I reply, showing her my paperback. None of that vampire bollocks you read. And less of the old, thank you very much.

There is silence for a short while. Chloe asks me to turn on the light. She then fixes her makeup in her compact. I sneak a glimpse. She could turn up to this gig in ripped pink pyjamas and a pair of minging Jesus sandals and she'd still come away with a tip, but she's a professional. She does things properly.

I don't like this bit – nor the next three hours.

It makes me feel bad and I tell myself it's simply business. It's just work and therefore not real.

I'll be right back, Terry, she says, putting a hand on my shoulder.

I don't respond and watch her leave the car and walk slowly up to the main entrance of the Benedictine. She brushes down the front of her skirt. Chloe is wearing a coal black two piece suit, skirt rising above the knee, every micro-movement that of a smart executive climbing the slippery pole. A French executive. Parisian class etched in every fibre, seeping from stockings. Heels so incalculably dark they absorb the light from around them, as if the leather is a tesseract made of a million theoretical black holes.

Her clothes are silent. Some clothes sing to you, some are so bright and garish they grab you round the throat, but not these. If they make any sound at all, it's that of a single, mournful note on a violin. She's even wearing black kid leather gloves. The only respite from the silence and darkness is a single red rose on her lapel and the white singlet underneath her jacket. The heels – six inches - stretch her calves to the maximum extent.

Chloe's not usually as tall as that. In the daylight. On the Enclave. Where we live. She's a different woman when she's working. Here, tonight, she walks slowly, confidently. In control. On her way to a board meeting. In Paris. She takes out her mobile phone and pretends to talk. Neck tilted, phone balanced on her hand like a praying mantis, the whole buried in the crease between her chin and her shoulder. Chloe always does this. I find the facade endearing, almost a Ritual. The fake telephone call.

I've never been able to take my eyes off her. Not since the

second time, sitting on her doorstep, the day after I saved her spilled shopping. The first time I was too busy rescuing her to notice, but the next…I could savour her. I had the time. That second occasion, she was a scruffy student. Cross legged. Brunette bob a mess. Two silver hooped earrings. Barefoot – mauve toenail polish, silver chain around her ankle. Sliced-up, paint-spattered, skinny jeans and a shrunken purple vest, no bra. Pastel, almost watery skin, the sun an uninvited guest. A rollup between her fingers, her phone in both hands. Her eyes, all eyeliner, shadows and burning suns.

>Manga eyes.
>The way Japanese cartoonists interpret the eyes of westerners.
>The way they draw them on *Marine Boy*.
>Looking at me. Sizing me up.
>Chloe has *Manga* eyes.

Most girls of twenty four wouldn't notice me.

I am a ghost to them. I am an invisibility beneath the threshold of perception, not even a hindrance in their vision, a Mote in their eye.

You get used to it.

Most blokes my age are used to it.

But not Chloe.

No.

She didn't take her eyes off me once, that sunbaked late morning in May, a million years ago.

Should have known. Should have known something was going to crack off there and then.

Tonight, I watch her approach the reception. She sways slightly, then stumbles on her high heels. When I see her do this, I want to exit the car, chase her, grab her, protect her (love her), but I sit stock still and she composes herself. I watch Chloe buzz in. After a second's deliberation and a nod to the wall camera, the door opens. She doesn't look back. I check my phone. If there's any funny business, she will press the tiny electronic signal alarm concealed in a heart locket round her neck and I'm in.

I protect. *I protect her.*

My name is Terry Valentine and tonight, I am a Protector.

Southwell Road

The time passes quickly. Three hours, as it happens. I read three chapters of the paperback, a pulpy novel I had read many times. I watch some drunks walk past the car along Stoney Street. A couple holding hands, seeking the hidden night clubs of the Lace Market. Happy students. Lost stag parties in clown suits.

At midnight, the old witching hour, a couple went at it in a doorway behind me, opposite the Benedictine, one of those rented office places, their secret liaison partially obscured by a spacious awning. They didn't see me. They were so enamoured they didn't expect to see me. Couples fornicate in public (with shameless expression and dramatic élan), so frequently these days, no-one bats an eyelid. In skips. In doorways. On the pavement. In the club itself. The girl, about twenty, tall and brunette. Bloke in smart suit. Out since five, the offices, the Friday night drink with colleagues gone haywire. Her legs wrapped around his back like Spiderman climbing a telegraph pole. I was impressed with his stamina – he didn't flinch for a second and she was no lightweight – but after a while it made me think of… of…and I turned away, turned the music up, put her relentless moaning out of mind. I didn't even see them leave.

I listened to The Beatles. Whole era on a greatest hits CD, Tried not to think about Chloe, tried to pretend whatever she was doing wasn't happening. Watched a punch-up at the end of the road – some homeless on the way to the Emmanuel.

It wasn't a particularly eloquent punch up. The three tramps were so sodden with cheap booze they kept connecting with air. It wasn't effective. What did Amis say in *Money*? Maximum violence instantly. These homeless blokes…in my day, we'd have slapped them once and moved on like ghosts. Nottingham is full of povs and homeless now, ever since the Tories cut housing benefit. I always give a quid when I'm asked, poor bastards.

Eventually, I watch her walk back the way she came. I check my watch. It's 1.30am. The rear door opens and closes with a comforting click.

Don't suppose you want to hear how it went? She asks.

No.

Okay.

Sorry.

Home, then, Mr Valentine. And don't spare the horses, I'm totally wasted.

That time of night all you see on the roads are taxis and buses and it's a smooth journey out onto Southwell Road and upwards. There are scattered groups of revellers, but nothing like when I was a kid growing up around here. It's ripe for regeneration, the new creative quarter. They don't call them flats any more – it's apartments, thanks to our Imperialist American cousins - and that's what's coming. As well as artist's studios and plush, chrome-furnished offices for the advertising and marketing industries. It's been fifteen years in the planning and still not a brick laid.

The recession. Big bad recession.

What's left is an old market and iron gates – disused shop fronts and waste strewn streets. The Writer's Studio, ostentatious and bold; the homeless charity shop opposite the burnt out wreck of Berlins, which I remember.

(Scrapping with Peterborough and Mansfield).

Two for one – all you can drink for a fiver. In the spring, tramps and wanderers come out of the caves and live in the demolished remains.

Well, they used to: They're building something on the site now, but I don't know what. Probably high priced flats.

Sorry, *apartments.*

It's still unseasonably warm. Chloe is talking to someone on her phone. Zena from Tiffany's, the secretary of the agent who sets up the appointments. They're laughing – Chloe has had a good night and is planning another. She's always busy. It's a boom time for the work she does, with all the women running the show in Nottingham, all the *nouveau riche*, the hardcore careerists with the stay at home husbands looking after Toby and Natalie; the politicians, the dedicated professionals, the middle managers and the chief execs. It's a woman's world now and Chloe's work never stops, but I know she isn't doing anything tomorrow as she has a party to attend, and I'm out on a special job with Pike. A nice couple of hundred for half an hours work followed by twelve hours on the pop and sweeties. I can smell her – her perfume is recently administered. It's potent, maybe even overpowering, but that's better than…than…the other thing. I never look at her after and I definitely don't want to talk to her, though I can tell she is dying to tell me.

She always is.

This is my eighteenth job for her and every time she says the same thing.

(*Don't suppose you want to hear about it, do you?*)

And each time I say no. There are blokes who would give their eye teeth for one sentence about what had transpired upstairs, but not me. It makes me seasick. It makes my stomach levitate. Daren't even look at her. Can't watch lesbo porn on the computer any more. And that pretty much means I can't watch *any* porn.

Every time I think of her I hear the ChiLites *Have You Seen Her* in my consciousness.

It's not clear how this state happened to me.

Don't know how I allowed it to.

I'm usually like iron, a proper hard bastard, but she's turned me into hot chocolate and a cupcake before bedtime.

She puts her phone in her handbag and begins to talk to me.

Job, Sunday. Are you free?

Of course, I reply.

In Gotham, which is, like, somewhere on the other side of Nottingham or something. Do you know it?

I do. It's a fair trek.

We'd best leave early, then. I always giggle when I think about it. Fancy Nottingham having a Gotham!

Why?

Gotham City, dufus. OMG, like, er Batman! Hello! Is there anybody home? That's where *Batman* lives.

Okay, I say, slightly embarrassed. I've no idea what she is talking about.

You are so behind the times, Mr Valentine.

Am I?

Totally. Don't you, like, go to the movies and stuff?

(*Movies?*)

Her phone rings again. It's one of her friends out at a nightclub. I switch off and concentrate on the road around Carlton and down toward Gedling as she speaks. There is hardly anyone out, but the streetlights are overpowering, almost neon, and you need to watch for the filth, who are always out and about looking for mobile soaks taking a risk. I drive carefully. I sneak a glance at Chloe, regret it, and then I fix my gaze straight ahead, on the road toward Burton Joyce.

Simultaneously controlling the raging sea trapped in my stomach.

But she saw me look.

Our eyes made contact in the mirror.

Like the abyss, her Manga eyes stared back at me as she spoke to her friend about some boy, some hot boy they both know. I didn't expect her to notice.

I thought she would be concentrating on her call.

(Fool)

I want to shut my eyes and I'm counting the minutes until we're home so I can pull the quilt over my head and forget any of this is happening.

I want to quit the driving job.

I want to leave town. I want to go and live on a beach somewhere and eat pineapples and think of nothing but the image of the serene ocean ripples before me. I want to burn myself, cut myself, watch the open wound bleed and bleed and…

…I want out.

Out. Terry Valentine is out.

(Torture)

This hurts.

Yet. I can't. I just… can't.

She puts her phone away after a seemingly never-ending torrent of loves and air kisses. Then leans forward.

How was your paperback?

It's good. I've read it before.

Will you tell me the story? Until we get home?

Really? I say, the nausea rising again.

I'd love to hear about Jack. We have time, don't we? Until we get home?

She leans back, removes her shoes and draws her legs underneath her on the back seat, like she does on her armchair at home when she is watching TV or reading a novel.

It's not really your kind of book, I say.

Everything's my kind of book. So, tell me…she replies and that time it seems more like an order, so for the last ten minutes of the journey, through Lowdham, Thurgarton and the pitch black chicane into Southwell,

I tell her about ***Jack's Return Home***.

How a Northern bad lad leaves town and becomes a top London gangster.

How he comes back home (Doncaster in the book, Newcastle in the film), to investigate the suspicious death of his brother. How he encounters a series of bigtime northern criminals determined to stop him finding out the truth using any means possible. Trouble is, they're all connected to Jack's bosses in the Smoke and they don't want him rocking the boat either.

Carnage ensues.

I tell her the whole story and conclude it as we pull up outside The Reindeer pub, where I first met her (her burst shopping bag, the rolling, cascading tins of beans and Italian tomatoes). She says nothing about the story and opens the passenger seat door herself.

Coffee? She asks, putting her shoes back on.

I want coffee with Chloe more than anything else in the entire world. I want it badly.

No, I'm tired, I say. Been a long day.

Okay, she says, and if she's disappointed she hides it brilliantly. I know she isn't, though.

Don't forget Sunday.

I'll be there, I say, opening the door to my flat as she walks away to hers, a few doors down.

She doesn't turn back. Not even the lightest air kiss.

I wish she would.

I'm glad she didn't.

David Brent

This the place?

He puts down his strawberry and custard doughnut, the sugar scattering on his tracksuit trousers like powdery snow. He checks the docket. We're in The Park. The house we're interested in is owned by one of Danny Mannion's mentors, Harry Fry, who owns three hundred places like these - a Victorian merchant's house broken up into three student gaffs.

Yeh, it's this one.

Tell me it's the bottom flat. My head's proper bad.

I'd tell you that, my friend, but I would be pulling your pisser if I did so. It's the top gaff.

Typical

Why's your head proper bad, Tezza?

Ale.

Don't tell me you've been on that shitty craft beer again? You know that gives you a headache and bad guts. Stick to the cider.

Overindulged. You know how it is.

Pike shakes his head. No sympathy for you, lad. C'mon lets go. Bring the kit.

I get out of Pike's pink Fiesta (a completely incongruous vehicle for the job in hand), and open the back seat, remove a black leather holdall, the type you see on bankjob films full of stolen cash. I look at Pike. In his rose-pink Adidas tracksuit and red Hamburgs, he is a sight, particularly as he's putting weight on again. His nausea-coloured belly oozes out the front of his waistband. I'm wearing a battered old dark blue Fred Perry and jeans. I hope I'm not as fat as he is.

As I shut the back door of the Fiesta, I look in the wing mirror. Make a note to rejoin the leisure centre gym.

We've been given a key to the main door and find ourselves outside the door of the student flat.

There is a strong smell of weed in the air. Deodorant and Perfume too. I see a little white kitten on the windowsill, with luminous, almost radioactive emerald eyes. It doesn't move, almost like a Chinese statue of a cat. All this means a woman lives here, who, perhaps, like I used to, enjoys a spliff. The door is as green as the kitten's eyes (but not as radiant). Pike knocks on it quietly. It opens immediately, which is not what we expect.

Hi, the man says. He resembles the bloke who plays Sherlock Holmes on the telly. He's wearing a milk-chocolate coloured dressing gown that's seen better times and his eyes are red. Can I help you?

Pike pushes past. I follow, ignoring the inevitable protests. I was right about a woman. A woman - his girlfriend? - is watching TV. Jeremy Kyle. She's mixed race, closer to black, immature and pretty, cream pyjamas still on, a dreamy, vacant, just-fucked look on her face, hair akimbo. I am immediately jealous, being quite partial to mixed fruit on occasion. The smell of dope is overpowering. It makes me wince.

Bit of a morning tune up, Quentin? Pike asks.

The man sits down. Chilling out for the day, he replies. Nothing on outside. We're about to watch a film.

He's posh – that accent is cut glass, privilege tattooed into his very essence. When I went to Uni, you still had accents. Now they're all like

refugees from Evelyn Waugh. Like this bloke.
Today, I'm muscle. Pike is administration.

He leads off, fingering a mug on the table.
No job?
No. Now, what's this about?
You know full well what this is about.
Oh? He says, playing thick.
You're fucking three months behind with the rent, Pike says. Four months if you count this one.
Oh yes. That. I've explained this to Harry. I'm temporarily…embarrassed.
You said you would pay him this month? All the David.
The David?
The *David*. The *David Brent*. The rent.
Oh. *The David.*
So where is it?
Mate, I'll be perfectly honest. There's, like, been a little bit of a problem, he says, gesturing pathetically with both hands.

Pike turns round toward the television. It's a sixty inch screen balanced on a stand. LCD. There are speakers. You could watch a good film on it – really experience it - and, I suspect, posh boy and his girlfriend would have enjoyed many a night doing exactly that, their own private druggy cinematic love experiences.

Without any warning, he boots it, knocks over the stand, and stamps on the television several times. It cracks in two under his weight.

Hey, that's a *bloody two grand TV*, posh exclaims, shocked.

Where's the rent, Quentin? Pike asks quietly, restrained, despite what we've all witnessed. It's all sex and violence on the telly nowadays. His girlfriend stares at him accusingly but doesn't move.

Listen, what's your name, sir…Mister…
No names. Where's the rent? It's cash or at least a nice trip to the bank. You're costing Harry big time.
I thought he'd take me to court. That's the legal thing…posh boy says, looking lost. I almost feel sorry for him. Only almost.
Court? You must have the wrong Harry Fry.
He says nothing, is even more bemused. Then he says, I haven't got it. Next week…I'll have the lot. Tell Mister Fry…
Pass the bag, Pike interrupts, ignoring him and talking to me. I do

so. He zips it open and removes a rusted pair of bolt cutters that were painted black sometime in the seventies.

Hold the girl, he says, gesturing to me, and she shouts, attempts to get away, but I pin her down into the armchair by her shoulders. She tries to bite me, and wails, but I slap her hard with the back of my hand. She's stunned. I stare at her as if I mean her serious harm and she knows to shut up. I find that my Buddy Holly spectacles help. They don't expect to be physically assaulted by a bloke wearing glasses. The information doesn't compute and it adds an extra level. Her boyfriend pretends to consider a Sir Lancelot impression but he is not very convincing. We don't take him seriously. We don't hit him either. That's not in the script. That wouldn't help.

Pick up one of her feet, Pike orders me and I do, her right one.

It's a lovely foot, coffee coloured, sleek and lean, with no verrucae, warts or blemishes anywhere, smooth to the touch. I suppress a momentary urge to stroke it, maybe even kiss it. It's a regal, majestic foot, built for sex and worship, but I feel…odd…

(Chloe)

…and I immediately suppress the instinct. She's crying now and struggling, her eyes wide. I don't want her to struggle, so I give her a dead leg, a solid punch on her thigh. Shocked, she starts to cry. I hold the upturned edge of my index finger to my mouth, tell her to shush. Tears roll down her face and she does so.

Pike places the clamp end of the bolt cutters over her little toe, turns to the man.

Where's the David, posh boy? I won't ask again.

Posh boy cracks, as anyone would.

Okay…okay…I've got something we can sell…don't hurt her…please…it's worth much more money than the rent. Please, don't…don't…

Pike pulls away, puts the bolt cutters back in the bag.

Let's see what you've got for me, Quentin, he says.

He rushes into his bedroom, comes back out with a small purple bag, which he gives to Pike.

His girlfriend jumps up and the two of them cuddle in the centre of the room, tears still flowing. They sit down. He's rubbing her leg to make it better.

I am surprised she can walk. I must be losing my touch.

Pike spills the contents of the bag onto the coffee table next to the girl's armchair.

Three glittering gold Sovereign rings.

Worth at least three grand, the terrified man says to Pike, pointedly ignoring me. Solid gold. The best. From Joburg. They're my father's. I'm looking after them for him. Tax. He's in mining out in Zim. Bloody old racist sod. Cut my allowance because of Nadia. You can have the lot. Just don't let him hurt her. Or me, for that matter.

Is that her name? Pike asks. Nadia. Nice.

Keep HIM away from her...he says, looking at me.

I'm not offended. Not in the slightest. I was simply doing my job. Scaring the living shit out of parents, sons, daughters, younger siblings and WAGS. Cheaper, quicker and more effective than small claims court.

These'll do, Pike says, pocketing the rings. By the way, who's the United fan?

I beg your pardon? He replies.

Pike gestures to the mug on the same coffee table. It's a murky, once-white Man United 1999 European Cup winning mug, well sipped, stained on the inside, resplendently emblazoned with the team photo (satisfied footballer grins) on the side.

Neither of us, he says, his girlfriend snivelling, cuddling his ribcage, staring at me as if I am Satan himself.

So, why the mug? Pike asks.

Oh, I don't bloody know.

Sorry?

It's not important. I borrowed it from one of my pals. I don't even *like* football. My family are *Harlequins*...

Pike picks up the mug. Turns round and faces the window. Removes his tackle and urinates into the mug. His piss, like warm limeade, splashing like raindrops into a puddle, diluting the remains of Nadia's coffee. He finishes, zips up and turns round.

I fucking hate the Premier League, Quentin, he says. It will be the death of clubs like Notts. We'll be round on Tuesday for this month's rent. Have it ready.

The man looks shocked. But...the rings...I thought...I...

The rings are *arrears*. There's the paperwork to consider. If you haven't got the cash, then Harry don't want you here when we come round again.

Pike leans down over the posh lad as if he is coaching some kids playing football on the park. He stares into his eyes and says, quietly: And if you trash the place, no matter where you are, or where you go, we'll find you. And my colleague here will be wearing Nadia's coffee-coloured toes around his neck. Understand?

Posh boy and Nadia both nod, sheepishly, ashen. I have a feeling they will be on the blow for the rest of the day. I also have a feeling they won't be here when we return.

I throw the holdall over my shoulder and without further patter, we walk down the stairs and out of the door into the sunshine.

Pub-bookie pub–bookie? Pike suggests, in Jamaican patois, as we get into the car.

Thought you would never ask.

Very nice characterisation, by the way. Even I was shitting it.

Do you think so? Thanks. I try.

Your round first.

It always is, Francis. It always is…

Pike and me do odd jobs like this for our friend Danny Mannion and his associates. I'm glad he's around. Big County fan. Two years ago, we were released from an eight year prison sentence for the outcome of a football fight in Squares where a rival hooligan died of a head injury.

I didn't mean to kill him.

I whacked him and he banged his head on the jagged corner of a fruit machine and died six comatic months later in some London hospital. The fact they started it, or that he was a frequently convicted top lad, a Face with a string of hardcore footie previous didn't soften the heart of the beak, nor has it ever lightened the Manslaughter millstone I carry around my neck. Pike wouldn't even admit he was in the same boozer, so they gave him the same sentence as me.

Tedious autobiography notwithstanding, let's face it: these kind of personal qualities don't look good on an application form for John Lewis.

Hand of Doom

Later, we're leathered, swaying and yawping like students and skint from our game of pub-bookie pub-bookie backing slow horses and even slower dogs between pints of cider. But now, it's time for sweeties. Pop on its own won't work anymore. I need more and so does Pike. The need itches at my bowels and I salivate at the thought. He tells me who has the gear.

Ricky.

We don't get on. Forest lad, which Pike doesn't mind, but I do. I hate Forest with a passion and Ricky knows it. We've got history. An unfortunate incident way back. A girl. Zhivagos nightclub. Top dancefloor. Disrespect. I was dancing with her first. I had first dabs. I tell Pike this. My oldest pal stares my way as if I am crazy and tells me to fuck off and think of the drugs. I shrug my shoulders and tell him okay, my head spinning and my guts churning through too much cider and Irish whiskey. The sweetie he gave me in the bookies didn't help much – an experimental anti-psychotic, part of a batch his mate from Thorneywood mental institution gave him to try out. As a dance aid. My eyeballs feel like floodlights, town is like a rave, and my brain is full of drum and bass on maximum volume, but none of this is enough. Not nearly enough. Ricky's place is on the top end of Radford, another one of those regenerated factories that once employed thousands upon thousands of Nottingham people. Now, they house thirty yuppies and fifty posh students from down south. And dealers like Ricky. No dogs, no kids. Calendar monthly rent a grand minimum. He lives on the top floor. In the state we are in, we need a lift.

Pike can barely press the intercom button. The interaction is pithy and fast and I catch it all. Ricky's voice is robotic – like a hyperactive dalek - and I understand that there is something wrong with the intercom.

Ricky? Yo, badman.
Who the fuck?
It's Pike, my friend says. We chatted earlier, bro.
On your own?
Tezza's my wingman.
Valentine? That prick.
Yeh. He's here and he's minted.
(*Prick?*)

If he's minted, badman...Enter, Ricky says.

A loud buzz (metallic bees leaving a robot hive) and Pike shoves at the door clumsily. We're in and in the lift no fuss and soon, we're in Ricky's place. He shows me no warmth at all when we shake hands. He's mixed race – Afro-Caribbean and white – but he's mostly English in attitude, which is rare round these parts, a place which makes Kingston, Jamaica look like Downton Abbey. He looks a little like Rio Ferdinand only shorter and better looking. About thirty five. Imperial Purple shirt and a gold belcher chain, black trousers, black socks. He's doused in after-shave – a bit like Chloe last night.

I check my watch – it's not even nine. There's no beer and even if there was, Ricky doesn't offer us one. He's watching TV, some rap channel and the blokes on there are giving it large. He taps one of his stockinged feet to the rhythm of the ripped off tune - *Sweet Leaf* by Sabbath is in there somewhere - on the massive sixty inch HD screen. His place, smart, modern, full of hyper-polished pine and minimalist paintings, smells of takeaway. Pork balls, chow mein, sweet and sour sauce. He gestures us to sit down and I am relieved he does. I plonk down on the sofa; leather, burgundy, five grand's worth if a quid, and I lose myself in the comfort. I don't smoke, so the spliff Ricky is rolling is off the menu. When it is finally constructed, wordlessly, a tight, expertly-rolled funnel, Pike takes a relentless toke, then another, filling the room with that acrid, herby, tramp's-sock smell. The rising fumes lick and caress my friend's florid cheeks. By the smell of it, they are smoking Beelzebub, Dutch, premium quality hybrid skunk. Stuff that sends schoolkids schizo. I used to love this. I am briefly envious.

Ricky offers me a toke with a respectful nod but I shake my head. That's not what I'm here for, but Pike is a monster who'd sniff an old rambler's thermal socks if he thought it would take him there. He gets down to business.

Need something a touch more *lively* than this, bro, but thanks all the same, he says.

What you talking, badman? Ricky replies.

Pike gestures to me. I pull out five twenties. I throw the sheets on the glass table.

The *shit,* bro, Pike says.

The new shit?

Yo. The shit. Take me somewhere in the sky, badman.

Ricky reaches over and takes the money. He doesn't count it, nor does he check it for counterfeit. He knows we wouldn't skank him. At this level, drug deals come with ironclad paperwork – it's not *King Of New York*. My mouth starts to water and I start to feel edgy and light in anticipation.

I love this part…knowing…*the knowing…*

This is some special shit, Ricky says. Straight from the pleasure factory. Custom made. Cost you all five of those purple notes, but you'll never forget the ride and you can take the rest home for tomorrow. Interested?

I'm very interested. Pike says.

This is the very, very best, Mr Pike.

Ricky walks into the kitchen. We hear some scuffling about and he returns with a pipe about two foot high. It's an intricate bong, custom-made. Moroccan. Possibly even from Mali.

I've seen them before.

Islamic Harem bongs. Property of the Caliph.

Two delicately carved full breasted girls, Scandinavian looking, eyes shut, locked in an ecstatic embrace, sculpted in silver. The women flicker in the spotlight. The pipe extension is as long as a grass snake with a duck bill end. It's a quality smoking vessel – nothing like, say, a black Tango bottle with a blue biro for a pipe. Class. Everything about this ponce box is class, I have to admit.

Ricky places it neatly on the table, the same kind of six foot long glass and tubular table I always wanted, but never quite managed. He removes something from his pocket, like a darts pouch, green velvet, with velcro keeping it closed.

You know what they call this, badman? Ricky asks.

What? Pike says.

The **Hand of Doom**, man. *Doom* for short. It's the very best on the market.

Jesus, Pike says, now getting seriously amped. Been hearing about this. That good?

The best, bro. The very best.

He removes a rock of pure white crystal about the size of a Minstrel chocolate. It is diamond white, almost clear. It's exquisite. I get a tremor in my cock when I see it. I am hypnotised by it. I want it.

Want it. I want it.

I've never seen rock like it, but then, this is the first time I've taken rock in a ponce box flat like this, with all the whitewashed walls, the pristine laminate, the tubular reflections and the many, many spotlights. The rock acts like a light filter and I see a rainbow spectrum.

Doom, Ricky says. Who goes first?

I nod to Pike, but he shakes his head. Mug's arrers, he says and points at me. I lean forward and take the pipe in my hand. I feel my bowels clench and my half-erect cock twitch. My face drains of blood, as if I am on a mountain and about to jump. There's something erotic about it too – something hot. I salivate again, my mouth wet and hot. I watch Ricky light the rock in the bowl and I wait a second, then draw, like sucking molasses through a tiny straw. I feel the heat hit my throat. Then my head fills. Within seconds, it hits me like an anvil. I lean back and enjoy the journey into heaven. I know the wonder isn't going to last.

This is *wonderful…*
Feeling. Power. Emotion. Chloe. Marge. My cock…

Doom gives you wood, bro, Ricky says, a million miles in the distance, deadpan. Viagra ain't never gonna cut the Colemans after the Doomboy gives it a tickle.

Pike's turn, then Ricky's. I scarcely notice.

The rap music on the TV is stunningly attractive and I hear every bass beat, experience every nuance.

I love you Sweet Leaf, but you can't hear…

I wish Chloe were here to experience this, but I know that's stupid. With Doom, anything is possible.

Anything is possible.
Anything is possible.

Heaven.
I am in fucking heaven.
Heaven. Heaven
Heav

The Proposition

Pike, me and a couple of others were doing house clearances off the books for Danny when I met Chloe.

Three of us were emptying a sickening terrace in Carlton - a dead old lady with no kids and thirty cats, most of which were starving because no-one on her street thought to go round to see if she was okay. Haggard, rotting corpse, bolt upright, favourite armchair, mouth wide open, a *King's Singers* Christmas CD on her seventies music centre, she was only discovered after the smell of corpse and dying cats began to affect her two immediate neighbours, neither of whom had previously given a flying bollocks about whether she lived or died. The place was a vision of Hell and I almost told Pike where to stick his job when he passed me the snowsuit.

Afterwards, Grice, the foreman, offered us a grand to clean the place up and Pike took it, typical him, but I passed. I remember Pike's words well.

Bollocks to you. I'll get Zbigniew and his mate to help me and they'll be on time unlike you, you unbelievable cunt.

Chloe lives four doors down from me in a tiny house circumnavigated by greenery so vociferous and abundant, her place could be some southern paradise a modern Scarlett O'Hara would employ a posse of slaves to tend. I sometimes spend hours looking out the window at her place. I can see her sometimes, on her pathway, on her ever present phone, nattering, smoking.

I'm glad she smokes.

She puffs away outside, like everyone else.

She actually enjoys a fag, so she's out there a lot of the time, allowing someone like me the opportunity to appreciate her, from afar, undisturbed, in all her flawed, undeveloped, ruined, glory.

(*Chloe through the looking glass*)

I encountered Chloe in the Enclave for the first time when I got back home from the dead cat lady's house. When I first saw her, she was carrying three bags of shopping. I had parked outside the pub and was idly considering a refreshing pint when right in front of me, the strap of one of her lime green carrier bags snapped.

Stinking of cat and death and desperate for a livener, I couldn't avoid Chloe's misfortune if I wanted to, which I didn't, and instinctively I offered to help.

Thanks for this. OMG, what a mess, she said, as tins rolled onto the road and potatoes followed them in quick succession. I chased them down. A pint of milk exploded like a fountain all over us. A bag of red grapes splattered.

I'm so sorry for being a pain, mate, she said, flustered.

Not a bother, I said. Those bags aren't much good. I've had the same issues with those bags. Here, I have a carrier in my car. Hang on a sec.

I returned to Pike's Fiesta, opened the back seat and pulled out a Tesco bag. Went back helped pick up most of her spilled shopping.

This is totally awesome, Chloe said. You're so cool. Thank you so much.

As I say, not a bother, I replied as I repacked the carrier with the stray items. I live over the road, but can I take you anywhere? I'll help carry.

I only live over there, she interrupted, pointing to the Enclave doorway.

Me too. That's my flat next to the door.

OMG, really? Awesome. You can help me take this stuff over. I, like, only moved in at the weekend and this was the first chance I had to buy some food.

We said goodbye and discussed the possibility of coffee and then she went home. As she did, I looked at her closely.

All the constituent parts of a tasty young ex-student girl were there. Five five. Denim jacket over a pink tee shirt. Jet black bob. Skinny jeans ripped in all the right places. Battered UGG boots. Standard issue student uniform, but with that face - nothing out of place, mathematically perfect, symmetrical, regal cheekbones and cherry red lips - she could never be standard issue anything, ever. I think I knew that then. I think I've always known it.

Certainly my innards did: I took one look at Chloe and my stomach felt like I was skydiving from twenty thousand feet.

We became friends, of a sort. I learned all about her and she learned nothing about me, which is par for the course. (I'm not much of a talker). She liked to natter, I noticed that about her, but she could also listen. It was obvious to anyone concerned that she was listening rather than waiting for her turn like so many people nowadays. Not that I gave her much to attend to. Generalities. Bollocks. This and that. I'm not going to tell her about the footie scrapping, or where I'd been for most of the last decade. Or my shit relationships – Marge, for example, who IS still about. Or why, after fifty years I'm still living on my Jack Jones in a two bedroom flat partially supported by housing benefit and doing odd jobs for ropey businessmen on the side.

Not that she ever asked, or would ask, but she was bound to think it.

I would.

You would, wouldn't you? Then, out of the blue, she made her proposition.

I remember the evening well.

Derby night.

First Saturday in June.

Now, The Derby isn't what it was since the upper class twits of the year moved it from a Wednesday, where it could have been a national holiday, like the Melbourne Cup in Australia, but it's still The Derby and I took the weekend off from the removals to watch every race.

Pike joined me for the Saturday and the two of us played the honourable game of pub-bookie, pub-bookie. The venue for this game was the Magic Spoons in the Market Square (for the pints) and Baldfreds, (for the bets). One time, you could watch racing in the pubs, but now it's all Sky and EPL and plastic crap like that, so we had to neck our pints and run twenty yards along the perimeter of the square for the bet. By the end of the day, I was munted and cried off the party Pike had planned. Didn't help his mood that Chloe had texted, asking me to come round.

Jesus, Tezza. Show you a bitta leg and you're like a fuckin' spaz. Weak at the knees. You got floaty belly? Course y'have. I can see it in your minces. That's it, go on, fuck your mate off for a tart, he said, bitingly, but I called him what I called him and we had a tipsy wrestle on the square and he put me on the bus home, telling me he was off to Crinkle's for some proper action, to finish the job off. Part of me wanted some of that, some of that proper stuff Crinkle doles out for us on occasion, but by then, Chloe only had to smile at me and I was buttercream spread out over a light and fluffy fairy cake even though we were just friends. To think otherwise would have been stupid and suicidal, but at that point, I was still able to think of her as a friend, still able to look her in her (Manga) eyes without feeling… feeling…well, what I felt later. Every time.

Chloe.
Twenty four years old.
Fifty years old.
Friendzone…
(condemned)
…and that was all it could ever be.
But on Derby night, when I got home, I was to be surprised. It was going to be something else.

Terry?
What?
Do you know what I do for a living?
Student? Coffee shop? Retrieving lobsters from Jayne Mansfield's bum?
What?
Nothing. Old sketch.
Totally don't understand it.
No idea, Chloe. What do you do for a living?

When she told me what she did, we were sitting opposite each other in her house listening to dance music on Radio 1. I was still under the influence, but it had been two hours since the last drink and I was sipping lemonade. Didn't want to spoil it. Booze had spoilt a few relationships for me. I wasn't going to let it ruin this non-relationship for a start.

Chloe – jeans, feet tucked up underneath her, a purple hippy shirt and beads, hair all over the place, no makeup – was half talking to me, half texting her mates on the phone, which was usually how it went when we got together. If you were a straight-laced sort of bloke with an attitude, you'd get offended at this, the phone thing, the texting thing, but that's the modern world, every zombie has the attention span of a gnat as they shamble about, and girls in particular cannot bear to miss out on anything going on, but I didn't mind. Not with Chloe. I sort of sat there and *basked*. I got the impression that night that Chloe had something to tell me, but I had no idea what it might be.

Her front door was open, allowing in a cool breeze, the dying sun's rays fragmented the arboretum into a spectrum of glistening leaf green. She scanned my face nervously and put her iPhone on the arm of her sofa.

Can you keep a secret?

Of course, I replied.

Serious, mate, she said, leaning forward, looking earnest, her eyes mournful, like a cat wanting all the milk in the house. This is, like, a proper secret. I could get into trouble. I'm nervous about telling you and stuff.

Chloe, you can tell me. I'm trustworthy.

And when I tell you, I'll need a favour.

A favour?

Yes. And you are so dead if you say no.

Okay.

Then she told me.

She spent ten minutes doing it and I didn't interrupt once. I was simultaneously enraptured and appalled.

Simultaneously blessed and cursed.

Hailed and damned.

I must have still been stunned when I agreed to help. I should have walked, especially in the light of how it all turned out for us. But I accepted her proposition (hailed and damned) without thinking twice and she came over and put her hand on my shoulder saying thank you so much Mr Valentine and I said (*you always were a dick*) no issues, no problem. Not a bother. Any chance of a coffee…

(Any chance of a coffee)

She told me the first job would be on Tuesday night, a regular customer of hers up in Arnold.

No drinks, no meals. Just…just…whatever.

Her boss would supply a car for the duration and would send someone round with it. Dress smartly and expect to be out for six hours or so. Maybe more. The money she offered me per week was enough for me to finish clearing the houses of the dead. Once I agreed to help her, she picked up her phone again and carried on texting and talking to me about the music on the radio, the pounding beats, the silky refrains as if we had just discussed a visit to her mother's for tea and tiffin.

She never batted an eyelid, Chloe.

Her behaviour was simultaneously perfectly innocent and dangerously psychopathic. And despite the alarm bells ringing in my head like Big Ben and his metallic cousins, I still went ahead and took the proposition.

Chemically Enhanced Singalong

Later that night, I drank my remaining Thor's Hammer cider and sampled a strip of morphine-based Co-Proxamol tablets while dancing naked around my flat singing The Beatles the top of my voice. My neighbour upstairs was not pleased, but I remember thinking my rendition of *Strawberry Fields Forever* was just about perfect. The pop and sweeties were all I had in the house, and with my wages going south on that horse, I had to make do. And I don't need any excuse to have a chemically enhanced singalong to the Beatles.

Between then and now, sandwiching all the shit that happened, all the good stuff, all the bad stuff, Chloe's been the only thing on my mind, no matter what happened to us, or what gear I took to get some breathing space, some peace, some contentment.

Guess I was in love even then.

It was later that I discovered her gaffer at the agency was a bloke named Neville Gant.

He and I were old acquaintances.

Or very old enemies, more to the point.

The Norman Calders

After last night at Ricky's place, I'm feeling completely disorientated and desperate for more confectionery. I should be thankful I am working. I spent the early part of the morning guzzling orange juice by the gallon and munching Crème Eggs. That Doom was superb stuff, but the comedowns get harder to deal with. Every time I go for the kill, I ease the pain the day after with a couple of hundred milligrams of Tramadol and when I get home, I'll take a jelly a mate of Pike's called Omar sorts out for me. I forget the last time I slept without some aid or other. And it has to be prescription as I can't smoke weed now. I hope Chloe doesn't have a job for tomorrow night. She rarely works two nights in a row, but it's not unheard of. I need to jelly out and sample a few quiet tins.

Early afternoon, a gang of us visited a doctor's surgery. Ordinarily, a doctor only sees one patient at a time at this particular health centre. On this occasion, however, it was an unscheduled group appointment to ensure, Sonny, a good friend of Danny Mannion's maintained his sicknote. His new doctor (the previous doc had retired) had made one or two ominous comments during Sonny's last appointment about the rejuvenating properties of an honest day's work rather than a life spent rotting on benefits, all that Daily Mail shit. It looked very likely, on balance, that the Man from Del Monte was going to say no to the sicknote.

Sonny, a hard working shoplifter and enforcer of Danny's doorstep obligations, who last worked when Wham were the only rappers in the chart, felt that those comments were inappropriate and upsetting. So he mentioned this to Danny over a pint. Danny agreed and asked us to join Sonny on his next appointment.

Sure enough, thanks to our presence, Sonny emerged with a long term sicknote safely tucked away in his tracksuit bottoms. Most of them went to the pub, but I was working and off to see Chloe I went.

I knock on Chloe's door and I hear a muffled invitation to enter. Chloe is wearing a bottle-green Kimono and painting her toenails. Dark purple. I only take a fleeting glance as I say hello. Her hair is immaculate – at least that's finished. Either I'm early or she's late. I check my watch and she notices with an elfin smile. Nothing pisses me off more than waiting for my woman to get ready to go out, but Chloe's my boss so it doesn't have the same emotional frisson. She can take all night and it would make no difference to the price of fish.

Unmistakably a woman's place. All flowers, cushions, pot-pourri bowels, nik-naks and accoutrements, almost more decoration than furniture. There's a smell of cooking I can't quite place. Her cat, Omega, is lapping at a saucer of milk in the kitchen and he doesn't even turn his black and white head to see me come in – I'm below him. He's a good judge of character and I resolve to give him a stroke when he comes over. I sit down on the cream armchair opposite Chloe. I'm wearing a suit as usual. Dark, three button. Skinny trousers, open necked white shirt. Black brogues I bought three weeks ago on Bridlesmith Gate. Made in Northampton. I hate wearing suits. She's lucky I had one – weddings, funerals and court; that's your lot.

I never wear ties.

I wouldn't work for her if she made me wear a tie.

Ties are for arseholes.

Chloe thinks a suit is appropriate and though she doesn't order me to wear one, there is an unspoken agreement between us that I do.

She is smoking a Benson and Hedges cigarette and for a second, I feel like asking for one.

I don't watch her smoke. I *daren't* watch her smoke this close up.

You look super smart, Mr Valentine, she says.
Thanks.
Different from, like, when we first met.
I had an excuse for that. Something to do with a dead cat or ten.
Omega stops lapping his milk and meows. Chloe smiles and maybe it's the aftermath of the Doom, or the stuff I took to beat the comedown, but I feel like smiling too. Chloe switches to business.
So, like, tonight, we're off to Gotham.
Yes, you said.
It's going to be a long night for you.
Is it?
My client is supposed to be taking me to dinner before we go to her place.
Dinner? I question. Where?
I so don't know, Mr Valentine. Take a good book.
I've got Jack to finish.
Yes. Sounds like an awesome story, she says, and I am not sure whether she is taking the piss. It is difficult to tell with Chloe. I watch her get up and walk to her bedroom.

Her legs are flawless, muscular and taut. Her calves are smooth and waxed and there isn't a blemish on her thigh, nor a single solitary scout from an offshore invasion of cellulite. Incredible legs. Their mere presence as they disappear into her bedroom is enough to make me want to be back at Ricky's place.

I want more Doom.
I want more of it than I can handle.
Failing that, I leaf through a paperback on the occasional table next to me. It's a girly paperback – some gargoyle thing by someone called *Louise Gornall*, some youngster's book - and I'm surprised Chloe is reading this.

Then I recall seeing her wander to the shops with her mates wearing her flip flops and ripped skinnies. She is a kid. All this sex and money malarkey is grand theatre.

I read the first page and put it back, cross my legs, listen to Lana, try not to picture Chloe dressing, try not to wonder what underwear she's decided to wear for her upcoming business. I shut my eyes and think of anything but her and before I know it, she's out. A single, simple black dress. Chanel. High heels. She walks over to the armchair and turns round, faces away from me. Would you zip me up please, she asks and I do so. Perfume I don't recognise caresses my sense of smell as I slowly join the two segments of her dress together.

Awesome, she says. Do you like Lana?

She's good, I reply.

I do. I bought *Ultra Violence* the other day, but I kinda thought I'd, like, play the original tonight, and stuff, just for a change. It's totally awesome.

I've read a novel called *Ultra Violence*.

Oh yes? She replies putting on her coat. What's it about?

I wish I hadn't said anything. Oh nothing…nothing much at all, I say. In fact, I'm mentioned in it. But I'm not going to tell her that. My claim to literary fame, apart from court archives, that is.

Crap! It so must be about something, she says, looking at me, eyes full of curiosity.

Just history, I say, switching deftly. What time do we meet the woman from Gotham?

In half an hour.

I'll never get us there in half an hour.

Chloe smiles. Mate, is this the face of concern? She finishes her cigarette and crushes the butt in the ashtray on the window sill. Take me to the ball, she says, picking up her clasp bag.

It's still warm outside, not even the hint of a breeze. We walk together to the waiting car.

Driving.

I try not to picture Chloe bouncing her shoe from the end of her stockinged foot. She talks for a time to her friends on her mobile and as we pass Bridgford, she starts to talk to me.

My client tonight is called Hope, she says.

Chloe hardly ever discusses her clients in advance. In fact, only once has she ever done so. My attention perks.

Oh yes?

She's from London.

Is she? Whereabouts?

Apparently, she's from the stock market and stuff. I don't know, like, where exactly in London she's from. I'm not, like, a googlemap. She's totally rich.

Aren't they all, I say, dry as dust.

Ah, mate, I mean rich. Neville...

(wanker)

...says she's proper loaded. Lives in a manor house. *Mega* rich.

Okay.

But not Wayne Manor...

Where?

You know...OMG! That's where Batman lives. I said...

Told you. Don't know anything about comics.

Knowing that, like, Batman lives in Wayne Manor isn't *comics*. It's, like, culture.

Is it really? I ask, slightly irritated, but her voice – roughened tonight by plenty of cigarettes – acts as a pacifier. I take a glimpse at her in the mirror and regret it.

I feel empty whenever I look at her directly.

She takes something from within me. Like a succubus eats souls. A lorry is about to pass me up ahead, his lights full beam, a corpulent red thing, and I suppress the instinct to spin my wheel and crash the car into its grille and die underneath it's giant wheels, (*so I never have to see her again*), but I drive on, the faint, imagined back draught of the passing truck a whisper.

You will have to come and look at my comic collection, she says, leaning back. Oh, and Hope wants to meet you too. When she spoke to Neville...

(arsehole)

...and discovered I used a driver, she insisted he – you – came inside and waited downstairs. Apparently she doesn't feel right when the help is outside. Get this...she's like, *oh I can't relax when the workers suffer*...totally true.

The workers?

That's what she said, Terry, and other stuff. Are you, like, mortally offended?

Of course not, I reply, turning down into a dark country road, pitch black. I need to concentrate. Anything can happen on roads like this one. She continues.

So, you can kinda escort me inside for once. I'm sure you can have a biscuit.

Lovely, I reply.

I don't like this at all and I don't like the way Chloe waits till two miles away from the drop to tell me. I feel betrayed and annoyed, but I keep it to myself. I don't...don't want... to hear her...working. At all. My pulse races and my heart pounds. I don't want this.

Is this compulsory, Chloe? I ask. Can I not stay in the motor?

Afraid so, Terry, she says, making last minute adjustments to her face in front of a golden compact. Like a Magritte painting, her eyes are obscured.

Only, I have Jack to read.

Mate, you can read it in the warm of the manor house.

As it is a warm night, I am not mollified. Her last sentence sounded to me like the end of the conversation. I don't push it, let the satnav take me to the gate of the Manor. Every now and again, I notice Chloe glance in my direction but I have no idea why. It could be anything. It could be nothing. I don't like it when it happens and I don't like it when it stops. She does it as I pull up on the gravel outside the giant manor house, the pathway floodlit by single high candle floods lining the immaculately manicured lawns. I thought she would be interested in the house, but no. She watches me all the way down and I am disconcerted by it.

The car comes to a halt on the gravel with a satisfying crunch. Chloe doesn't move. I am expected to do my full chauffeur bit, which pisses me right off tonight. I turn off the headlights and open the driver's door, walk around the car, my leather soles making noisy imprints in the gravel and open her rear door.

Ta, mate. she says, and as she gets out, I notice her stocking top constricting the inside plane of her exquisite, porcelain thigh. She comes near me and I can smell her perfume and it makes me tremble.

I don't want her to look at me.

I just don't.

She waits. I shut the door and auto lock. She reaches for my arm and holds it with her left hand. Without further comment, we walk across the gravel to the door of the giant Tudor Manor house, like some posh married couple; its windows, each an eye, a wide, gaping eye with no lids, looking at us, at least one of the windows hiding a single pair of human eyes within (there always is).

The door ahead opens. Silhouetted in the light is a woman and I suspect this is Hope come to greet us. As we walk closer, details become clearer. She is holding a goblet style glass, half full, presumably of wine. Her hair is ash blonde and curly, a picture of the big-haired eighties. She is wearing a white dress and she is barefoot. I put her at forty, but nowadays, you can't tell a woman's age anywhere between thirty and sixty, thanks to face cream, Botox, gyms, slimming pills, healthy diets and endless sex. One thing is for sure, she's stunning and I am glad I don't have to speak. I leave it to Chloe to do the small talk and the necessary.

Hope? Chloe says, holding out her gloved hand.

You must be Chloe? She replies, and the two shake hands. She doesn't acknowledge me.

Yes. I'm Chloe.

So luscious, she says. Come in. I have wine.

The house is furnished exactly as you might expect. Half olde worlde, the antlers hanging on the wall, the Persian carpets, and the umbrella stand, the chiming Grandfather clock, the endless parade of family portraits up the staircase and along the corridor ahead. They may not be her relatives, but the nouveau riche buy places like this and keep it all intact; dead animals, dead portraits, busted panels, locked and secret rooms, torture chambers, tiny Priest hideaways, the lot. The place smells of leather, walnut, polish, candles - and beef.

Cooking.

They aren't going out for dinner. Hope's either sent out or her chef's done the business.

Hope's figure is even better in the light. There isn't an ounce of fat on her, not an ounce and she walks with skill and consideration. I think of what she and the woman walking into the living room are about to do and I feel the dry and powdery sawdust in my throat embrace my windpipe like a vice.

Sit down, she says. Not you...she points to me. You wait in the games room. Do you play billiards?

Hope is drunk. That sentence took a millennium to say to me and lifting up her arm to point at me must have been an effort. She's used to ordering people about and it gets my back up. I suspect she's been on the vino collapso since tea time. Despite that – and it must be some masochistic class thing - I'm taken with her. Viscerally. That voice. Her dress is see-through, she has a smooth, almost hand carved figure, planed to the millimetre, with lines like a waxed surfboard. Her hair tumbles over her exposed shoulders. Metallic eyes, cold and unforgiving, more green than blue, somewhere in between. I wouldn't cross her willingly. Scarlet nail varnish on her fingers and toenails contrast with gold jewellery that flares and flickers in the fiery light projected by the open fire. I notice an incongruous black G-string underneath the dress. She isn't wearing a bra, her nipples substantial, like spinning tops, pointed and attentive. I am envious of Chloe and then I feel sick again, crush the thought of what…

…I nod, without looking at Chloe (*this is her arena*) and Hope escorts me to the door.

Games room is there, look, okay, she says to me with a slight slur and I can smell her perfume. She's bathed recently, probably drinking her wine in the bath.

Sure, I say.

Without further interruption, Hope shuts the door and the sudden shift from the heat generated by the warmth of the fire into something else – a world of frost and emptiness – is striking and I feel momentarily blinded.

I walk down the corridor a few yards and open the door. There is a man playing billiards. White shirt, black trousers. The billiard table is well lit, but the room is not. There is a flickering open fire. The walls are lined with oak panels and mounted upon them are the heads of more dead animals (Stags, a Bear) and paintings of old men. Old politicians from the Georgian and Victorian eras. Red flock wall paper and huge planks of dado rail. Old school. That smell of beef and old cigars. A billiard ball clicks against another and the man ahead walks around the table to retrieve the cue ball from a spacious pocket. He is taller than me by a foot, and he is moustachioed. Rare nowadays except for goateed metal heads and charity events. His hair is brown, like the hide of a horse. Plenty of it, with sideburns. Thin, but not emaciated-thin: Wiry thin, the type of frame that can pull itself up a brick wall or swing on vines from tree to tree. Military. He is in his stockinged feet as he traverses the table. I feel momentarily awkward until he breaks the silence, without looking at me.

Do you dabble?

Once. Not for a long time.

Might be in for a long night, he says. What with those two and their girly games.

I am offended straight away and I feel sick.

Play a match? He asks, offering me his cue.

Okay, I say, and I remove my jacket, hang it on a mounted coat rack by the door.

Billiards is more my game, Squire, he says to me. I don't know why it went out of fashion. Snooker balls are over there, if you prefer the modern version.

Billiards is fine, I reply.

Ignoring the man's cue, I select my own, a perfectly balanced and tipped instrument of despatch from a rack of ten next to a window draped in red velvet curtains.

I'm Terry, I offer.

Conn, he replies, taking another shot. not offering his hand.

He has a London accent. He walks to the other end of the table and replaces the three balls on their spots. I'll kick off, he says.

Mug's arrers I think, mischievously, but say nothing.

Conn and me play the ancient game of billiards mostly in silence. He is a superb player and at the table most of the time. On the rare occasions he does speak, I find out he works for Hope as her Man of Business. That's how he described himself. He's a West Ham fan, a one-time season ticket holder. Ex-military. Guards. I was right. In other words, he's the deal. Hope must be seriously minted to have a Mr Troop on the books. I'm out my depth. He's not alone either. We are interrupted every now and again by other blokes – skinheads, mostly, big bastards.

Their interruptions are probably for my benefit. Assuming not everyone visited the billiards room, there must be others so it seems that Hope employs a small army of geezers. Proper muscle too. Conn, who never makes eye contact with me (or with the others), could be tasty. I wouldn't want to cross him.

If Hope decided to play hardball with Chloe tonight, I'd have my work cut out to fulfil my obligations, but, just in case, I scan the room in some detail and there were enough household items I could use to make a show.

That's the advantage of following County, especially when I was a kid, when every arsehole was a hooligan.

The eighties: The era when you went to a mass brawl and a football match broke out.

Notts.

Always outnumbered, always underestimated. It gave me, Pike and some of the others, (*Bully Brothers, Cucumbers, Leonard, Mellaw, Clarkson, Clifton Tom, Breaker, Beanie, Sparks, Whiskey Jack, Peeler, the Mad Postman,* the names come cascading back in seconds), a split-second psychological advantage.

There's enough armour in the games room, including the cues themselves, (*Wolves*) and a set of pokers.

Luckily, Chloe didn't raise the alarm. Up…up…there doing whatever…whatever she does. So we play billiards and after a couple of hours, Chloe comes downstairs. There is no sign of Hope.

Time to go home, she says to me, not a hair out of place.

I'll see you out, Conn says. Good game.

Cheers, I reply. Enjoyed it

He puts away his cue and I do the same. There's something not quite right with Chloe. She's looking at me as if she is trying to establish

a psychic connection. As if she is trying to tell me something, but it doesn't work and the three of us walk down the entrance hall to the main door. I notice a portrait above the door. A Cavalier, from the time of The Restoration. Flowing mane, a dark blue tunic, a thick, moustache, arrogant eyes. He is holding a golden tipped walking cane. I stop for a second. I'm a sucker for History ever since I studied it at Poly back in the day – and any bleeder who likes the horses can't fail to owe a debt of gratitude to Charles II. Chloe watches on quizzically, but says nothing.

Conn, who's that? I ask.

Who?

The Cavalier. Above the door. The portrait.

That's Sir John Calder. One of the richest men in England at the time and one of the greatest landowners in this part of the world. A favourite of the King. He built the original manor house, though it has been substantially restored, obviously. Some of the features, the originals, you can still see. The Oak timbers, the wainscotting and whatnot. A member of Charles II's court. Charles was often up here in the East Midlands for the sport – hunting, racing. Particularly the racing. Out at Oadby where Leicester racecourse is now. Sir John owned over a hundred racehorses at one point. That was something which made him one of the King's favourites. You like the horses, Squire?

I do.

Me too. Grew up with Park Top and Nijinsky.

Fantastic animals. I'm a Dancing Brave man.

Proper horse. Starkey was a dimwit that day. One of the worst rides I have ever seen on a racecourse. The Brave deserved better.

You're not kidding. I had a proper wedge on

Kids don't care for the noble sport nowadays, do they?

No.

Crying shame. Anyway, Sir John spent time in exile as a child after Cromwell laid waste to the country. He was restored to the seat here when it was feasible. Liked a good time. Liked a good old knees up. This manor is his legacy.

Cool, Chloe says.

Indeed, Miss.

I guess that's too good a portrait to throw out too, I comment.

Especially a family portrait, Conn replies enigmatically and opens the door. Good game, he says and stares into my face.

For the first time I notice his eyes. Illuminated in the spotlight. They are almost black, rather than blue, as if azure marble had been treated after being burned in a charcoal pit. They are narrow too. In the darkness and the concentrated light of the billiard table, I hadn't noticed before.

They are the eyes you might see on a Judge.

I've seen eyes like that before.

I realise immediately that Conn is an establishment stooge, an acolyte of the Order. He'd kill because the crown was threatened.

That's what he is. This is one of the blokes, I realise, who'd end up working for MI5 or for one of the richest women in the country. In other words, the complete opposite to me.

The absolute opposite. We look at each other for a little longer than is absolutely necessary and there are unspoken words shared below the level of perception, even our own perceptions. The moment freezes in time. We become the subject of a portrait there, in that hallway.

A Still Life of which there are three major influences:

Conn: London. Corporate shill. Establishment. Order.
Sir John Calder: Empire. Establishment. Master of all he surveys.
Terry Valentine: Nottingham. Anarchy. Freelance. Loser.

Chloe, the obscured fourth element, coughs slightly, as if she is aware of what is going on, and the moment is broken.

Ma'am will be in touch, Conn says, smiling, opening the door.

We leave. I say nothing and escort Chloe to the car, across the gravel. It's cold, unexpectedly, and I take off my jacket and put it round her shoulders, a gesture she accepts and she keeps it on until we are down the road, the car warming swiftly in the darkness of the night towards Southwell.

Don't suppose…

I do, yes. Tell me.

Awesome, Mr Valentine. This IS a bonus…

Spare me the gory bits.

Oh, I shall do. Way too *gross*! She replies, laughing.

You're not kidding.

I have to tell you what went on up there and stuff. OMG, it was crazy. I feel so uncomfortable about it, I'm so glad I can talk. May I smoke in the car, Mr Valentine?

Wind the window down. Don't burn the leather.

She lights a Benson and Hedges. I watch her caress the tip with her newly painted lips and take a deep drag.

You'll never guess what she said. OMG. OMFG.

What?

Hope. She's totally crazy.

Were you safe?

Absolutely, yeh, So, we get upstairs and we do what we do and after, OMG, she's like, I'm totally into you, Chloe and I'm like, oh fuck, I don't need this, I totally don't need this, and she's like, I can't help the way I feel about you and, like, I've fallen in love with you and stuff, like, at first sight.

That bunny boiler stuff's not good for business, I interject.

OMFG, this happens to me all the time! Crap!

I'll bet.

So I'm, like, okay, and I'm thinking, crazy bitch, whatever, and she's like, do you feel the same way, did you feel it, did you get the electricity between us, it was so intense, and I'm like, yeh sure, thinking whatever, it wasn't that good, not compared to...well...you know.

I get it, I say, hoping for no stomach churning detail.

So she's, like, tell me you feel the same way, and I'm like, no, I'm sorry, you're cool and all that, but, hey, it's business and you're paying for this and I'm like, no I don't jump fences with my clients and she's, like, OMFG, I'm so sorry, I thought we...we...I've never felt anything like it, emotionally, I mean, on the heart level.

Ah, I say. That pesky heart level...

Totally. OMG, she's like, bursting into tears and asking me to forget what she said and how she'd, like, spoiled everything between us. I'm like, thinking WTF, back right off with the love stuff, bitch, but then she's going mad at me and, like, she switched superfast and started calling me a whore and gettingnasty and I'm so kinda...

(bitch)

...reaching for the Terry button on the dresser, but then she's, like, I'm sorry, I'm sorry.

She was on her way, I offer. Drunk, I mean.

Drunk? Man, she's *crazy*! Crap, I totally don't need this shit, and I'm, like, speak to Neville if I've not pleased you, as a client, and that was a totally asshole thing to say because she picks up her table lamp and smashes it against the wall.

You should have called me, I say.

I'm, like, *chill right out*, and she's sobbing and, like, begging forgiveness as if I've known her all my life. *Like, we were married.*

Jesus.

So, I'm like, let's call it a day and I'll come back and see you, which is a total lie, and she's like, will you? *Please say you will*? And, like, I get dressed and say yeh. She mentions this party and I'm like, uh-huh and oh yeh, and all I kinda wanna do is GTF out of there.

Good move.

Crap, I can't work out whether she was pissed or totally crazy. It's, like, *way* gross.

Probably both. Next time, call me.

She leans between the seats. Lowers her voice. Aren't you pleased I dealt with it, Mr Valentine? Aren't you proud of me?

I'm proud of you. But remember what you pay me for.

To look after me, huh.

She smiles and throws her cigarette out of the window after one deep drag that I thought would never end. She takes off her shoes and lays down on the back seat.

This business. It kinda takes it out of you, you know.

It probably does, I reply.

Tell me about that bloke.

Who?

The bloke you were playing snooker with.

Billiards.

That as well. He was kinda dishy.

Chloe...

Just kidding, mate.

Good, I reply, freezing cold and bony skeleton fingers letting go of my sweetbreads. The road is empty and I am making good time. We'll be home soon.

Home.

And when I get home, I think, I'm going to drop three jellies and drink half a bottle of Talisker and I may even

(stab at my thigh with a compass)

sleep all morning and then call Marge and go round and see her and do something normal for a change, take her to the Pitcher for a Czech lager and

(slice chunks from underneath an armpit)

stay at her place, have a bite to eat and make

(death)

love all night, just like we used to,

forget Chloe for a

(fat chance, fat boy, cut yourself up)

bit and be normal for a once, mix with normal people, normal, normal, everyday folk down in Nottingham, none of this

(why not remove one of your eyeballs, like you tried at North Camp when you)

strange, surreal, mad, lesbian

(eyeballs, eyeballs, eyeballs)

Chloe shit

So, Mr Valentine. Tell me about Jack again, she asks. I liked that. I liked it a lot.

I do. I tell her.

Marge

Marge opens the door and lets me in.

It's hard to tell whether she is happy to see me, indifferent, or pissed off. As usual, I can smell the plant before I see it. She likes a spliff, Marge, and I only wish I could join her. If I did, I'd be back on the fags again and brown bread in ten years. I've been out all day with Pike, explaining to a restauranteur on Danny's behalf that supplies to his restaurant have to be paid for and that hundred and eighty day terms of payment are unacceptable. At least they are to a catering firm partly run by Danny Mannion. Sadly, the owner disagreed. Said business had been tough, diners hard to come by.

Pike had been enforcement today (with Johnny V on admin and me on driving and removals) and to spice up negotiations, he screwed opened the lid on a canister of petrol in the vicinity of the owner's youngest son, about ten, while simultaneously discussing the Human Torch (who, by all accounts, is a superhero in the Fantastic Four).

Getting the message loud and clear, the restauranteur paid sixmonths worth of arrears and a year in advance on a new contract.

I loved Marge – still do, in a way – and we were together for six years, throughout all the good times, down at Notts. I had offers, but not once did I let her down. I don't recall precisely why Marge slept with Bryn and I don't want to ask her again. No point crying over spilled milk and the only thing you bring up when you rake hot coals is cold ashes and dying leaves.

I walk in and sit down on her sofa. She's watching some soap on SkyPlus, maybe Emmerdale, and she walks over to the kitchenette and fetches me a can. Lager. I prefer cider, but this will do. She's smoking Beelzebub skunk, the stuff the blacks around St Ann's use, straight from the Indies via Rotterdam. It's powerful gear. More than one bloke after smoking too much Devil has ended up in Thorneywood Mount raving about the moon landings, England's faked World Cup win in 66 (filmed at Shepperton studios) and Bush blowing up the Twin Towers.

I watch her take a deep drag. She's wearing a light blue towelling robe and pajama bottoms. She sits on the armchair opposite and pulls her legs up underneath her. She puts the joint carefully into one of the grooves in the heavy onyx ashtray on the arm of her chair. The place smells of skunk, perfume, air freshener and burned toast

A tall, posh glass of white wine nestles on a pine occasional table in front of her. Ash blonde, blue-eyed, an hourglass figure (admittedly with a touch of elasticity round the belly), and legs you'd frame if you could, long and slender, I'm lucky to find her on her own. I've visited when she's been in company before and it can get awkward.

It's *been* awkward.

A good looking woman, Marge has never been short of male company, but you always get the impression none of them are ever good enough. They never last. I suspect I was one of the longest lasting in her life. I'm disappointed that she hasn't sat next to me. I need her tonight. Not for sex, but for something else. I want to lie between her breasts and I want her to stroke what remains of my hair, while telling me it's alright. *It's all going to be alright, Terry. All of it. We'll all live Happily Ever After.* But she's sitting over there, a million miles away, on another continent, and she's watching the telly, clearly stoned, so I decide to wait. She knows what I need. I don't need to tell her, it's etched all over my face like a bad prison tattoo.

I ask her if I can take my shoes off. She nods, puts down her cigarette and comes over to take them from me, like a Geisha. She's proud of her flat and proud herself as a woman. My priest-black socks are new otherwise I would have retained the shoes. I lie down on the sofa and wish I could have a cigarette.

She's forty-two, but could be thirty, so I guess smoking has done her some favours. She has tattoos on the underside of both wrists but I try not to look at those – she would never have tattooed herself if I had stayed with her. I don't approve of tats on women, even though I have the Clockwork Orange Isosceles, off the poster, with NCFC underneath, but then, Marge would have done what she wanted anyway. Her flat is warm, like most women's places (*Chloe*), with the heating full on and damn the consequences. I'm relaxed. I love coming to Marge's place and she doesn't seem to mind. Only time she complains is if…well, if…she's got a fella on the go, but she's been single since Easter when she finished with that bloke she was seeing for being too controlling. He tried to stop her going to a club with Cheryl and Keeley and that was a mistake (even though it was probably shrewd strategy, knowing those three), because she kicked him into touch instead and never spoke to him again. Marge told me that she was done with blokes, which left the door wide open for me to chill out when I needed to.

It's the end of the soap and Marge comes over and tells me to shift my legs. I do and she sits down at the other end of the sofa and puts my feet on her thighs. She still doesn't look at me, focuses on the adverts, some bollocks, some nonsense, and she strokes my stockinged feet idly. She smells intense up close; all the times we were together she smelled like that, but now, she is all woman, all grown up, rather than the angry, passionate kid she was then, in her mid-twenties, back in the nineties.

(Chloe's age)

I've told her about Chloe. On a couple of occasions. I've recounted my intimate Chloe thoughts, my Chloe observations. I'm not sure she likes me doing so, but I do. She listens quietly and sometimes, like tonight, she strokes my feet. Sometimes she lets me share her king sized bed and I think tonight might be one of those nights. She lost her job, she told me, and now she was back on the JSA, so Monday was like any other day and we might lay there and talk and…and…the thought of sharing her bed makes me anxious but as she strokes my feet and watches the news, I am…am…

…more confident that I can…

…confident…

(Chloe)

I do want to know what Chloe does.

Upstairs.

With her clients. It obsesses me. I want to know. I want to call her up now. I want her to tell me in graphic, intimate detail. I want her to inform me, educate me.

I want know to about the fluids and the frictions, the moves and the shakes, the…moans…the…ecstasy (*her ecstasy*)…the cums, the explosions…the thermonuclear fission in her belly…I want to know her…know her… but I cannot, I cannot.

(Chloe)

Some men like to think of their woman in bed with another man. When they are together, when they are intimate, but I can't allow that to happen. That way monsters lurk. Some men carry it through and pay men to sleep with their wives while they watch and they get off on it. It turns them on and even though some of them go a lifetime without actively seeking a willing accomplice, it's in their heads, the ploughing, the moans, the woman's fevered pleasure, the third person fuck, the watching, seated, at the end of the bed; hiding, through the keyhole.

They call it Cuckolding and without it, without that impish thought, that weird impulse, some men cannot get it up. It furnishes them with power, almost as if the virile substitute ploughing their wife on the marital bed is a battery of some kind, a power source. Some women love it, others do it because they are told to, others (*Chloe, yes*) are ambivalent.

If you were married, I say to Marge, would you agree to sleep with a man because your husband wanted to watch you fuck?

She grins. Oh yes. I love a little bit of swinging. I do. Especially if the new fella were possessed of a proper whanger.

Would you still respect your husband in the morning?

I wouldn't gi'it a second thought, Terry. Why? Are you getting kinky in your old age? Shall I ring Cardus up? He's got a cock that about came out me trap.

I'm contemplating something. You know, having a think.

Well, don't think too 'ard. You know it ain't good for ya, duck, she says, giggling.

I'll shut up, then, I reply, amused and connected with her good humour.

We sit there for a while watching some shit on the TV and then she turns to me.

I've had a threesome, you know.

Have you? I reply, half wanting to hear, half not, feeling the nausea rising. It's always the case. *Devil and Angel. Angel and Devil.*

Two blokes and me.

Two blokes? You naughty girl.

Yep. A Choc Ice, it were. That's what they call it, she says, taking a draw on her joint.

A what?

A choc ice. A few year back. When I were havin' me mad days.

A choc ice?

One black bloke, one white bloke.

Oh.

Brilliant it were. Loved it.

Do I know them? I ask, feeling mildly sick and also turned on, despite myself and despite my current problem.

Nah. They were from London or sumut. Never saw em again. Never even asked em for their Facebook. It were a one night stand after a party on The Green. I went back wi em to the Holiday Inn in town. Never forget it. Fuckin ell, they about killed meh. Couldn't walk for a wik.

You had a one night stand threesome?

Marge looks at me down her nose, like a teacher querying a response from a pupil that she didn't understand. She takes another toke of her spliff, the pungent, mysterious grey smoke obscuring her face and rising up to the low, new-build ceilings.

Sumut wrong wi that, Terry? She says.

It's a bit forward. Did you at least get their names?

She laughs. I did, but forgot.

It's OTT, even for you, I say.

Prude, she replies, stroking my shin. I like me blokes, what can I do?

Join a convent. Ever slept with a woman? I ask.

She shakes her head.

Not yet, Tezza. Know anyone who's up forrit?

Yeh, okay, I say, regretting bringing up the subject and batting away the irony with great force. Marge picks up the signal and takes another sip of her glass of wine.

(Forty two, single, still fit, still attractive and still crazy after all these years, why shouldn't she sleep with who she likes? It's a free country. It's you with the problem...)

(Chloe)

Would you get married? I ask.

What, again?

I forget she has been married before, shortly after me. A bloke from Clifton who promised her the world and gave her a string of black eyes instead. I wasn't in contact with her at the time, for obvious reasons, or I'd have had a natter with him (with moral support from the lads, if necessary).

Sorry, forgot.

Nah, she said, ignoring my apology as if it never mattered in the first place. I'm buzzin wi my own company. Unless you fancy steppin' off bench?

You kill me, Marge. I can scarcely look after myself.

She laughs too.

Then she moves my legs out of the way and stands, brushing some skunk leaves from her pajamas.

I'm bolloxed, she says. Coming forra lie down? You can talk me to sleep, like you used to.

I tell her I will and get up. I walk to the window. A few revellers wander from pub to pub outside, but not many. In the old days, Sunday night was the buffer between a great weekend and the horrors of work. Town was rammed back then. The football lads met up to discuss the Saturday battles. The girls dressed up for a half a lager and black. Nowadays, many of the pubs shut on a Sunday. It's still mild outside in this most Indian of summers.

Oi, Marge interrupts. Warm the bed up for meh while I go for a pee.

Obediently, I walk over to the bedroom, undress, and get into bed on crisp white sheets. Marge's place is average at best and sometimes, when she's on one, (the booze, the dope, the men), it can be a real shit pit, but I have never seen Marge's bed unmade and there are always ironed, virgin white Egyptian cotton sheets. I luxuriate in them. Marge is next to me, wearing her red G-string. She is burying her head into my shoulder and her arm lies across my chest like an anchor, a comforting weight.

(Chloe)

Briefly, inevitably, Marge's jewelled and pale hand travels down my belly and tries to manipulate matters and I allow it to happen, enjoying the feel of her delicate palm…but…but…(oh no)…as usual…it doesn't work…

It's been weeks now.

Ever since I took

(what she does)

the driving job.

(Chloe)

At one time, I'd come visit Marge on a Saturday and we wouldn't get out of bed till Tuesday, except to go to the pub or the Indian. Every position, every room in the house – and I've known her twenty years, so don't believe that bollocks about new being better. I think if she married some geezer I'd still sneak round like this. I'd make sure she married a lorry driver or something, one of those overnight ones. It's a love thing for Marge, I always think (and maybe it is for me, too), so my currently recalcitrant babymaker stays *(Chloe)* on strike, flaccid and pathetic, the anxiety as a result starting to rampage around my head like the Ebola virus through a river village with each stroke of her hand. Realising what's going on, she kisses my shoulder and holds me close to her and I am relieved.

This is what I am here for, to chill out and relax, get rid of the horrors of the weekend.

I wonder what Chloe is doing for the last time that night.

I hear Marge's breathing begin to slow and deepen, like a desert wind on my neck, and I follow her into the deepest of sleeps.

The ringtone of my mobile wakes me up at eight. Marge is still asleep, now with her back to me. I reach over to the bedside table and pick it up. With an uncomfortable start, I see it is Chloe. I answer.

Morning, mate, she says.

Chloe, I reply, yawning and wishing I could go back to sleep. I have never been a morning person. It isn't in me. Those people who run ten miles before breakfast have my admiration. Give me the night anytime.

She gets straight to the point.

Take me on a trip tonight?

Where? I sit up and prop myself on the pillow.

This is the only time I ever really want a cigarette, the first one of the day. When you quit, you are only ever giving up one cigarette – the first one and the best. Marge stirs. I put my free hand on her shoulder and silently, she moves into me with her behind.

Leicester. Are you up for it? I know it's kinda a long journey.

Leicester's not far, I say.

I've, like, never been. Is it nice?

It's like everywhere else.

Good. It's an interesting job…Neville…

(arsehole)

…called me up first thing, which is, like, kinda unusual, but it's awesome money and if you can take me, we'll be quids in. Only trouble is it's an all-nighter. You'll be, like, in the car for hours.

Okay, I reply. I don't mind that.

How much?

She gives me a figure. It's considerable. Part of me wants to say no because of Neville *(twat)* and I don't like Leicester, but I can't turn down the money. I get a share for the driving – and the implicit assurance of security that comes with it.

I don't want to go to Leicester. I've got bad memories of that train station, that time we were ambushed by the Squad. Two of us were sliced up bad and I got one of the worst beatings of my football life in that subway, and we never got revenge back at our place. How could we? Thousands of Leicester zombies. *One nil Gary Lineker, you zombie bastard.* It's a tough drive too – I would need the satnav and I hate those. Man should be able to navigate. It's in the genes. But there's no excuse for saying no, in the end. I might take Marge out for dinner with the proceeds, if I can get the pointless notions

I have about Chloe out of my mind for a few hours.

Count me in, I say.

Awesome, Chloe replies. Mine at eight. Where are you? Your lights were off last night.

I look at Marge's slender back and stroke it.

I'm at a friend's place.

There's a brief silence and I know Chloe is grinning. A friend, huh. Well, I'll see you tonight, mate.

Okay.

Loveya Terry, she says mischievously, sending my stomach into a cartwheel routine, and with that, she puts the phone down and its only now I see that Marge has been listening all the time.

Women, huh.

A woman can lead three lives and a man would never know the first, but women can spot the changing wind ten minutes before it happens. It's that's seventh sense. No wonder they're all fucking each other nowadays.

Chloe? What did she want?

Work tonight.

Brilliant, she says, and gets straight out of bed into her dressing gown.

Cuppa, she asks, without looking at me.

No sugar, I reply.

Even though there's nothing between Marge and me, nothing on paper, no rings, no commitments, and I'm not the only bloke who shares these pristine white sheets, I know she's pissed off and maybe I should have let the phone ring. I'm stupid.

Always have been.

Should make an honest woman of Marge, I think as the nicitinous afterburn of her first cigarette of the day travels like a silvered ghost along the ceiling and into the bedroom.

And then once more, I think of Chloe.

Syzygy

As I always do, recently, at moments like this with a safe option facing me clear and stark like a traffic light, like a string of motorway signs.

SAFE OPTION HERE
SAVE YOURSELF
SAVE EVERYTHING

(Pointless)
(Completely, utterly pointless)
(Has there ever been anything more pointless)

Chloe.
My next door neighbour.
Twenty four. Half my age.
So attractive to me it's an effort to breathe whenever I think of her.
So beautiful she stops time in its tracks.
My employer.
Bisexual student.
Lesbian prostitute.
It's no wonder I'm fucked.

Marge and me drink our tea and I get dressed. I avoid smoking cigarettes for the seventh year in succession while she has three in a row. She talks about her brother, Dave, who is now a Major in the Engineers. Her mum is sick again, but she's having an operation on her knees so she'll be alright. Her mate Christie is pregnant again with her new fella, her sixth (four different dads – ever the optimist). Jobcentre are calling her in to sign on every week and Marge is not happy about it. I sit and listen to her and watch her foot bob up and down, recall the times I had those pearly polished toenails in my mouth. She tunes up a joint full of Devil, no tobacco, and tells me she's busy for the next few days but leaves me an in for the weekend. I tell her I might be working and she nods her understanding.

Call me, she says, looking at me with those blue eyes of hers, a brief moment of vulnerability. I lean over and kiss her lips and she returns it – she tastes of cigarette smoke, butter and mouthwash. Every part of me wants to get back into bed and lose myself in her, but I can't, I'm prevented, I'm hamstrung, and I walk out the door without looking back

It's cold out in the Lace Market.

People go to work. The tram passes by full of commuters. The sky is silver and you don't need to be a weathergirl to know the heavens will shortly open their floodgates. I pull up the collar of my coat and head to the nearest Ladbrokes for the morning dogs.

Land Of The Baby Squad

So Jaden's like, you're kidding, and I'm, like, say what? I'm telling the truth and he's, like, he really doesn't believe me and I'm, like, *totally* gone out with it. I've had the most amazing experience and Jaden's, like, thinking *I'm a liar*. I'm totes pissed off with this. Wouldn't you be? He's such an asshole.

The ghost? I reply, keeping my eye on the lorry up ahead that is subtly wavering from side to side. I wonder whether the driver has been on the bottle. It's more likely he's overlooked his tachometer and should be resting.

The road from Southwell to Leicester is a dual carriageway and I'm taking no chances, driving like a dowager on jellies on the right hand lane, a steady sixty. There are geezers overtaking on the left at a hundred, a hundred and ten, and I want to be well away from that lorry if the driver falls asleep. It's a giant truck, some vast white and blue Polish thing, on the way down to the Channel. Those drivers, paid per load, don't take much notice of the law.

Chloe leans forward.

You *do* believe me, Mr Valentine, don't you?

That you saw a ghost in the Saladin?

That's, like, what we've been talking about for the last ten minutes, dufus.

Of course I believe you, Chloe. The ghost was a lady and she was dressed in blue. You were talking to a pal on your blower and there she was.

You sound totally unconvinced, she says, coquettish, smacked arse, sitting back again. She folds her arms and if she were standing up, she would stamp her feet, I am sure.

Never been more convinced, I reply and Chloe, heartened, carries on nattering in the same vein. I slightly tune out. I've met Jaden before, a few times, a local, a friend of hers, slightly younger, up at the college. Fancies his chances of some horizontal action, but she's already told me on the QT he's in the Friendzone (like me), sadly for him, because he's got big puppy dog eyes whenever he sees her and she's aware of it and sometimes, I think, she plays on it, but then they do, don't they, women; give you a little bit with your supper and leave the rest in the pantry. Poor Jaden. He must be a real cynic not to agree with her about the ghost. If I were young, and agreeing with a woman like Chloe about some drunken hallucination in a posh pub helped remove her panties, I'd have said whatever was necessary.

So, I was like, Jaden you arsehole, have you ever seen a ghost and he's, like, they ain't no such thing as ghosts and I'm like, getting totally pissed off with him so, I'm, like, it's time for my beauty sleep and I open the door and he's like, can I come round again, and I'm like, I'm busy and I want to be friends with someone open minded, like, so come back with a new attitude, like, I so don't need friends with closed minds in my life.

For not believing in ghosts?

Mate, it was his *face*. Like, he looked at me as if I were dumb.

Okay, I say, even less convinced Jaden knows what he is doing with women. I am now at least hundred yards behind this truck, but there is a roundabout coming and I am turning right toward Oakham. I know that lorry is going to prang somewhere down the M1 and I am relieved.

Putting Jaden and the Blue Lady to one side, I ask about tonight's client.

Who? She replies.

She is wearing the Chanel black dress with black stockings and long black boots.

Her lips are crimson red and her eyes are heavily made up with mascara and shadow. Her chestnut eyes, like a cooling sun seen through smoke, cannot be dimmed and I notice them stare at me in the rear view mirror. I can feel her stare on me and the gaze goes straight down my spinal cord, upsetting my stomach and tickling my groin. Each night I drive her to work, she looks more spectacular than the last time, though I am aware that it may be something to do with my descent into an unfortunate morass of obsession rather than anything else.

She's so exquisite, you'd kill for a kiss, if that is what it took, and I know that's something I have to deal with before I go absolutely fucking crazy.

Your client.

Oh, them, she says. It's not *a* client.

What? I reply.

Try the plural. *Client-Z.* That's why the money is so good.

Explain, I say, punctilious and direct.

I'm, like, being paid for a double.

(*Choc Ice. Oh God no, please, not a...*)

A married couple. Neville...

(*Prick*)

...said they run a company that makes airliner seats and safety equipment and stuff. Like totally unawesome stuff like that, which made them millionaires. Apparently they swing and, like, the wife wants to try...

(*I don't want to hear it*)

(*no*)

(*yes you do, yes you do, yes y*).

...out her girly side. She's a lesbo virgin.

Yeh, but what about the bloke.

Him? He kinda wants to watch his wife and me, like, in action and stuff, she says, matter of factly.

A cuckold, I say.

Yes, she replies. That's what Neville said he was. Like, he said he'd pay the same as if, like, we were going to get it on and stuff, like if he was a punter. I wouldn't let him touch me, but for the amount they are paying, I'm totally up for a show. What do you think, mate?

Make sure you have your alarm handy, is my only response and Chloe can tell by the tone of my voice that I don't want to get into the practicalities. I turn down into a country lane. A mile to go. It's completely dark now.

I will do, hon, she says and begins to get ready, compact out, a little more lipstick.

If it were down to me, I'd get a proper job, Give the pop and sweeties a miss. Forget the horses, kiss Marge goodbye and marry Chloe, live happily ever after. Be the last human being she would ever go to bed with, but it isn't up to me and I'm purely the driver and onsite security. I'm nobody. I'm invisible.

Listening to her plan makes me feel even more so.

More of a nobody. Even more invisible.

I wonder whether Chloe knows this.

I wonder...

I won...

Almost from nowhere, the satnav beeps and we find ourselves swinging into the driveway of yet another country house populated by lesbian millionaires and swinging tycoons. My bowels turn to ice water. I don't want her to go and the feeling (which I have to suppress, for oh so many reasons), that I should stop her gets worse with each trip. Mandibles made of frost grip my heart and I want to be sick. I cannot guarantee I won't when she is inside, doing whatever she does with whoever is in there.

I pull up.

Seriously, I say, turning round. Set the alarm and I'm in there. Be careful.

Chloe smiles, leans forward and my heart disintegrates. You're like my dad, she replies. I love it when you get all fatherly.

Do you indeed, I reply, churning.

I'll be fine, hon, honest, so let's all think of the money, honey, she says, seconds before she gets out of the car.

I have not been invited in tonight so I am trapped in the front seat with my sandwiches, litre of orange juice, silver flask and paperback. I feel empty and cold, even though the night is temperate and the rays of moonlight amplify the impact of the floods along the gravel pathway.

I watch her walk to the door. The way she sways is hypnotic. She looks fabulous. And then, she stops, a few metres short of the front door.

Turns round.

For the first time, she glances at me from a distance and she smiles, faintly, raises her hand and waves. A tiny wave, no more than a tremor. Then, she walks toward the door, which soon swallows her, the belly of the corporate whale. I cannot see who has let her in.

I am too stunned.

We have been doing this dance for weeks. I have lost count of the number of jobs Chloe has done for the prosperous sapphos of the East Midlands entrepreneurial incorporation, but I do know she's never waved at me before and it's a key moment, one that takes a while to fade in my mind's eye and my belly feels like fairy cakes and hot chocolate at bedtime once again.

Marge calls me on the phone while I wait, staring at the lit window above, clearly the master bedroom, like some stalker. We exchange pleasantries. She tells me she has a job interview at Debenhams and I wish her luck. She talks about her sister, Elizabeth, with whom she has enjoyed lunch. Her voice is lovely. I have always like Marge's voice. It's not as creamy and husky as Chloe's but it still smoulders, still has a light, silky afterburn after each sentence. She asks me if I want to come out or a drink. I say yes and ask when. She replies at the weekend. I tell her where I am and she goes quiet on me and then she says she will ring me and hangs up. She's been doing that a lot lately, I recall, as I stare at the shadows in the master bedroom window and try not to think about Chloe.

Marge.
I should pack all this in, get a job at an agency, the Post Office, or on the line at Boots and shit. Marry her. *Marge*. Margaret. Named after the Queen's sister, apparently. Call her Margaret or Maggie or Mags and she'll walk away from you as if you had shit your boxers. Yet, Marge, she's happy with. I want to call her back but I know I've bolloxed it up because she doesn't approve of my job with Chloe.

But its not that.

Marge is no stranger to bedrooms around Nottingham and beyond and she wouldn't think twice about clearing her debts by sleeping with a rich bloke, so I guess it's something else. Some female intuition.

She's right.

Chloe. Jesus. I could no more quit this caper than…than…

Sweet Jesus Fucking Christ.

It goes quiet, the light still on upstairs.

I'm reading *Jack's Return Home*. I've reached the bit where Jack is shaken out of bed by his old pals, the gangsters sent up by his London paymasters to fetch him back, and then the **alarm goes on my phone,** a high pitched squealing. I check the clock.

Chloe has been in there for two hours.

This is the first time the alarm has sounded since I started.

Shit. I almost kick the car door open and race across the driveway.

The front door is locked…shit…and so I sprint round the side of the house to the back. The back door is locked too, but the door has glass panels and I can see the key in the lock. Immediately, the security light illuminates the rockery and I spot a hand sized rock. Picking it up, I smash the panel, clear the jagged fragments and open the door from the inside. Chloe is shouting amidst other voices and it's coming from upstairs. They couldn't have known about the alarm because they knew

I was outside. They're taking a risk…the bloke, the husband. *Twat*. I see a staircase and I ascend it two steps at a time, heart racing, familiar icy fingers grabbing hold of my sweetbreads

(Hartlepool…Luton…Brentford…Peterborough)

as they used to, my bowels loose…shitting it…oh jesus…and I hear the source, a room at the end of the corridor. As I reach it, a woman - redhead, curly, forty or so - opens the door and says *NO, it's got out of…got out of hand* with a wild look on her face, and I push her out of the way and there's Chloe curled up on the bed, naked, whimpering, and a bloke, a wiry bastard, blonde and thin, naked, meaty hard on, looking at me gormlessly *(oops)* as if he was about to get into bed for a nice nap, my appearance interrupting his sordid thoughts and inspiring a face of great surprise, especially the moment before I floor him with an exquisitely delivered (**TIMBERRRRRRRR**) punch that connects with an impact like the cracking of plastic.

Groggy, he tries to get up, but I stamp on his head, bend down on one knee and hit him again on his nose, which becomes a nasty mess.

The woman behind me is shouting at me to stop, so after one more substantial hammer blow to pacify him, his nose detonating, blood and sputum dripping onto the (lush) cream shagpile master bedroom carpet, he curls up in a ball, holding his face, tears falling like a little boy caught with his fingers in Mum's purse.

You've done it now. Can't beat up customers, she screeches, kneeling over her whimpering partner. Neville will have you, he'll have you, just you wait. He'll *have* you.

Chloe is getting dressed. She's stopped crying (tough old girl).

It doesn't look like he's raped her, but there are a couple of bruises on her back and a mark on her face. Her back is *(oh no)* scratched too but she covers it with her jacket. Quick as a flash, I pull out my digi camera and shout **oi, blondie**, and he glances instinctively, and I take a photo of him, clear as daylight. It's a superb pocket camera, a Finepix, 20mp, and blondie's rapist face is framed for eternity in the viewing screen at the back.

Bingo!

Grass us to Neville, love, and I'll visit the press with this and they will inform everyone in the East Midlands that hubby here is a rapist.

He's NOT…

I hold up the camera. Not important whether he is or not, love, I say, wiping my face clear of specks of his blood. Mud sticks in a smear and slander contest. I'll bet he's got a decent job and status, judging by the Merc outside. Might not survive the word Rape. A couple down the league table from **Nonce**. People don't like emotive words like that. Rape. Nonce. Rape. Nonce. They tend not to forget either. Rape. Nonce. Rape. Nonce. Hard words to forget, love.

What's a Nonce? she asks.

Kiddy fiddler. A Jimmy Saville. A *beast*. The worst form of humanity there is.

You won't say a thing about that, she responds, a face of pure evil, the grimace of a harpy, her fiery, crimson mane akimbo, her teeth bared. Neville *knows* folk.

I bet Neville doesn't know hubby here is a rapist. I bet Neville doesn't have *that* information on his client file.

She slows down, changes tack. She's half naked, hair all over the shop, her middle aged woman's tits drooping almost to her spready belly like enormous sacks, with huge terracotta nipples, but she's got a substantial pair of black panties on and – weirdly – a pair of thong sandals. She's no oil painting and it's hard to picture her with Chloe, who is something special.

He just…just got excited. Wanted to…

…that wasn't the deal, I cut her off. Chloe doesn't work with men. You knew that.

We'll pay…we would have. We'd paid a lot more.

OMG, I wouldn't have let him touch me for diamonds, Shirley, Chloe interrupts, putting on her shoes awkwardly, like an ostrich. I so don't work with men. I totally told you that before we started. We discussed that…

This time, the woman says nothing, pure hatred on her face. I conclude this interaction as Chloe walks to the door.

Here's where we go from here. You don't use Tiffany's again…Shirley. If I find out Neville has been informed of this unfortunate business, I'll come back up here and do a little bit of flyposting. A little bit of *brand marketing*. A proper **Blondes Have More Fun Being Rapists Marketing Campaign,** as it were. I'll have leaflets printed with his new mugshot on it. Then me and the lads will spend next Sunday afternoon dropping said sparkly leaflets through the letterbox of every house in the area. Before you know it hubby here won't be able to go to the shop without local kids whispering the word Rapist. And when some of the dads find out that they're living near a rapist? Maybe some bored old *Squaddies*...

You wouldn't, she says. You wouldn't dare...

...might accidentally on purpose spill petrol through the letterbox onto your doormat. And you've got such lovely lush carpet too. Chloe?

Yes, Terry.

Did Blondie touch you? Did he come near you?

He slapped me round the face. Kneed me in the back.

Did Shirley touch you?

No.

I take a couple of steps toward the prone husband and kick his shin. Hard. Brogues. He feels it. He won't be playing football or squash for a while, that much is obvious. I bend down conspiratorially. Be thankful your tiddler didn't make contact. Imagine what I'd have done to you then. Shirley? Let's be sensible. This ends here.

Evil bastard, the woman replies, holding her husband close to her, as he rubs his shin, still weeping uncontrollably.

Later. At home.

I flop on my bed, turn off my phone. I am too wired to sleep and too depressed to go out. The monkey I received for the Leicester horror was no comfort and I throw the money clip on the sideboard. Battering Blondie felt like a loss. I can't sleep because of the voice inside me. I reach over to the top drawer of the bedside table and take out a Temazepam. I only have one tablet left.

Omar.

I'll get Francis to call Omar. He's got the sweeties. Pricey, but you have to be in your sixties, demented and half-dead to get jellies from the GP nowadays and they're the only sweet that works. They succeed every time. Exactly what it says on the box.

A mental note is etched and a jelly disappears with the remains of a can of Tango I cracked open before

Leicester.

Bastard.

The pop is flat and I wince. The very minute the jelly disappears.

Don't need...hate Leicester...

Bast...

The other night I had a nightmare, which may or may not have been caused by the jellies (or the Doom, or the beer) and I get anxious. The dream was a bad one, but the only element I can recall now is the nuclear explosion, in still life, except deep, deep magenta, like wine and blood blended. In the dream, I was wandering the area where my Mum was born, in Basford, the old Shipstones brewery and I could see people staring into the distance. A cobalt sky, vast in a way British skies never are, extending well past the horizon into a singularity, the cosmic void. There was no wind. I watched as the vista changed and I was on top of a hill, under a bridge, well away now, as if I had walked into a vortex, a shifting time lapse. Nottingham, now a hundred miles away.

The atomic cloud: torso thin and bloody, its mushroom apex enormous, immeasurable in scale. No soaring wind, no fiery afterburn, no devastating blast. The cloud stood in the distance, part of a Still Life.

I turned and there was my son, next to me, someone I had not seen for a decade. Now a man. He didn't notice me or if he did, he had made the decision to ignore me. Marge was there, or someone who looked like her. She also stared straight ahead without engaging my attentionand I was vividly aware of the need to touch someone. To hold someone's hand, someone I loved while the city of my birth evaporated.

And there was my mother, in her turquoise headscarf, almost muslin, concealing the jet-black hair of her wondrous youth. All of us, together, in the midst of scattered others, a minute, fragmented, population I didn't know and would never know, scrutinising a photograph of the apocalypse. The unimaginable blast frozen in time, watching it all vanish into the abyss, with faces of disinterest, the erased stares of the already dead…

I awoke with a jolt which twisted my neck.

I don't want that again. I can still see that cloud in my mind's eye.

I spent that morning considering the blast, its implications, its precursors and its antecedents, but I was unable to. I put the dream down to the jellies and the recent stress of driving Chloe.

I get off the bed and strip down to my boxers, go to the bathroom and turn on the shower. I luxuriate in the (*should have killed him*) pounding, superheated jets and I watch (*battered him*) my shoulders and arms flush and sizzle (*cut him up*) in the heat. It's not hot enough (*rape*

Chloe, rapist deserved a kicking, a bad, bad kicking) and I turn it up to eight. It scalds my forehead and I grit my teeth (*you're soft, soft, soft*) but it's no good and I turn it off, towel down. I lie back on the bed and the phone rings. It's Chloe and I answer straight away, my heart doing a somersault like some sixteen year old kid with his first crush.

Thank you, Mr Valentine, she says and her voice is like the smoothest marble lathered with all the ointments in the east. The

Sultan never had a concubine who talked like Chloe.

S'okay. It's what you pay me for.

No, I mean for not *seriously* hurting him. You didn't just save me but, like, the whole situation. Your quick thinking.

I must be getting diplomatic in my old age.

There is a gap, a slight gap, almost imperceptible and I notice straight away. I wonder whether she's on her computer.

But then she says, you're not old, and yawns and I know she's in bed because I can hear her pillows ruffle.

Thanks, I reply. I feel it (*you should have fucking battered him*)...right at this very moment.

I wanted to tell you that and stuff. You were awesome.

Being complimented is not my thing and I blush slightly. Luckily, I don't have to answer because she continues. Shall we go to the Tranquility for a beer? My treat.

Without even thinking I say yeh, sure.

Awesome. We can have a natter about books and stuff.

Great, I reply, not quite believing it, not quite registering what was happening. Disconnected. Dissociating.

I like the Tranquility, she mused. Comfy and nice beer. I had a pint of that Thor's Hammer Special Edition last week.

That's lethal, I say.

Tell me about it. I was, like, well out of it after one pint.

It's point eight.

What?

Eight gravity. Lethal, especially if they've had it in the barrel for a while. It develops. Gets stronger.

Chloe ignores that bit and continues. Kinda quiet too. Good for a quiet chat. I was there last week with a couple of mates from Uni but they're all away this weekend. Except for Jaden, who is, like, well out of my good books and Brian, who I don't normally mix with without his partner, Kate. Don't know him all that well, so I don't know why I call him one of my mates. Um, besides, I want to know about what books you read. We could sit outside. In the back yard. That would be well cool.

It would be, I reply.

Yeah, she says. Is seven okay?

I'll be here. Probably sleep till then.

Me too! I'm sha...tired out. Must get some actual sleep. Laters, mate.

Part II: Valeria Messalina

The Sea of Tranquility

I'm not really a lesbian, you know, she says. Not that its, like, any of your business, nor is it an issue one way or another. I could be. I sleep with women for money. When I think about it, I spend way more time in bed with women than I do guys, and some of the women who pay me are gorgeous, I mean totally awesome. Wowohwow. And they are, like, wonderful in the sack. I could be totally queer. I don't feel as if I am. Being a lesbo doesn't complete the puzzle.

What puzzle is that, then?

The puzzle that is ME, silly, she says.

Oh okay, I reply, nonplussed.

Quite a few of my mates at Uni went lesbo, Chloe continues. Family too, like, my aunty in Brighton is a proper Terry Castle dyke. A butch type, y'know. Braces and flared jeans and stuff. Remember Jim? He came round the other week while you were waiting to pick me up.

Yes. Jim.

Gay. I know loads of gay men.

Oh.

So, like, whether I'm into girls or not shouldn't make any difference whatsoever.

No. I understand.

What I don't understand is why she is telling me this, but I simply nod. Chloe has had three pints of real ale and I suspect she is a touch merry. While I contemplate the meaning of what she's said and, more importantly, why she's telling me, and whether she is telling me the truth, I decide on a diversionary tactic. Another? I ask, standing, throwing back the foamy amber entrails of my lager.

Do you think they have more of that Constipated Duck? She replies.

I think they've run out. They had the last time.

Crap! That beer is awesome. Why don't you drink some proper ale? She asks, pointing at my pint glass.

Brings me out in boils, I reply and walk to the bar. Chloe has been sitting opposite me.

As I pass, I tell her I will buy her a pint of Bishop's Tipple and she nods, tells me she's going to the toilet. I follow her with my radar gaze. I watch her sway, her graceful movements, a modern, slender, ballerina. All curves and contours. Her hair, jet black, head tilted slightly to one side. Looking at her phone, like they all do. She doesn't walk in a hurry she ambles, monitoring her screen - and though they try to hide it, I notice a gang of five-a-side footballers Chloe's age do a double take as she walks past. One of them earlier took a long look at me. I could imagine the whispered old-enough-to-be-dad jokes.

(Come on, son. Come and have a go if you think you're hard enough).

In her paint spattered jeans, ripped and sliced in all the right places, olive green vest, visible scarlet bra straps on her freckled shoulder, gold thong sandals, toenails rendered with ornate flashes of crimson, she could be every student there has ever been, only a million times more stunning.

The pub is half empty, but there's been a rain shower so we've been sitting inside, in front of the main bar, near the fireplace. To our left, an old couple silently sipping halves of Mild. To our right, two middle-aged blokes, in spectacles, accompanied by an Airedale terrier that everyone pays homage to as they leave. In quiet moments, the youthful complement of bar staff take turns to offer the dog treats, biscuits and such. He's a fine looking dog, looked after to the nth degree. Chloe has already paid her own homage. I suspect the two blokes are gay, keeping in the swing of Chloe's revelations, but I may be wrong. It's a couple's pub, either that or a sporting and travellers rest.

I like the Tranquility.

It's a haven, as its name suggests (though, I am told, it is named after the sea on the moon). All fake walnut and fake mahogany, brass and cornices; Victorian paintings alongside Edwardian advertisements for brown sauce and snuff. Seemingly, the staff have been trained at some customer-focused boot camp to be hyper-friendly, even when faced with some of the most entitled human beings on the planet.

Case in point: Abbey serves me, blonde hair, bosomy, fresh, wearing a pair of immaculately clean black framed glasses, trendy, an energised, sunswept smile that suggests she's absolutely delighted we chose her pub to spunk away the thick end of fifty quid on a Monday night.

I order a cider and a Tipple and walk back to the table. Chloe is in the corridor on the phone. Idly, in the lamplight of the admiring stares from the five-a-side gang, she soon rejoins me and sits back down. She whispers cheers to me with those full lips of hers and I see her eyes, the same dark chestnut as the beer in front of her. I look away at the Airedale. He stares back at me. He barks and wags his tail. The two men carry on chatting away unconcerned and then Chloe puts down her phone. She doesn't tell me who the call was from, nor do I ask.

So, where were we, she says. Oh, yeh, I'm not, like, a full on lesbo. I like my men.

It's basically a game, then.

OMG no. I like sleeping with women too. Don't you, Terry?

When I get the chance, I reply, laughing, but I understand the question is rhetorical and she flies on with her discourse, occasionally sipping at her Bishops Tipple.

My service is, like, a professional service, though it's, like, awesome that I get some job satisfaction out of it! I make, like, distinctions. Work and pleasure. They don't mix. I keep them well apart and stuff. Like, I worked that out when I started the game last Christmas. With some of the women I met, I had to do it. No confusion. I'm a professional. My clients are kinda guaranteed that. They can switch off too and get their money's worth.

You switch off in case a punter falls in love with you? Like Hope did?

Basically. It happens a lot, believe me, Chloe says, nodding earnestly. I'll tell you about it sometime. I'd have told you already if you'd let me.

Okay. Yes...

It's like a mental strategy. I cut off.

And blokes?

Oh, I fall in love all the time with men, OMFG.

It's probably the genetic impulse, I say, archly.

Kinda, she replies, and glances at a newly arrived text on her phone, then continues, hardly breaking stride. I don't do business with men. Never have. Totally doesn't appeal. Way too complex and – I'm, like, giving away trade secrets here, old geezer – I absolutely have to love a man to let their *thingy* anywhere near me.

But, of course, I reply, highly amused by her unexpected candour.

Neville is always trying to get me to sleep with his male clients – like, bribing me with large sums – but no, I always say no and always will. I work with girlies and that's, like, my brand. That's who I am.

That's my trademark.

I see.

Oh *do you*, Mr Valentine, she replies, tilting her head to one side. Do you see?

Another text comes flying from cyberspace and she does that incredible thing girls do with her two thumbs and a reply has already gone by the time I come to terms with how fast she is. I take control of the conversation.

Can I ask you a question, Chloe?

Of course, mate. Ask me anything you like?

Why are you telling me this?

Chloe is momentarily taken back. I thought you'd like to know, she says.

Oh, okay.

Have we not reached this level yet, Mr Valentine, she says as she leans forward, almost accusingly.

Which level would that be, then?

Friendship. The friendship level. Like, I thought we had reached that.

I raise my glass to her. She picks up her pint and glasses are clicked.

I guess we have reached that level, Chloe, I say. How did you start?

Being an escort for girls?

Yeah. This caper us two new pals are involved in, I say.

Chloe checks surreptitiously to see if anyone is listening but, as usual, everyone is absorbed in their own personal worlds. No-one eavesdrops like they used to, not with reality shows on the TV. She takes another sip; I will have to top up her beer again and she is going to have the mother of a hangover tomorrow.

Can I sit next to you? She asks. I don't want anyone to hear this.

Without waiting for my answer, she comes over and sits on the spare seat next to me.

There's now no space between us and I can smell her. Her perfume, her skin cream, her sweat, the nicotine and tar on her fingers and clothes, her clear nail polish, her machine washed *(her sex)* skinny jeans, the ale on her breath, the retained meniscus of the shaving cream underneath her freshly-shaven armpits. Every now and again, because she is tipsy, her eyes blink subtly faster, but even with her lids down, protecting her from the wind and the rain and arrows of the night, those eyes are still more radiant than an exploding sun. It's only after a few seconds of her being next to me that I feel my heart stop still and I am in danger of dying.

So, here we go my new pal. Here is the crazy tale of, like, how I became a provider of sexual services and stuff to the female business community of the East Midlands.

And stuff, I reply, more to get my heart going again than to anything else. I sit slightly away from her. She crosses her legs and the overhanging foot bobs up and down, perfectly formed, like a glacier in an open sea, edged at one end with ten volcanoes aflame with lava and crimson fire. I resolve not to interrupt as she speaks

Why Chloe Went On The Game

On a train home last Christmas, on my way to see the folks in Rochdale, I sat next to a businesswoman. The train was rammed and I was totally lucky to get a seat. That Nottingham to Manchester train is crap, even at weekends. The businesswoman, Rebecca, was totally gorgeous, I mean OMFG, lush. Wow! About forty, straight straw-blonde hair down to her shoulders, superb business suit and high heels. Immaculately made up, blue eyes. Awesome looking woman. We get talking straight away. She's, like, local, you can tell by that accent you've all got, Terry! Anyway, after a while, she revealed she was, like, a proper lesbo. Never, like, slept with a guy after that first time when she was a kid, in an unlocked Chemistry lab, after a school disco. Decided she didn't like cock after. Anyway, after Sheffield, we're like, getting on well and out of the blue, she's like, offering me TWO GRAND to spend the night with her in a Manchester hotel. Blunt as anything.

Two grand? I say

Two grand! I mean OMFG. Well, I was, like, OMFG, and then she was, like, I'm serious, no strings attached, two grand in your handbag, cash money and I was like, OMG OMG, and she was, like, think about it, we've got three stops. I'd like to go to bed with you, if you want it. Well, Terry. At the time I was in crazy debt up to my eyeballs, and I'm like, WTF. My stomach's going over. I'd, like, never even snogged a girl before - even in a nightclub! All my friends have done that! I can't even recollect sharing a bed with a mate. I'm going bright red and I'm like, OMG, what do I do? She's, like, old enough to be my mum and I didn't want her – like, how could I? Not downstairs, if you get what I mean. In my loins...

I know what you mean, Chloe, I say, helping her out.

Awesome! Yet, I'm like, what an opportunity. And she's stunning. Not a grotbag like some of them. A proper model. It's like Christmas – Christmas at Christmas, if you know what I mean, mate. I was sorta unemployed at the time – my Mum had sent down my train fare and I was, like, sharing a flat in town with Kerry and you could tell she was after moving her weirdo of a boyfriend in. So whatever happened, I would have to move out in the new year. I couldn't even afford proper Christmas presents for my mum and dad and brother.

Some dilemma, I interrupt, captivated.

So, what do you think I said? I'm like, yeah, okay, and she's, like, oh that's lovely, and that was that. I never even told her I was a lesbo virgin! I thought I'd play it cool. So, like, I called my mum up and told her I'd see her tomorrow and Rebecca's like, thank you honey and patting my jeans, and, like, the next thing you know, I'm pussy deep in Prada and panties with one of the most successful players in Nottingham. Man, she made sure she got her money's worth, OMG.

I looked away to let her know I didn't want to go any deeper with this and she grins and giggles, but she doesn't push it. She's flowing nicely.

So next morning, Rebecca drove me to a bank, withdrew two grand and gave it to me still in the bands. She's like, Chloe, you're worth every penny, contact me when you get back to Notts, and she's, like, giving me her business card. So when I get back to Notts I call her up, go over to her place, and it's, like, **Lesbo Dawn: The Sequel.**

Great film, I say, laughing and Chloe taps me on the arm, also seeing the joke.

So, like, I spend three days straight in bed with her – she even calls in sick to her own company – and then she's like, telling me something important. You're lovely, Chloe, and there are lots of successful women like me all over the Midlands who like girls. You could make yourself a few quid and I'm like, WTF? And she's like, yeah, I could introduce you and before you know it, I'm in bed with women in Derby, in Matlock, in Sheffield, and most of all, in Nottingham, which is full of professional lesbos. OMG, it's unbelievable how many there are in Notts. All her colleagues and customers. Not all lesbos either, as you know. Some bi, some curious, some kinda straight, most married. Some had lesbo thingies when they were kids and stuff. All of them have their own money, that's, like, what they all had in common.

And because of Rebecca, I'm, like, earning a grand minimum per night, plus train tickets, a meal, a drink and tips. My debts disappeared in two months! I'm popular too, so she tells me, so its getting so I'm in need of a manager and so Rebecca – who I'm still sleeping with, like, three or four nights a week, which kinda sorted out the flatmate problem – introduces me to Neville and **Tiffany's Escorts.**

(Cu...)

I resolve to prevent my inner self having a pop every time his name is mentioned, but it's hard. It's so hard. I hate him with a passion, and I can tell Chloe knows because she tells me.

I know you don't like him, Mr Valentine. I can see it all over your face, but I need him to organise my schedule and Rebecca was, like, far too busy to do it herself. In fact, once Neville got to work, I saw less and less of Rebecca, which, like, was kinda sad. I don't talk to her at all now, which is so not cool. I miss her.

Chloe's whopping brown eyes moisten when she tells me this. I wonder whether her cheerful protestations of straightness are entirely accurate, but she swiftly moves on, as if she had overstepped the boundaries of her own revelation.

And that's that. Here we are, Mr Valentine. After that night in Grantham, I, like, needed a hand and you appeared in my life and that's totally awesome.

She raises her glass to mine and we clink again.

Me too, I say. Totally awesome.

We'll go out next week and you can tell me how you came to be my driver, she says, and then she leans over and kisses me on the cheek, before she picks up her phone.

Makes a smoking gesture with the two fingers of her right hand and scoots out of the bar much faster than she did last time.

(I'm never going to wash my face again)

I can still sense that kiss and I am momentarily stunned.

Not the arid kiss of a maiden aunt, but the luscious, wet kiss of a
(lover?)
dazzling woman.
Not the butterfly kiss of a child, but something else
Another type of kiss.
A completely different category of kiss altogether.

Tiffany's Escorts

We walk home, feeling mellow. Chloe is definitely squiffy and she holds my arm as we walk past the Burgage, where Byron used to live and where the Funfair comes twice a year. She's nattering away about Jaden and Carla, her friend who works behind the bar at the Saddlers, and about this and about that and I'm smiling, luxuriating in her voice, enjoying the lightest of her embraces, the presence of her delicate hand on the arm of my quilted jacket. It's nippy now, the moon obscured by thick cumulus clouds fast transforming into an unbroken sheet full of rain. Tonight is going to be wet, you can get a sense of it in the air.

The rain wouldn't stop Chloe though, she's off on one, gesticulating. talking ten to the dozen, the impact of four pints of five G strength real ale.

Would love a bag of chips, she states as we walk past Southwell's only chip shop.

Is that all you want?

Can I have a battered sausage too? Quite fancy one of those.

Of course, I say and we walk in, the heat hitting us. There are ten minutes to go until shutdown time and luckily, there is one battered sausage left on the tray. I'm not hungry.

When I get inside, I am going to finish off a bottle of Malt, drop a Jelly and listen to some late sixties sounds, Byrds, Crazy Horse, that kind of thing and a dinner would take the edge off the buzz. I'm chilled out, feeling wonderful, enjoying the company of a much younger woman and making each minute last for an infinity. The woman behind the counter is no stranger to the fruits of her own fryers, but she's lovely with it and she hands Chloe her bag of chips and sausage and we walk back toward Eastgate, past the quaint shops and boutiques which characterise this most prosperous of towns.

At night, in the darkness, with few people around, the lamplight coating the tarmac of the road with an amber glow, reflecting from shop windows guarding luxury stock without listed prices, accompanied by the smell of some of the most expensive Indian food on the planet at the Taj Mahal.

I feel relaxed, the only time I do in the town. Most of the time, I feel like a fish out of water here, but not at night. Not in the darkness and the cold.

Having Chloe next to me – munching her chips with a fork, still nattering, this time about what she is going to do with her degree when she gets some cash behind her (she is a BIG saver of all this money she's earning, either that or…) – completes me, even though we will never be intimate (of that I am sure), I can always hope, I can always…always…

(pretend)

that there is a sliver, a crack in the membrane of reality where we could be together,

Chloe and Terry, an invitation to the wedding, love from…just us, just us and…and…

(fantasy)

…we approach our place, slowly, my pace almost funereal, like a slow march, not wanting it to end. I notice a shadowy figure standing at the gate to the Enclave and I know instinctively who it is and so does Chloe, who finishes her chips in double quick time and throws them in a skip on the road outside one of the student lets. It's all over, all the good vibe. I feel my blood run cold and my face contort.

Neville.
Chloe's managing
(Pimp)
agent.
Six foot four, suited and booted, immaculately turned out, a
(street corner gangster)
businessman on the way up.
(property of neville)
(school bully)
Marcus Garvey Businessman of the Year 2011
(forestoldschoolforestbridgeforest)
(property of neville)
Nottingham Topic Centrespread.
(pimp)

I knew him of old and he knew me. We have history. One day, when I was a kid, Neville and three of his mates beat the shit out of me for being a Notts fan on a street behind the Boots Social Club. He stamped on my head. Sliced up my new light blue round necked Adidas tee shirt, a birthday present from my mum, and laughed while he did it.

(Area 3 Businessman of the Year 2012)

We went to school together and whenever he could, he made my life a misery.

I used to shit myself thinking of Neville Gant.

Course, that's all forgotten now.

All in the past.

(just kids)

(what do kids know!)

(forgive and forget, mate. It's all Nottingham now, innit)

Three weeks after, he smashed my eight year old brother on the head with a plank as he walked to Cub Scouts. Knocked him out and ran off. When I tried to have him back at school, he broke three of my bottom teeth with a knuckleduster his dad had given him and stamped on my head again. Smashed my glasses. Again. The cops were called but even then, I'd never talk to cops. He was eventually expelled from school – I wasn't the only geek he beat up - and I saw him every now and again round Notts on nights out. He had worked his way up. Boxing. Boxing promotion for underprivileged young men. Inner City restoration in the wake of Thatcher's riots. Grant funded business during her latter days, Heseltine money. DWP. Ethnic minority training contracts, employability, Jobclub, ethnic minority business promotion; then computer sales, PC services. He'd changed. Clever. Got baptised. Someone once said to me that he was violent at school only because he was Afro-Caribbean, because *it was important that he was able to protect himself in a racist society*.

Ironic.

At the time, I wore national health glasses, collected stamps, watched Notts and cycled to school on a racer my dad restored from a scrapyard. To this day I don't know why he beat me up. Perhaps because he could. Perhaps because of football when the Red bandwagon started to roll.

(Nottingham Forest European Cup 1977 and 1978)

Or even music. *(Northern Soul. Northern Soul. Northern Soul)*

Or perhaps it was because I was a dweeb.

(Not anymore, motherfucker)

Imagine my surprise when he turned out to be Chloe's boss. It was something of an eye-opener, but then, I doubt he publicises his role in Tiffany's Escorts in the Court and Social section of the Nottingham Topic.

I wonder what he is doing here and have not come up with an answer when we reach him. I struggle to hold back the hatred. I've changed since then. Neville knows it. He usually keeps his distance. I'm volatile, partly because of what he did to me. He probably hurt my head that time. Probably shook it up

(turned you into a nutter)

a bit, mangled the mesh. I ought to tell Chloe, but why would I bother her? Chloe breaks away from me and goes up to him and gives him a hug, something which makes me want to kill him, and then myself. I knew then that I would be taking more than one jelly later tonight, and possibly engaging in other of my usual stress relieving activities too. Neville doesn't even acknowledge me. Not that I expect him to.

Chloe, darling, we need to have a natter, he says.

Best come inside then, Hon. I'll make some coffee. We've been to the pub, haven't we, Terry?

Yeah.

Delightful. Neville replies, his voice impossibly deep. I'll pass on the coffee, but I shall take a glass of water, if I may. I have news.

After the pleasantries are done, the glasses shared, the seating arrangements made, the obligatory ignorance between Neville and me settled and normalised, Chloe sits on the arm of the chair next to Neville, which pisses me off and makes me want to do a Hungerford all over the place, every house, every pub, every takeaway to the sound of Jimi Hendrix's *Machine Gun,* but I sit there, blank faced, the night ruined.

Every now and again, Neville glares at me with those dark eyes of his. There is no love lost at all, but while we exist in different universes, everything is groovy, but when we get too close together…when our orbits collide…

Hope Calder has been in touch, darling, he says.

What does she want? Chloe replies, quietly.

I'll come straight to the point. She is having a party on Saturday night followed by brunch on Sunday morning.

All the top people are going, all Nottinghamshire's great and good. Stars of TV and media, financiers, bankers, the usual movers and shakers. By all accounts, it is going to be a huge event.

So? Chloe says.

Well, dear heart, Hope…

No. Absolutely not, Chloe interrupts, knowing what is coming.

…hear me out. I know what you said to me, darling…

I meant it too. I don't mix, like, business with pleasure and she is way over the top. I told you what she said. Crap! I told you, Neville…*I told you…*

Chloe was about to let the booze take hold and go into auto pilot, but then Neville stopped her in her tracks. *Ten grand* were the two words he used to do so and even I stopped my hatred of him for a single, internal step.

What did you say? Chloe asks, sitting back down on the arm of the sofa.

Hope Calder called and offered you ten thousand pounds to be her escort for the evening and morning this weekend, from 8pm on Saturday to 1pm on Sunday, after brunch.

He then nods at me, and I can see it is begrudging. Terry here gets two and a half grand. Little me gets a supernumerary amount for brokering the deal above and beyond the commission you pay Tiffany's, which, Hope assures me, will be paid by her instead of you, if you agree to the deal. Tiffany's will also be rewarded. She has offered to pay for ten of our girls at a grand a piece to make the guests happy, no questions asked.

And I have to do what? Chloe asks.

Simply be you, dear heart, he says, so slowly, I can barely wait for him to finish without falling asleep. Simply be you.

OMFG, Chloe says, after a while. Ten grand cash?

In advance, Neville says.

OMFG. Terry…what do you think?

It's not up to me. It all hinges on you. Ten grand is a lot of cash for sixteen hours work.

What if she gets all gooey again?

I'll be there. You've got your alarm.

You see, Neville interrupts, you've got young Terry there in your corner, he says, perhaps the most cynical, disdainful, disrespectful sentence I have ever heard in my entire life and my hackles are so up they're ripping the collar of my polo neck, but still I keep shtum.

Chloe gets up and takes a sip from her litre of bottled water. She leans on her worktops as Neville carries on.

Hope Calder is one of the richest women in the country. The family came over in the Norman invasion. Some French name, I forget. I'm told the knight who fathered the dynasty were on the same boat as the Bastard himself and I'm sure Terry will tell you that the boat with the Bastard at its helm was the single most important boat ever sailed, isn't that right, Terence?

Without those Norman boats coming over, I say, flat, without looking at him, we'd never have built an Empire and nothing would exist as it does today. No America. No Industrial Revolution. Nothing.

Well done, you! The Calders have been friends of aristocracy and politicians ever since. As a result of said patronage, her family own a good portion of prime Rutland and Leicestershire agricultural land. They own mines in eighteen different countries. They own textile factories in all the right places – Indonesia, Guatemala, Laos – with some of the lowest unit labour costs on the planet. Banking. Shipping. Minerals. Finance. Recruitment. They trade in every commodity known to man, including every precious stone you can think of. You name it, they have a finger in the pie. Money flows to them like a river, dear heart.

And Hope runs it? Chloe asked.

She's the Chairman of the Board. The eighth richest woman in the country.

She could hire anyone she wants for this weekend, Chloe says, quietly. This is, like, way too weird for me.

It appears, Chloe, she has taken a shine to you, my darling. Neville gets up and puts his half-drunk glass water on the table next to the sofa. She needs to know by lunch tomorrow. I would consider it a personal favour, Chloe my love, if you were to consider this proposal positively. My other girls – your team mates at Tiffany's - will have a delightful Christmas bonus too.

I'll let you know, Neville, she replies, not looking at him.

He walks over to her and gives her a cuddle, which she returns. My stomach goes into orbit and my head turns all weird and violent inside, but no-one would ever know.

Neville breaks away and says goodbye.

To Chloe, not to me.

Omar Jelly

The westbound tram arrives and hundreds of people swap places between carriage and platform. Not as many as there used to be before they ring-fenced the tram from the all-day travel ticket that ninety percent of Nottingham's commuting public use to travel to their hellholes in the City. I stand and read the Racing Post on the corner of the Market Square. Pike is late, but he is always late. The Indian summer is passing and the season is reverting to type, so I am wearing a scarf for the first time in months.

Last night, I slept for an hour if that. I wanted to get out of bed, get in the car, drive into town and slice Neville so bad I'd spend the next ten years in North Sea Camp. I have never hated anyone as much as I hate him and I was so wound up this morning that I called Pike and told him to contact Omar.

Need a jelly and I need it bad.

He said okay and here I am. Knocking myself out tonight is the only option. Cannot stand another night pacing up and down like that, picturing...imagining...

...hating...

...picturing...

(Chloe)

(Neville)

...hell...

...hell...

...hell...

...jellies...

...hell...

(Hug)

...hell...

I am studying the form. Redcar races today. Most of the racing they put on up there is unwatchable. The Teeside course is fundamentally a mile long straight, subject to mystifying draw biases and arcane ground variables. On the round course, a racehorse needs to be drawn low, on the rail, as the turf seems firmer there than anywhere else and centrifugal forces around the bend at the top mean that horses drawn high are forced to travel a quarter of a furlong further than the others. Most of the horses are slow and the trainers spend so much time messing around, they don't know whether they are cheating or not at any particular time, so as I'm completely wired to the mains, I fold up the paper. The chances of Pike and me being able to work out the score today in order to win a grand is remote. I want the jellies and I wish I could walk into a shop, pay my fee, and walk away with them, but buying contraband drugs – prescription or recreational – nowadays isn't as simple. It's now a social thing, particularly men our age.

Pike is walking up toward the Starbucks and he has someone with him, a tall geezer with a goatee and a long white jacket, a thin white Arab duke I am pleased to see, the ostensible purpose of my visit to town. It's Omar. He's ambling along as if he owns the city, the Sheikh of Nottingham City, land of a Thousand

Nights. Next to him, Pike is wearing a lemon yellow Adidas tracksuit, topped off by his Hackett cap. Ready as he ever is to steam into an imaginary posse of Swindon or Rochdale except those days are long gone and everyone who goes to Notts kisses and cuddles in the seats. It's not the old days. You get more aggro at the Panthers now, and Ice Hockey is a cunt's pastime for people with learning disabilities.

We shake hands in turn. Pike is upbeat. Gentlemen, rather than discuss our business in this monstrous atrocity of a British autumn day, he says, I suggest we decamp to the Magic Spoons for a swift pint, and we agree, particularly as the pub is right next to us, though I have no idea why Pike is talking like this, unless it is to impress Omar, whose swarthy, olive countenance is a picture of abundant health in comparison to our pallid complexions. The rain spits in our faces and I am glad to get inside, past the porch next to the patio dining area, past the old blokes in anoraks who smoke foul smelling roll-ups and stare at the passers-by going about their daily business. Even at ten past eleven, the place is jammed. Average age of the punters in there is fifty and with that I'm being charitable. I feel youthful. The gaff, like most Magic Spoons around the country, but particularly this one, stinks of ennui, misery, hopelessness, depression and despair. The place also smells of bacon, and ignoring the environment, I realise that my mouth is watering; I'd not eaten since yesterday. Pike knows I drink Thor's Hammer when I am in town. It's a serious, druggy, tipple that strengthens continuously in the barrel. Omar also samples the thick, amber-coloured West Country concoction. Approves the first sip.

He leads us to a table right at the back next to an old couple who look a little like old time comic couple Arthur Mullard and Queenie Watts. They sit nursing pints of session bitter, arms folded, staring into some infinite point in space. How many times in their married life have they done this? A million times.

A million times a million.

We three talk bollocks for a while – football, racing, gossip, news – and then Pike, impatient as ever cuts to the chase and addresses Omar.

Enough of this idle chat. Terry here can't sleep and he's in the market for some nice Rowntree's jelly. Can you assist my very good friend in this matter?

Indeed, I can, he replies. I happen to have several strips in my top pocket right now. Don't need them at present. I am in a delightful phase of my life, in the company of a nice local lady from West Bridgford.

Bread and Lard Island, Pike replies. Nice ladies do tend to come from Bread and Lard Island.

Yes they do, and my Cartier is helping me to sleep quite nicely, Mr Pike. I am a bad, bad sleeper usually.

Sorry, Pike says. What did you say her name was?

Cartier.

We look at him.

Cartier, Pike says. After the watch?

Are you guys taking the piss? Omar retorts, smiling.

Us? Pike says, gesturing. Heaven forbid!

That's good. Cartier is a wonderful lady and we are in love.

Anyway, one week in the summer, perhaps early July, I went three nights without sleep and I started to believe everyone was out to get me. It caused considerable problems at the University. That was it. Went to the see the doctor the very next day. He couldn't have been more understanding. Next night, I slept for fourteen hours. These tablets do the trick.

Omar speaks English with an Arabic tinge, but it's not completely Eastern. He's spent the last few years much closer east in Bristol and you can select the soft, elongated vowels as much as you can detect the essence of Cairo.

Therefore, I don't need my prescription at the moment, he continues. As you've discovered, Terry, unless you see an old family doctor who doesn't care because he's about to give up the medical caper for a life making galleons out of matchsticks, the average doc has tightened up on the distribution of jellies quite considerably.

You're not kidding, I say. Where I live, safecracking is easier.

I understand why, Omar says. Jelly can be lethal. Illegal in eight countries and restricted in fifty more.

He removes the two cartons from inside his jacket pocket. Long white boxes the size of a pen case with a light blue lid on each end. **Temazepam** written in plain black letters.

How much? I ask

To you, a pony a box.

Fuck me. Pike says. Twenty five quid?

Fifty quid the pair. It's the going rate. I've got an offer on them from a Libyan at the University. He's all right but he's always boring me with Quantum Mechanics this and Archimedes Screws that, because I made the fatal mistake of telling him I once studied engineering. Always talking about reconstructing Libya. Boring bastard! He wants me to go and work with him over there but no way will that ever happen. I hate Libyans. Camel shaggers! Fifty quid is the price, sir.

I am but a humble student and my lady and I are off to Ascot.

Yeh, okay, I say. Fifty it is.

Omar offers me his hand and I take it. He wants me to haggle but after last night, I don't need the stress. I simply want the jellies. I peel off two twenties from my roll and take a tenner from my wallet. I place the money on a stool and Omar takes it, leaving two long boxes in its wake. Standing, Omar tells us he's going to buy more drinks. He disappears to the bar with his confident swagger.

I know full well that Omar has told us a pack of lies. There's no insomnia issues. He has the inside track on a supply of contraband NHS medication from somewhere up North and he has had it for years. Every time you buy something from him, you get this Moroccan bazaar spiel and sometimes I think even he believes it. It certainly helps if the Filth pull him, not that he's taking much of a risk. Six months suspended and a sizeable fine would be my best guess at the maximum penalty and that would be for theft rather than dealing. I have never heard if Omar deals in Doom or Horse or Base or Chang or anything like that, but for all I know, he may do, as I don't know him that well. He's more Pike's friend and he's said nothing. I have no idea whether he has a girlfriend called Cartier or not.

Let's drop one, Pike says, as Omar walks to the bar.

Now? I say.

Yeh. I need to chill out.

What about the horses?

It's only Redcar.

Nah, I'd…

Tezza, stop being such a cunt. Let's get out of it. It's a horrible world we live in. When are you working again?

Friday. All weekend.

Plenty of time. Let's make a day of it. Start with a couple of jellies, all warm and toasty, have a few beers with Omar, bang a Lucky 15 on with Baldyfred, treat ourselves to a couple of KFC family feasts from Viccy Centre, and we'll go back to mine. Top it off with a can or two, roll a couple of fat ones, and watch Real Housewives of Orange County.

Francis, you know I can't.

What?

Smoke. I gave up years ago.

I'll do one without tobacco in.

Sorry, no good. You keep forgetting.

Well…how would you like some special chocolate fudge cake?

Chocolate fudge cake?

Fucking lethal, Pike says. I mean, I had half a slab the other night and I didn't come down till Sunday. I was Freddie Laker.

Cake's fine, I say, popping out four Jellies and passing two over like a croupier pushing chips towards a winning punter at the roulette table.

Pike spoons his and pretends to shake them, like dice, a little ritual of his when he takes pills, and he swallows them, concluding his pint of cider in order to fully wash them down and release the calming angels within the jelly tots. As if I had never done this before, as if I was copying my elder brother, I do the same and finish my pint too.

Omar is still at the bar, in a crush, and immediately I feel anxious that we won't have any beer for a while and then I feel anxious that the jellies will put me to sleep, which they aren't supposed to do in this context. I am confused, momentarily and wish I was over at Marge's (or Chloe's) place but I batter down the compulsion and keep the voices suppressed. Pike is grinning, his fleshy boat, all cheeks and stubble, now glowing in the artificial light of the Magic Spoons.

Then, I've got a real treat planned for later, he continues. You're going to love it, Terry. You are going to fucking adore what I have planned.

Omar is back with three pints of cider. Thor's Hammer. Each pint an oversized shard of amber crystal encased in glass.

Blimey Harriet, he says. I thought I would never get served. Who are these beasts? Whatever happened to the spirit of the British Empire, he says, rhetorically, referring to the defeated, near-dead regulars of the Magic Spoons. Pike offers a toast.

Better Times Ahead, chaps.

Better Times Ahead, I say, quietly.

Allah Is Good and Wise, Omar says and the three of us down half a pint in one.

Flash forward. Night time.

I'm on auto pilot.

A taxi, Pike nattering away like a clown entertaining kids at a party. Abuzz. Radford. A row of early twentieth century terraces. Cheap rent for the immigrants, the students and the lags on probation. Always feel nervous down this end of town, but my oldest friend is in his element. This was where he was born and raised and he knows the avenues and alleyways better than most. Here, you can buy mangoes straight off the SS Africa for a quid, Polish cheeses for a brace, and a set of dentures for less than the price of a stolen bike. The price of crippling an enemy with a paving slab is fifty quid, an assisted wank from a tart behind a skip is a tenner and drugs that keep you up for a week are easier to find than a job. This is the bipolar opposite of where I live in the sticks, where a councillor losing the nine iron from his bag in the pub is front page news. Sometimes I feel the urge to return to Nottingham so bad it leaves me bereft.

Pike is buzzing and chirpy despite half an orchard of cider and a crate's worth of Beelzebub. He calls a number on his mobile phone as we stand in the middle of the street. It's ten and quiet. I don't feel the cold and I'm scared of the darkness, but I don't let Pike know this. I'm stoned, pissed, jellied and seriously out of my comfort zone.

We're in front of a terraced house and the door opens. It's a proper English shanty house. Pike bounds two stairs at a time and I follow up three flights.

Another door. A girl answers.

Terry! She says and cuddles me.

I stare at her. *Who the...*

It's Rachel, lover. Rachel Melon. Remember?

Yeh, sure, I say.

But I don't recall her and I feel awkward and then....

Fucking hell. I DID once know Rachel Melon.

Not very well (I have hardly ever known anyone well), but she was a girlfriend of a pal of mine at the match and then she hit the party scene. Base. Yeh, Base, that was her toot of choice, what the kids call Crystal Meth now. John Portman. That was his name. Her fella. Nicked at Sheffield Wednesday in the pub up the hill behind the home end. Proper battle, six against six up and down the hill. Nil-Nil draw on and off the pitch. Good bloke, Johnny. One of the lads. Rachel devastated him. Gutted and filleted his heart. He hit the drink. Took six months to pull him round. He had all the plans. Marriage, kids, house out in Wollaton. Love in the moonlight and a triple dose of Happy Ever After. She's fifteen years younger than me. Back in the day, she was something of a looker. Nice blonde bob. Long legs. Top dresser. All the names, all the brands, a Bridlesmith Gate girl. Good teeth, welcoming smile. Keen on drum and bass, the night clubs, the downfall of many unsuspecting local girls. Dealers hovering like wasps. A little something to keep the party going? Back to my place for something special? You know the rest.

Where did she work? Um, don't remember. Proper job. Career, prospects. Johnny Portman. Then one night, she meets a dealer. In one of those cool clubs in the Lace Market, in the back streets. Populated by the Nottingham Glitterati. *St Germain* on the decks. Cool as motherfuck. Freebies and flattery. Places to be seen, people to be seen with. The first step on an inevitable continuum ending here at Crinkles, crossing broken hearts, long-forgotten kids, a season ticket to the NHS, simply terrifying domestic violence and a fifty gigabyte database of Cash Generator sex with men you probably wouldn't want sex with sober.

Some women can't get enough of drugs.

It's in their wiring. A buttress against the emptiness in their souls. They think they want excitement, sisters are doing it for themselves, but they're running away from their bad boyfriends, their bad dads, and their bad history. The void.

Why don't they SEE me?

These women should never touch drugs. Dealers spot them like vultures spot dying fawn. They're susceptible – physically and emotionally - and they always have been. Pop one anti-inflammatory for their corns and next thing you know, they're blowing plasterers in the passenger seats of transit vans for the price of a rock.

Nottingham is full of women like that.
Sex doesn't get them hot.
Drugs do.

Pike whispers to me. This is one of Crinkle's many bitches. Heyup, Rachel.

She glowers at my friend with disdain. She cuddles me. I get a whiff of her armpits and I know she's not showered for days; sharp knees and elbows, a missing tooth, left side. Hair still blonde but streaked with grey. The whites of her eyes tinged scarlet. There is nothing behind them, the portals to something no longer living.

Surfing vest (*Pipeline, the North Shore*); tight, hip chick denim shorts that cut her in half.

Five stone wet through, her body a stick drawing. Some diet. Crystal meth had knocked years off her body and added twenty years' worth of wrinkles to her face.

Missed ya, she croaks, as if she was my sister or long lost lover or something. She's trembling as she cuddles me, deeply, her arms wrapping round me like cobra babies.

Leave it, Rachel, Pike says. We're here for sweeties not one of your famous blowies, and that inspires Crinkle to shout something in a distinctive urban patois. Rachel backs off, sits down on the sofa.

I should be angry at Rachel Melon's decline, but I can't feel anything. I am completely zoned, disconnected, stoned, drunk. Three other girls in Crinkle's flat and they all look like Rachel and they're out of it, zoned out sylphs, the sirens, the fairies on the water lilies. They could be any age; pointless speculating.

Blank, detached, off and away.

Skin and bone, they look like shadows of people burned into the walls after the thermonuclear bomb destroyed Hiroshima.

Crinkle himself is skinny. In his beanie hat, with his multiple earrings, double sleeves of ink and greying goatee beard, he resembles the lead singer of a garage band.

He's no looker.

Without the drugs he supplies to these women, he'd be lucky to get a tenner reacharound in the gents from the pub slag.

Crinkle is another one of Pike's friends who I barely know, but I'm itching to be his friend tonight, I'm itching to join Crinkle's women on their rocket to another planet, in another solar system. His place is a stinking shitpit that makes mine look like the throne room at the Taj Mahal.

Have a seat, bad boys, Crinkle says. The fruit pastilles are sweet and juicy.

He gestures to the girls aggressively and they get up, sit on the floor. Pike stumbles over one of them and sits down, pulling me with him. Posters of Tupac, Fifty Cent, Jimi Hendrix and several other people I don't know, (*rappers, hip hop*), confront me on the wall opposite. Like many young men in the city, Crinkle worships black culture. In his head, he's a Rasta gangster bad mammajamma even though he's whiter than I am. There is a mirror to my right, a giant sheet of silvered glass that brings to mind a magic door into another universe. I resolve to look away from it. One of the sylphs continues to gaze into the looking glass even after Crinkle's harsh instruction. She's hideous, all scars, welts, angled bone and discoloured, misshapen teeth. A hollow wreck moulded entirely from regret. She stares at the image of herself in the mirror perhaps to make sure she still exists.

Crinkle sits on the arm of the sofa, Pike's side.

Cool. You got THE sweetie, haven't you? Pike slurs, making sure.

Crinkle grins, showing yellow teeth. If you got the coin, Doctor Doom awaits, he says, slowly and almost in a whisper.

Sweet. Hurry the fuck up, he says, peeling three magenta coloured notes from his roll.

So it begins.

Pike passes me the pipe and leans over me as I place it between my lips. I smell his breath and, for no apparent reason, his Hackett cap stimulates a drunken memory. The epic battle against Luton down the Lane, the glorious day he booted a MIG in the face, causing his hapless victim's nose to burst like a catherine wheel, painting the antediluvian bricks of the Navigation Inn like a modern art masterpiece.

Francis Pike. My oldest friend. My only living friend.

(I want Marge. I want Chloe. I am drunk and I am scared)

This is sublime. Pike says. Ain't kidding. This'll do the trick, boy. Silver, an old school hash pipe about three inches long. The bowl is a grinning skull with rubies for eyes. They used to have mesh over the top of the bowl to stop the hash rocks spilling, only this time there is no mesh because there's no sharing, no three tokes pass it on, there's one tickle of the Id for thirty quid. I watch Crinkle place the rock in the bowl wordlessly, his eyes beetroot, his teeth the colour of old newspaper interspersed with erratically displaced soot clusters. He's a relic from the zombie apocalypse happening around us daily, in the high street, an Armageddon of decline that no one can define, but is there nonetheless. The Armageddon elephant in the room. The zombie Ragnarok all around us and taking place in a high street near you.

Zuvembie. Zuvembie.

They walk! They walk!

Crinkle is the Bokor, the keeper of the Doom, the Resurrector of the near-dead, a dark Shamen who raps as he beats up his defaulters with crowbars, slices the cheeks of his enemies with a Kyocera blade he calls the Kingmaker, sells Ketamine on that corner near the Theatre Royal to pre-loading students on the way to the Ocean, and makes the sylphs beg on their bony knees for leftovers from his Wizard's sack every night of their lives.

I don't know why I'm here, in this vile pit, this inferno, this ravine of self-pity, this abyss.

But then I do. Yes, I do.

Pike is insistent, (as he always was, even when we were kids, its a nobble, it's a buzz), and he lights the Doom rock. It sizzles and crackles and gyrates and rattles, like a burning cellophane crisp packet. I draw a five second drag, watch the rock burn to nothing and it hits me, from nowhere, like a fucking hammer a HAMMER a HAMMER and I fall back onto the sofa cushions.

Rachel Melon joins me, the Doom ripping most of the synaptic junctions in my brain into tiny pieces and lies on my chest. She puts her withered, skeletal, Auschswitz arm around me and she says yeah, yeah, yeah, Doomboy, Doomboy, Doomboy, and my eyes shut and

this is
What
Angels
Must
Feel
Like
As They Ascend
To The
Golden Gates

and I put my arm round Rachel's emaciated body and she holds me tighter, squeezing every inch of the hit from the incendiary rock.

In the near distance, on a cloud somewhere, I hear Pike laugh and laugh and laugh and he lies next to me too, on my chest, kisses Melon, tongues; filthy, skinny, tragic, catastrophic Rachel Melon and I laugh too, the hit filling every inch of my body, my soul, my brain, my cock, my existence with energy and the three of us laugh and laugh and lau

Parklife

I'm going to say yes, Terry.
Okay.
To the party. I'm going to do it.
Okay.
It's business, isn't it. I can handle it.
Yeah. Okay.
What do you think? She says, punching me lightly on the upper arm. You can't say okay, silly. Please feel free to express an opinion, old geezer.
I laugh. Chloe smiles and I fall in love with her all over again. It's torture and utopia in a single fragment of time.
(My God...My God...)
It's your decision. It's your body.
Ya think? Chloe says and bashes me with her wooly hat.
I do, yeah.
Well, pardon little me for expecting, like, a deep conversation, Mr Valentine.
As I say, it's your decision. Has he been in touch?
Who?
Neville.
You really don't like him much do you. One day you will have to tell me why.
I say nothing, smile thinly.
Nope, he's not been in touch, she says, but the way she says it, I'm not sure she's telling the truth.
Okay.
He's leaving it to me. And if you say, like, okay one more time, I'm firing you and letting Jaden drive me to the party, dufus.
He couldn't give you a croggy on his bike.

Chloe laughs. Too true, mate. Besides…

…what?

She walks over and puts her arm in mine. You'll look after me if, like…

..it goes a bit pear, I interrupt.

What?

Pear. Pear shaped. South. Tits up. Wrong.

Totally. If it all goes wrong, Mr Valentine.

I thought Jaden might be a karate expert.

We're still not talking. Ass! Guess it's going to be down to my old dependable Mr Valentine, doesn't it.

It does indeed, Chloe.

We are in the park right below where we live. It's emerald green in the sunshine, but there's a nip in the air that calls for coats. Chloe is wearing her wooly hat and Uggs, almost like the first day I saw her. It's quiet. We're walking toward the old church graveyard and the flower garden behind, though there's nothing doing in the autumn – even the trees are regenerating ready for the spring. I am so confused by what's going on in my head. It's too bad. It's too weird. My head is suet pudding and my bowels are on fire. I don't know whether the drugs are helping or not, or whether they are making it worse. I don't show Chloe how I feel. I smile as she natters away, her lustrous voice soothing me like some buttery linctus.

Doom.

Jesus.

A more aptly named drug there has never been. I want more and want more of it and I'm calling Pike the minute I get home. Tonight. Need it tonight. We've got a small job on tomorrow and I'll be needed, a regular old girl Chloe sees up near Cedar Forest - a retired deputy manager of a bank whose impotent husband's tragic death led to the blossoming of her long-suppressed amazonian tendencies, but that's early doors and never more than an hour before Chloe…Chloe…finishes…you know – but then it's either the party or another weekend job. Marge wants to see me and I can fit her in on Friday no issues, and I plan to tell Chloe this.

I don't want to see Marge. I want to see Chloe again. And again, and again, but I know its madness, we're a mix of boss and employee and *(friends?)* and I'll never get what I want from her (*love*) and so

Marge is essential. I'm calling her when I get home too.

Walking in the park is Chloe's idea. Talking through the weekend. I don't know why she can't do this on the phone. Her mere presence makes my stomach fall through my arse, head like after a ride on the Waltzers at the fair.

I want her.

I can't have her.

I need her. *It kills me.*

I guess it's the other girls, she says.

What about them?

The ten other girls. The Christmas bonus. That's, like, what clinched the deal for me.

Okay, yes.

You know, I would have given anything for a grand two years ago. I couldn't buy presents for my family. That's, like, superhard, y'know.

I can imagine.

And, like, some of the girls down there have got kids. Babies. A grand will make sure those kids have a good Christmas and stuff. It's totally unawesome when you've got no money for Christmas.

Yeah, it is.

What are you doing for Christmas, Terry?

(Christmas?)

(Doom. Doom and more Doom)
(Boxing Day match cmon you pies cmon you pies)
(King George)
(Marge.)
(choc ice choc ice choc ice choc ice)
(Marge)
(one on top, one on bottom, her fevered cries)
(Doomdoomdoomdoomthehandofdoom)
(Wolverhampton. Favourites down the card to pay for the entire festivities. Henderson at Kempton. Easterby at Weth)
(Chloe, by the fire, Manga eyes, stroking her feet, dark purple toenails, box chain, watching Jimmy Tarbuck, Bruce Forsyth, Jools Holland, a gentle kiss every now and again, the glittering Christmas tree sprinkled with the spirit of the birth of baby jesus)
(warmed up kebab)

(Pike, Crinkle, Crinkle, Rachel Melon)

(this serene purpleness is the property of Crinkle property of Crinkle property of Crinkle)

(jellies, Tramadol, warmed up KFC family feast, bottle of Talisker)

(my long lost son)

(a bestwood crack den with the chaps)

(making love on the rug, tears, everlasting love, our eyes meeting, never ending love, love ending never)

***(Doom. Doom. Doom. Doom. Doom. Doom. Doom.** Buckets of it. Buckets)*

Not sure yet, Chloe. And you?

Home for a week. See Mum. I've told Neville. Christmas Eve. My mum's looking forward to seeing me. I've not been home for months. I've been such a bitch!

You've been busy, I say.

I'll be able to take home lots and lots of presents for my nieces and nephews too. Can't wait. I love giving presents. C'mon slowcoach, let's go to Pietro's for a Latte. My treat!

Can we have muffins? I ask, somewhat pathetically.

You can have two, Mr Valentine, and she holds the arm of my quilted jacket with both hands and smiles at me and I melt like an ice lolly on a beach in August.

Wayne Manor

The queue of cars outside Wayne Manor, as Chloe and me decide to call it, extend onto the road. Up ahead, stewards clad in HiVis waistcoats guide the guests into the grounds. One I recognise from last week, a meaty skinhead with piggy eyes (who is the spit moral of a Swansea bad boy I sparkoed outside the Gordon back in the day), a real dribbling troglodyte, a bouncer template, a bloke who spends his weekend nights trying to get into the flowery panties of sixteen year old chav girls in the queue for the nightclub, and/or beating the shit out of drunken strays from rural stag parties down in the big city for the weekend.

Other stewards are clearly brought in for the day. They'll be multi-tasking later when the party warms up. Trays of sweetmeats and sherry. Cubed pineapple and cheesy chunks might be thin on the ground tonight. The guest list is premium Nottinghamshire A-List. The cars are proper motors. Jags, Mercs, Range Rovers. Up ahead, I see what I think is a McClaren. I'm briefly envious. I've always a decent motor. It's throwing it down with rain, but it's not winter rain, it's warm still, for autumn, and it's not turning the fields into mush. I don't need to amp the windscreen wipers.

I've got a brolley in the back, if needs be, to keep Chloe dry. We are six or seven cars back, but Conn walks over, as if from nowhere, submerged under a brolley, like a giant upturned oystershell, all in black, and I wind my window down.

He tells me to pull out and follow him. I break from the queue and follow him to the gate. The face of the driver behind us is a picture, some grey haired bloke who could be the twin of Bob Holness. He's not a happy bunny. I'll have a T please, Bob. There is a second channel with no queue, and Conn gestures us down there.

VIP treatment, Mr Valentine, Chloe says.

Seems like it.

It must be love, huh.

Or all that dough she's forking out.

That Conn…he IS a bit…

Don't, Chloe. Just don't.

OMG, you old geezer! Anyone would think you were jealous!

Me?

Yes, you.

Nah, not me.

Are you jealous? She whispers conspiratorially with a grin on her face.

Let's stick with business, shall we, I reply, embarrassed.

Chloe smiles. She's in fine form. She must be because she's been nattering all the way down. She's wearing a dark raincoat which covers her party dress.

I watched her dress earlier. The party has a roman theme and Neville had sent up a package of clothes for Chloe; a toga, with a headdress made of a lattice of palm leaves and strappy gold thong sandals. The skirt of her toga barely reaches her thighs. *I look like a total slag, Terry. OMFG, what would my mother say about this. Crap! I may as well go to the party in my scanties and stuff,* she said. I avoided looking at her as I calmed her down, told her to think of the money. I could hardly bear to look at her. Especially her feet, which, like her fingernails were painted the darkest of purples, like black grape. On the third toe of her left foot, a silver toe ring sparkled. Her hair, black as night, reflected the light from the bulb above her and her make-up was perfectly applied. Her Manga eyes, her crimson lips caressing the khaki filter tip of her cigarette as she smoked. *I'm like beginning to regret this,* she says. *I'll bet the whole party will be gross. And Hope's going to be slobbering all over me like a lovesick grandma. You should have stopped me. Mate, I'm SO blaming you for this,* she said as she dressed.

We park up in the car park outside. There are already thirty or forty cars there and it's only seven fifteen. I make sure I park where we can make a fast exit if necessary, nearest the fence (even if we get blocked in we can break through the light wooden fence and race across the fields toward the south side of the road we came in on). I ask Chloe to pass the umbrella and she does. Then I leave the car and walk round to where she's sitting, open the door and let her out. She smiles at me.

You will look after me tonight, Mr Valentine, won't you, she asks?

Of course. That's what you pay me for.

Don't let me do anything stupid. Keep an eye on me.

Okay.

Thanks, mate.

You're welcome.

Then she does something that knocks my head off. She gets up on tiptoes and she kisses me on the cheek again. She did this in the pub and I can't get my head round it. I smile, try to retain the essence of the brief meeting of her soft lips and my dry skin, and arm in arm, we walk toward the main door through a red roped partition, like one of those film premiere entrances in Hollywood. Hope Calder hasn't missed a trick. There's a concierge who resembles a Ghanaian game show host, all tux and fake smiles up ahead and he books us in and then a man appears from behind the concierge and takes my brolley and our coats. I look at Chloe and for the first time ever, she seems nervous.

Bless her. *Bless her.*

I want to turn back and take her home, but then the look of anxiety passes and she begins to smile. She whispers to me that she will think of the money and asks me once again to look after her. There is classical music and it sounds live, a string quartet, all violins.

Conn appears, this time without the umbrella.

Miss, I've come to collect you.

Yes.

Ma'am has been awaiting your arrival. I'll take you.

Cool, she says, not meaning it at all.

Hang on, what do I do? I ask.

You can watch the party with the rest of us. I'll meet you in the billiards room, Squire. Tell you the rules.

Will I have rules to follow? Chloe asks.

Miss is a guest, Conn responds. There are no rules for the guests. Only the help, as ma'am says. Follow me.

Chloe leans into me. I can sense her breath on my cheek.

Laters, Terry. Don't eat all the biscuits.

Conn escorts her up the stairs to Hope's suite. I cross my fingers and I am soon on the clock. Ignoring Conn's instruction, I explore the early stages of the party. Most of the doors to the rooms are open and I wander in and out largely unnoticed. There seems to be no central gathering. Each room has a waiter popping in an out with trays full of drinks or food. I was correct about the sausages on sticks. The music – the source of which I had yet to discover – is being piped into each room, bright, breezy classical music. Guests chat and laugh. So far, so party. Everyone is wearing a toga. Not the same toga, like some multi-cellular entity, but togas, in plural. The clothes vary in size and in colour, except, I quickly notice, for the women, who all wear pristine white. There are many that are the colour of twenty pound notes and there are a few which are jet black, like Chloe's business costume. I briefly wonder what this diversity means, but it escapes me. The masks they wear vary too, in colour and in size, some half face, others, eyes only, but they all obscure the eyes of the wearer, and the beholder, for that matter. It would be hard to recognise anyone here.

What did Neville say? Nottinghamshire's great and good. Councillors, MPS, top coppers, businesswomen, the judiciary, oligarchs, architects, solicitors, media figures, advertising gurus, marketing analysts. Entrepreneurs. Thatcher and Blair's children. The nouveau riche. Then there would be the landowners and their wives and daughters, the estate agency barons and the property moguls who rebuilt the centre of the City. Mall owners. The BBC would be here, the Tobys and the Natalies, the sons and daughters of middle class careerists subsidised by the license fees of terrified one-parent families in Lenton. There's serious money here. I can smell it, and it temporarily makes my guts turn over. The whole place stinks of cash, of decisions, of self-interest, of colossal hypocrisy and narcissism. I'll never get my hands on a tiny percentage of what these people are worth. I have always hated the rich for precisely the reasons they love themselves. If I had been a little bit luckier, it could have been me, but I doubt it. Too much integrity. Never met anyone rich who had integrity.

I walk out into the hallway and I immediately see Sir John Calder's portrait. I walk over and stare at it. His eyes burn into me and I laugh inside.

Times haven't changed since the Restoration, have they, Sir John.

(It's the way things are meant to be, Mr Valentine)

The Norman Conquest. Feudalism.

Calder's eyes are Norman eyes, the eyes of the rake and the pillager.

(It has always been the same and it always will be).

Nothing's changed. The Normans: Slayers. Invaders. Feudalists. Tyrants.

(The rich fiddle, while the poor burn, Mr Valentine. Twas it ever thus.)

Conn's men, at least one in each room, in tuxedos and black brogues and bow ties, merge into the background slightly underneath the level of perception. They are maskless, but for the type of people here, they won't need a mask anyway. The women might meet them on a girl's night out in Browns or in the Lace Market, a bit of rough, a change from the whimpering, flaccid, once-a-fortnight hubby looking after the kids back home, the same dick, the same moves; they may even fuck the better looking ones after a few too many gin and tonics, but they certainly won't interact. They're merely the help. It makes me sympathetic to the Cause, and then I tell myself that most of Conn's troops are bound to be arseholes, bouncers and ex-hooligans who probably support football teams I hate, so I put the class war politics on the back burner.

I do my best to merge.

I am alone, a separate entity tolerated, not invited by anyone except Chloe.

I check my phone occasionally for the alarm status. No sign. No news is good news. I wonder what's going on upstairs and…and…I go into the billiard room and wait. It's empty. I pick up a cue and lay out the three balls and begin to play in order to pass the time.

I am desperate for a drink, but something about working for Chloe makes me slam on that brake pedal. I don't even think about Doom or any of the other stuff I've been taking lately. The sweeties. The midget gems. The sherbert lemons I started taking after the football fighting ended. The confectionery we all started taking to fill the void, though nothing could ever fill the excitement gap of a good twenty on twenty football fight in the street. Not drugs, sex or the birth of a child. Nothing. There is nothing to beat it. After a punch up like that, a life like that, every Saturday afternoon, everything that comes after is a film made in black and white and with a soundtrack made purely of silence. All that's left is a shard of crystal rock in a skull encrusted pipe.

Some of the boys kept the day out going. The boozing, the day out. *Haxford, Nick, Chas The Mod, Swifty, Beech, Clifton Tom, the TITS gang, Eddy S, Dave W, Jules, Preece,* some of the old ARA lads, but mostly, the bad boys went away, left it to the young NYC lot to behave badly. The coppers. Well on top now. Boozing was never enough for me. The beer was fuel. Energy, petrol, not an end in itself.

I needed more. I *need* more.
I need sex.
I need violence.
I need fucking DOOM.

I don't know about the aftereffects. Don't think about it. If I do, it's in the abstract and I feel no pain or irritation.

No addiction. No comedown.

At least none I'm aware of.

Unless of course I'm permanently addicted to the buzz.

I'm so chilled that I wish Conn was here, an opponent, an opposition, though the last time we played I took a colossal beating.

Every now and again the door will open. Always an accident – party guests lost – and none of them even bother to say excuse me. I can still hear the music and I warm to it as I relax, canon, glance and drive to my heart's content on the billiards table.

Then, after half an hour or so, the music stops and I hear footsteps outside. I hear shuffling and some applause. I leave my cue across the corner of the table and I go outside. The guests are lined up along the wall of the hallway and they are staring at the stairs. Lined up along the stairs are Conn's men. There is a hush in the air. The guests speak only in whispers. The portraits observe too, even Sir John Calder ceases his sneer and attends.

Something is about to happen and I know what it is.

The music began once more and at the top of the stairs, out of my eye shot, I hear movement. I walk past the guests who all begin to applaud. They don't notice me, but a meathead does, one of Conn's gang, and he gestures to me to get out of the way. I glare at him and then, when I have a decent view I lean against a wall and watch as Hope and Chloe walk down the stairs, holding hands.

(Jesus)

Chloe is wearing a purple and gold cat mask which covers half her face so I cannot see what she is thinking.

Hope sports an Imperial Purple full length dress and her blonde hair piled high in ringlets.

She is unmasked (*of course she is*) and surveys the assembled throng, now easily a hundred and fifty to two hundred strong. They are applauding gently, nothing excessive. Chloe wears her white toga – not even she, the Empress's Consort – escapes the vanity of

(Valeria Messalina)

the Roman party's hostess.

(*of course – who else could she be!*)

The two of them glide effortlessly downstairs. If I were one of the guests, I'd want to know the story with the girl with the hair as dark as night and cherry red lips. No one would know she was bought and paid for except Conn's men…unless…unless they all knew and it was like some sort of…some…sort of joke.

(Chloe)

(Messalina)

Hope stands three steps down, still holding Chloe's hand. She addresses the togaed throng.

Thank you all for coming, my friends. I am delighted you could make it. I'd like to introduce you to Katie…(*applause*)…who is with me, so we will come round to chat and say hello. But before that, I want you to know that my house is yours and all that is in it. Food will be served in the dining room shortly and I want you all to dance and dance and dance the night away with us. So please, let us make this the best night of the year. Eat, drink, make merry. Love you all…

I'm too far away from Chloe to see what she is thinking but she's safe with all these people (and me) and I work it all out in a second and I wonder whether Neville knew about this.

Whether he knew the plan.

Ten grand for someone's love.

Not sex.
(Chloe)
Love.
(she fell hard, like you)
Nineteen hours
(you'd pay it, if you had the bread)
of pleasure
(you'd pay double that for one night with Chloe. Treble)
a party
(Valeria Messalina)
 a gathering of friends
(empress, whore, cuckolder, poisoner, plotter, murderer)
the reflected glory of fledgling beauty
(I, Claudius)
(you'd chop off a leg for one kiss)
a ten grand night that would last forever.

I notice lots of single girls around the place, attractive, much younger than most of the guests, and I guess they are Neville's geishas on a grand a piece. A terrific night's work. They deserve it.

A story from when I was a kid comes back to me. Messalina, who was a nymphomaniac according to the biographers and historians of the time, was so driven by sex that she challenged the most popular prostitute in Rome to a duel, to see who could sleep with the most men from nightfall to sunrise.
The Empress won with twenty four.

There doesn't look to be many single blokes here, though it's hard to tell who's who when everyone is wearing masks. And rich people tend to hunt in pairs, that's one thing I have learned, Mr and Mrs Peabody, Mr and Mrs Getty, Mr and Mrs Singh, so the girls must be decoration.
If it weren't for Chloe I might have had a chat, especially with a blonde by the staircase who is similar to Amy Smart out of *Crank: High Voltage,* (the sequel, where she's got some size on her, like Marge), and who looks like she could be the feature attraction at a sex amusement park, but I'm a pro and I'm on the job.

I can't understand this thing I have about Chloe.

I usually go for blondes. Marge is blonde. Zoe was a blonde, Nat was a blonde, and they all left me bleeding black, but this Chloe thing...this...thing...

No.

In a train, the entire party heads for the ballroom, which is right at the back of the house. I join in, so far uncharted territory, southbound, past the billiards room. It's a vast place, Wayne Manor, and the ballroom is a cavernous theatre; laminated, mahoganied, enchanderliered, becandled. Rather than a string quartet or an orchestra, modern music is piped in from somewhere.

The assemblage begins to boogie.

It's Motown or something like that, Gloria Gaynor, Diana Ross, school disco stuff, and the atmosphere starts to heat. I stand at the back and let everyone get on with it. I sip a glass of lemonade but wish I could risk something stronger.

My employer and the girls from Tiffany's are the youngest there and they form a dancing core at the centre of the dancing complex, even though this music is straight out of their parent's – maybe even grandparent's – record collections. They look good. Easily the best there. Proper dancers with rhythm and rhyme, a lack of self-consciousness. They've been briefed. I watch a couple of them grab hold of a couple of gents, who may be the single ones, and they don't miss the opportunity to boogie with girls half their age. I wouldn't either. I watch Chloe and Hope dance. Hope is not wearing a mask and the look of joy on her face is both uplifting and sinister, if you know the story. She's not a bad dancer, engaging with the beat and matching Chloe twirl for twirl, move for move. There's something dark about Hope, but at this moment, she is all light and effervescence and when Caesar's Empress parties, so does everyone else. They play *You Sexy Thing* by Hot Chocolate, then *Rhythm of the Night*, then *Can You Handle It*, then *Tracks of My Tears* and *Midas Touch* (ping) with each song, more people bop until there is just me and Conn's army watching on from the terraces.

At the point where I am tapping my feet, enjoying the spectacle of the masked romans dancing, Conn appears on my shoulder.

Quick game? He asks, all (*Hammers, QPR, Brentford, Charlton*) London charm and (*dishiness)* disguised efficiency. I nod at Chloe and he follows it up with, oh, she'll be fine, she's captured Ma'am's strawberry good and proper, and he says it in such a way, with his body positioned at such an angle, that it is no longer a friendly request. I aver and follow him to the billiard's room, the upbeat feminine defiance of *I Will Survive* fading into memory.

We walk past two of his men.

Do you know, Kipper? Conn says, standing in front of a bloke who is as wide as I am tall and with heavy lidded eyes plus an ill-fitting bow tie.

I can't say that I do.

He's Forest, is Kipper, aren't you, chap?

Kipper nods. He hasn't taken his eyes off me once. His face is a magnum opus of silence and stillness. His arms by his sides, his belly ample.

Recently finished a stretch in Lincoln, haven't you, Kipper. A little bit of a disagreement up at Chesterfield in 2007. Promotion season for you Trickies?

I'm Notts, I say, firmly and immediately.

County? Notts County? I thought it was all Reds in Nottingham. I thought Notts were all old men?

I'm Notts, I repeat. Conn's treading on thin ice and I struggle to stay relaxed, but as fast as he got us into the problem, Conn gets us out.

Oh. You won't know Kipper then, will you! Carry on, Kipper. Conn says.

Kipper doesn't reply. He doesn't even break his blink pattern. He's not meant to. This little vignette is for my benefit. I know he knows I'm Notts. I know he knows I've been down for a stretch. This is Conn talking in Man Code using Kipper as a tool. Only, he's made it clear that I'm the tool. *You follow a shit team and you've been completely disrespected, you Northern woolyback.*

I'm not sure Kipper's in on the joke. He probably is.

Hope Calder's
(Valeria Messalina)
urbane Man of Business has pulled a trigger with me – people always take the piss out of Notts, because there aren't many of us and we're overshadowed by Reds – but I keep the resentment under my Tux.

Pike would probably have planted everyone in sight.

In the billiards room, now hot through an open fire crackling away, he pulls out the three balls and breaks off without asking for a toss. I watch as the balls start to ebb and flow on the immaculate bottle green baize. Again, as time passes, I find my periods at the table tend to be brief. It's a practice match for my opponent, who clearly knows his way around the table. He's probably semi pro. I dread to think what he would do to me at snooker. We don't say much, a few generalities and then, at the end of a three hundred and fifty break, he smiles at me.

The door opens too, simultaneously. It's Kipper and another bloke who looks like Kipper and

(but then, most of them look like Kipper, they always do; it's like an outtake from Being John Malkovich *only with people who look like Kipper, all heads and shoulders and tuxedos and eyes like pissholes in the snow)*

they take their positions on either side of the door.

Now then. We need a word, Conn says, putting his cue away.

I retain mine. This could get tasty (*Jolly Colliers*, Rotherham, *Pack Horse*, Bury), and while I have been on the clock, I had always hoped that was going to end amicably. It's unlikely that I can take three of them, but I could blind one of them and damage the other before Conn takes me out. Inside my jacket I have a Stanley, lubricated, with an unused blade and I could probably do some damage to Conn, but I don't fancy my chances.

Okay, I say, with a subtle ambivalence.

It's about Miss Chloe.

My employer.

Yes. Your employer. My employer has taken something of a shine to your employer.

Has she now. Taken a shine to my employer.

Indeed she has. Ma'am is enamoured. Her strawberry is proper crushed.

Yes, I know. My employer mentioned it.

Now, I couldn't give a monkey's about my employer's tastes. I've been with her for seven years now and I've seen them come and go. The ladies – always the ladies; ma'am has always worn the sensible shoes, if you get my meaning. However, his is the first time I've seen her like this. Genuinely. It did my surprise ducts up like a kipper, no pun intended. She can't sleep, she can't eat. She can't stop thinking about Miss Chloe.

Okay.

I think she's in love, Squire. Have you ever been in love?

(Zoe. Nat, Marge...Chl)

I don't reply. I don't need to.

You know how it is, then. How incomparable it is – and how painful it is when it goes tits up.

The other day, Ma'am didn't get out of bed all day. Devastated, she was. After their tiff. The last time Miss was 'ere. Totally broken, she was. You recall how that is, Squire. You recall how that works.

Again, I don't reply.

Now, Miss Chloe is a kid and yet to understand all this malarkey, all the affairs of the heart, I would imagine, but Ma'am thinks that if...certain conditions were met, your employer might perceive the situation her way.

Conditions? I say.

My apologies for being blunt Squire, but the first condition would be that ma'am would like you to leave. Right now.

Oh yes?

Clear the path, as it were. You'll get your five monkeys, no bother. Miss Chloe can stay a little bit longer and the two lovebirds can get to know each other better. You know. *Love Story*, a walk in the grounds on an autumn day, a visit to the Bookshop on the Corner, a glass of champagne by the fire, just the two of them. Threes a crowd. You understand that.

And Chloe? I reply. I'm employed to look after her. She's not going to agree to this.

Conn grinned, that supercilious, arrogant grin, the one he had on his face earlier, with Kipper and the Forest thing. His cockney patter was starting to get on my nerves. He was coming across like a proper badman. His words measured and planned. I show him nothing. Lean against the wall with the cue in my hand.

She's won't know you've gone. You can explain all that later. Some medical emergency. Some issue with your mother. An unavoidable problem with the pets. You, Kipper and Mister Finch here are going to put on your hats and coats, walk out into the car park, get in your motor, go for a quiet pint in the Feathers down the road and talk about the good old days at the City Ground and we'll all live happy ever after. Don't worry about the boys. I'll send a car for them in about an hour.

Conn? I say.

What?

I'm Notts. I keep telling you.

His mask slips - as cockney masks tend to when confronted.

As if I give a fuck. You could follow the smell of your own shit, for all I care. All northern cunts are the same to me. And your clubs. Forest. Notts. I have no idea and no one else does either. What league are you all in? The Vauxhall Conference? The Beazer Homes league? What?

I ignore him – he's not the only supercilious West Ham fan to have given me this shit over time - but my grin matches his. If I were a cockney, I'd definitely be Milwall rather than an Iron. I grip hold of the cue a little tighter. There's one thing, I say.

What's that?

You've forgotten about Tiffany's. She's a paid employee. You've paid till tomorrow then she has to go, whether I'm here or not. It's not a choice she can make.

Laughter erupts all-round the room. Even the impassive, gimlet looks on the faces of the bouncer sentinels break a little. Kipper, in particular, laughs audibly, a deep bassoon laugh, almost a growl. I grip the cue even tighter.

You don't think we'd be going through this little embarrassment if we hadn't discussed the matter with your *employer's employer*, do you? When we mentioned it to him, he says, yeh whatever.

The laughter increased.

Whatever? He said that? I comment.

Like a teenager. *Yeh whatever.* That's what Neville said. The implicit assumption being that I don't give a fuck what you do as long as I get paid.

Okay, I reply. Conn's laughing and on a roll.

But what nifty Neville doesn't know is that, the plan is, Chloe can move into the Manor and we'll never see that pompous black cunt again and he definitely won't be getting another shilling from my employer. He definitely won't get an invite to the wedding.

He'd grass you, I say. He'd go to the papers.

Are you crackers? He's a businessman. He's got thirty other girls working for him – ten of which are outside at the disco. Why would he balls it up like that? And what crime, exactly? What exactly would he grass? You're not thinking, Squire. Do you know what he said when I told him what I planned to say to you?

I can imagine, but tell me.

He said...

...Conn is playing to the audience now. Kipper and Finch are chortling along as if they had been told the world's funniest joke. He keeps glancing at them...he said...and I quote...*Valentine?* I don't give a fuck about *Valentine,* dear boy. Feel free to...get this...separate the cunt's balls from his midriff and leave him bleeding in a ditch. Now that's not nice, County, is it? That's not nice at all. Feel free! Who says that nowadays?

I've no idea, I say, noting that he's calling me County now, proving me right. The laughter subsides a little to be replaced by silence. They all stare at me. There isn't a lot I can do, but I figure they won't want a fuss, not with all these guests, the great and the good. They won't want to see me being dragged out of here. They won't want a fight. They're gambling.

They expect me to agree.

Conn expects me to walk out quietly and easily.

I don't know where he gets this idea from.

So what's it to be? Conn says.

If I don't agree?

Oh, don't be so loopy, County. Just fuck off. Your employer will be fine. Leave. Be a good boy.

Conn? I say standing up straight.

What?

You know I can't do that.

Oh.

You've always known it. Stop wasting time.

Conn nods subtly. I know, County. You're right. I've just wasted an hour of my life. Kipper?

He nods, a non-verbal instruction, and the muscle walks towards me.

This is going to hurt. I tense, pick up the cue, and hold it longways, plan my strategy. *Smash Kipper over the head and slash his bumchum down a fat cheek. Fountain of plasma. Gives me a few seconds. Need to get out of the door and into the main party where the guests are.*

Then, Kipper pulls a cosh out of his pocket and Finch reaches for...*oh shit, a claw hammer*...this IS going to hurt...I think about running, jumping through the window, walk backwards, those hard faces the last thing I see and, as I am about to reach into my jacket pocket for my Stanley, the door opens, loudly, with a bang.

Chloe.

She seems drunk, swaying. Kipper and Finch obscure their weapons and Conn stands to attention. She skips straights to me.

(in that toga. Jesus)

I've been looking for you everywhere, old geezer. Come and dance! Stop playing this silly snooker game. Your oldie music's on outside. And bring your pals. OMG, this is a *totally awesome* party!!

I put down the cue, turn to Conn.

Cheers for the game, West Ham.

You're welcome, County.

Better luck next time.

He grins back and nods. What else can he say? After all, the night has yet to begin.

Hot Stuff

Chloe grabs me by the hand and we almost skip into the ballroom. The music is pounding and the ballroom is packed, a giant rectangle of hardwood and polish underneath three magnificent mirror balls reflecting every inch of light from below, plus intermittent, rotating floodlights of every colour of the rainbow.

Effortlessly, Chloe guides me through a sea of dancing people, sweat and perfume and she's grooving to the beat. *Car Wash* by Rose Royce, from school discos as a kid. Dry ice filters through like the spray of a geyser and before you know it, we are in fog.

Before it happens, I see Hope. Dancing with a bloke who, judging by his hair, may be from the East Midlands News, definitely some media type, with a mullet haircut fashionable when he was still on the way up.

The whole place buzzes.

I'm still hyper from my near beating. Relieved.

I can't dance. I haven't done this in years. I've got the rhythm of a ten ton truck. I was definitely the type to stand at the bar with the chaps talking football until ten to two and then get steamed into the handbags, tongues meeting like clashing swords. (*Turners,* Mapperley Top). The old ways, before blokes were forced to dance because of the new competition. We get to the nucleus of the dancefloor and the music changes. I recognise it and Chloe, who approves of the music shift, moves into overdrive. Donna Summer. More school disco music. The only time I ever used to like disco music. School discos. I do a weird shuffle, trying not to trip over my own feet and make a fool of myself, one foot in front of the other and watch Chloe. I watch her. Wide eyed.

Oh my.
Oh my.
White girl can *dance.*

I may as well not be there, which suits me. She's in the beat, her eyes closed, and her arms in the air. She twirls and I notice for the first time that she's barefoot. She may as well be naked.

Hot Stuff.
I need some Hot Stuff baby this evening.
Hot Stuff
I need some Hot Stuff baby tonight

I do something with my arms and she smiles, moves towards me and grabs me, puts her arm around me and moves her leg up and down my thighs.

Then she does something with her behind that I didn't think was anatomically possible. She doesn't stop looking at me, all lips and flashing brown Manga eyes. Her look is ecstatic and it's all I can do to stop an embarrassing reaction. Up and down my body she goes, up and down…a dancer, the queen of the dancefloor, the princess of the night

Hot Stuff.
I need some Hot Stuff baby this evening.
Hot Stuff
I need some Hot Stuff baby tonight

so hot, so supple, so mobile, I cannot take my eyes off her. She's almost dislocated. I can barely move. My mobility isn't necessary as Chloe gyrates up and down my body. I can feel her tiny panties on my thigh and she is singing as she moves as she moves up and down, simulating some hot, sugary, syrupy, oozing, steamy, enmeshment of our bodies, as if we are coated in molasses, our

Hot Stuff.
I need some Hot Stuff baby this evening.
Hot Stuff
I want some Hot Stuff baby tonight

souls the essence of decadence. This is every dance ever danced, the dance of Salome, the dance of Bathsheba, the dance of Jezebel

(what must she be like in)

puts her finger in her mouth as if she is sucking a lollipop and licks it as she slides down me, lingering, tasting it. I hardly move, can't move, paralysed. I know what she's doing. She's fucking me, fully clothed and standing up, without fucking me, some eastern thing, and I know she is a

(bad bad girl)

but then I know (*thank god for rationality*) that's what all these girls do now in the clubs nowadays, they've even got a name for it, so I keep the ego under control and my cock in my shorts and enjoy the fairground ride, watch her slide up and down my body, one hand on my shoulder for balance and one around my waist for grip, allowing her flawless, firm, pale body, in a toga, to do its thing…it's sublime and wonderful thing.

Singing to me now

wanna bring a wild man back home

about wild men and hot stuff, about what she needs and I wish she wouldn't and I wish I could dance so I could match her move for move, but actually, I'm a dirty great useless pole and she's

(wonderful)

showing me what she can do and I am hypnotized and then, the music fades

Hot Stuff.
I need some Hot Stuff baby this evening.
Hot Stuff
I want some Hot Stuff baby tonight

She pulls away, laughing, probably drunk, high on the party and I don't want her to for a second. Miraculously, as if my thought had influenced the DJ, some form of magical thinking, the music change brings on *Ain't No Stopping Us Now* and she holds me again and we sway from side to side. We talk. I take the lead in this.

Thanks.

What for?

It was getting tasty in there.

With dishy Conn?

And his merry men.

What's the problem?

Oh nothing. Tell you later. Football stuff, I lied.

You old men. Football!

Yeh. Football.

Lucky Hope was dancing with her ex and I fancied dancing with you, isn't it.

It certainly is.

She didn't mind either.

What?

Me dancing with you. I asked her whether I could.

You did?

She's the client.

And she didn't mind?

Totally not, Mr Valentine. Go find him, she said.

Seriously?

Absolutely.

Okay.

Mate, I meant what I said outside.

What?

Keep an eye on me. I've seen Hope talking to some people. I think they might have something like that Leicester thing. With Shirley.

Really? I don't think so.

Maybe you're right. I don't want anything like that.

Hope's got you bad. She's serious about you. That won't happen.

Maybe, yeh. Like, I dunno…it's a hunch. Just…just in case. Keep an eye on me.

She raises her finger to her lips. Then she lightly fingers the necklace alarm. Don't go too far away from me, old geezer. Hang on, Hope's coming.

Okay. I'll keep an eye out. Be careful.

I will be.

Hope is standing next to me.

May I cut in? She asks, and her face, while elegant, hides all sorts of pain and anguish and death.

She knows I know.

She also knows I know now what she wants from me and I detect a glint of malice in her eyes.

(The Empress)
(Empress)
(Valeria Messalina)

Conn is on the other side of me now and I wave at Chloe. Hope and she bop away as if I had never happened, as if I had never been there. I walk to the right hand side of the floor through a horde of dancing couples. The two goons are there and they don't look happy.

Conn walks in front of me

I don't suppose you are leaving.

You heard me the first time.

Conn makes a gesture, a sweeping gesture with his left arm.

Let's go back to the billiards room?

You must be crackers. Our billiards days are over.

You can't stay in here. This is for Ma'am's guests. That's the rules.

Tough shit, I say and tense up.

Now, Conn has no idea what to do. He can't cause havoc with all these people here and I'm not moving. He thinks about it for a short time and then smiles, magnanimously, being as he's been stuffed.

Enjoy the party, County. But we'll be waiting for you afterwards. And your employer isn't going anywhere.

I wink at Kipper, who isn't amused in the slightest. His gormless bumchum pal – Mister Finch - isn't either. Conn gestures to them and they walk towards the door, leaving me at the side of the dancefloor. I knew I'd be safe now until the morning, as long as I stayed near people. It was likely that more of Conn's goons would be watching me wherever I went. Which was both a good thing and bad.

Later, while Chloe and Hope are talking to some people, over drinks, in plain sight, I find myself in the corridor looking at a scale map of Wayne Manor hanging on the wall in between two nameless old portraits. It's an enormous place, extended, spreading over a hundred acres with the Manor itself at the epicentre. In case it gets heavy and we have to make a swift exit, I memorise the locations, which is easy to do.

It's a sixties ordnance-type map, so the road we came in on is there, as is the wood we passed in between it and the manor. There's a stable complex spreading to the left – I'll bet that's where Conn's army stay when they are on the job – and several old buildings. The place had probably been extended over the years, maintaining the original features. I stare at it for a good ten minutes and do my best. Then, I stopped a waiter and asked him for a tonic water, which he fetched in double quick time and after a sip, I walk back into the disco and watch Chloe. She's having a great time, in character, hanging on Hope's every word. Every now and again, Hope will put her arm around Chloe's shoulder – a gesture which could be interpreted in many ways. Defensive, protective, proprietorial. It annoys me, but its ten grand and I suppress my usual madness and carry on watching, listening to the music.

A woman, with a curvy, slender body, carrying a flute of champagne approaches me.

She is also barefoot, though her legs are not in Chloe's class. She's wearing a Victorian Plague mask, with the long beak. Shorter than me, coming up to my neck. I smell cigarettes on her and she's swaying. I keep my eye on Chloe dancing (Bee Gees, *Jive Talking*). She's having fun, in character. Plague mask is talking to me but I cannot hear a word she is saying. I lean down to hear what she has to say, but I still can't hear her, the music is so loud. Shrugging her shoulders and making a *comme ci, comme* ca gesture as she does so, she walks off and starts talking to another bloke, this time in a Red Death masque.

A bloke stands next to me, tall, wearing a simple robber's mask and he too starts to talk to me, but again, I cannot hear a word he is saying. I lean over and he repeats himself. I still cannot hear him and he walks off. Then, my stomach starts to rumble and in the blink of an eye, as if someone had left open the standpipe plugged into my guts, I start to feel woozy and weak. I could throw up. My eyes host a cascade of exploding, brightly coloured stars.

I look at the glass in front of me.

Drugged. No. No. No…

Bastard! They've drugged me.

Conn.

(Drugged)

But why? There's nothing they can do. It's too obvious to pull me out here. Daft. Daft.

I lean back against the wall. As I do so, I see Hope and Chloe begin to walk, with an entourage, out of a side exit. They are laughing and joking, nothing wrong at all. I tell my body to move, to stride forward, to follow her and I want to shout and bellow, but I cannot.

I am powerless.

The bastards have

Part III: Ping Box

The Bastards Have Drugged Me!

I stumble forward. Conn, Kipper and Finch appear from nowhere and pretend to be concerned as my head begins to pound. A woman is now in front of me, without a mask. She peers into my face and I hear the word drugs and I hear the word doctor immediately before I fall to the floor. Conn doesn't expect this and there is a crowd. I can only hear two voices though…Conn and the woman, cockney and Devon, somewhere like that, in Nottingham at a party at Wayne Manor,

He's fine, don't worry ma'am, enjoy

very sick…

we'll take him out for air. Don't worry at all.

Stop telling me not to worry. Did you hear me? I am a *doctor.*

Sorry ma'am

He needs to lie down fast. Are there drugs here? He looks like

Drugs

Drugs

Drugs

Drugs

(Doom)

Dooooooooooooooooooooooooooooooooooooooomherrrrrrrrrreeeeeeeeeeeeeeeeeeeeeeeeeeeeeeeeeeeeeeeeeeeeeeeeeeeeeeeeeeeeeeeeeeeeeeeeeeeeeeeeeeeeeeeeeeeeeeedoommmmmmmmmmmmmmmmmmmmmmmmmmmmhere?

No, no drugs.

Is there a room he can

freshairfreshairhe'llbellrightallrightallrightallrighrightllrightallrightallrightallrighrightllrightallrightallrightallrihrightllrightallrightallrightallrighrightllrightallrightallrightallrig

hright

allllllllllllllllllllllllllllrighhhhhhhhhhhhhhttttt

I'm a doctor, he needs more than freshair a roomaroomaroom

Yes…I shall sort a room.

It may be worth calling an ambulance

No need for that. Don't waste health service resources. I'll look after *after after after after after* him. Lots of water. Ask one of your goons to get my medical bag from my car. The Lexus.

Lexus.

Fucking boring party anyway, all this disco music. Haven't heard such shit music in thirty

And I try to tell them to look after Chloe, but they can't hear me because my vocal chords don't work and my ears are shutting down and all I can see is some distant point in the Universe and then, the rest of me sh

Unawesome

The words – her words and mine – speed by in fragments.

This is not a dream.

This is not a nightmare.

I've been shafted.

The car journey home was an exercise in uncomfortable silence.

I tried to explain, I told her the full story, but Chloe was having none of it.

(Conn)

There seemed to be nothing I could do.

When we get round to her house and into her kitchen, she lets loose.

This is not a dream.

This is not a nightmare.

Terry, I'm sorry. I can't trust you.

But...I was drugged.

You left me.

Chloe...

You totally said you'd look after me. You didn't.

Look, what happened up there?

As if you care. You were drunk and asleep. You've been taking drugs. I've noticed all the time. When you are not working. You take drugs. You took drugs last night. You totally did. You were supposed to look after me.

But...but...you know that's not true. Conn drugged me. If it weren't for the doctor, they'd have taken me out and battered me too. She saved my life.

What doctor?

What do you mean, what doctor?

There was no doctor. Conn said. You're making this up because you popped some pills and you were wasted. You embarrassed me. You left me. Conn said he saw you take pills. He told me. He said.

He's lying. Lying. Listen to me. Chloe. Listen to me.

I don't want to hear this. You're telling lies. You were on that bed when I saw you. Drugged up. Look at your eyes now, mate. They're like headlights. You're on drugs.

Chloe…those people…

You were totally supposed to look after me. You promised me. I thought we were friends. I thought we had become friends. All you had to do was stay off the drugs at work. For one single night. You were supposed to look after me.

They…my…my…tonic water…pills…

According to Conn, when I went looking for you in the morning, you were fast asleep. I asked him to take me to see you. I saw you lying there. You looked a total wally. On drugs. You'd been sick. I don't know how you were able to drive me home.

OMG! We are supposed to be so careful. And there were Police there…

This time, I say nothing. Chloe is super angry. Ranting. I have never seen her like this and her staccato, machine gun delivery is unusual. I have never seen her stressed. Her arms are folded and she's not even looking at me. She could be about ten. She won't listen so even though my heart is racing and I know how this is going to end up, I know that Conn has done enough to wipe me out of the equation (God know what *else* he said). I could plead and I could reason but it would be pointless. She stares at some point on the floor, near her doormat. I think she's crying, or about to. Off she goes…

I could have had a horrible night. OMG, there were some totally weird people hovering about upstairs – like that bloke in Leicester – I told you, I told you - and where were you? Fast asleep. Drugs. Drunk. And we're supposed to be working together.

Chloe…

I am SO angry with you. You let me down. Totally. I can barely bring myself to speak to you.

I told you what happened.

That old thing! OMFG, not one person in there can confirm what you said. They all said you were out of it. Conn told me you had been at the vodka more or less since we arrived too. In the billiards room. You promised me. You're not supposed to drink while you are working. You agreed. We discussed this.

I know…we discussed it.

I'm like, not repeating myself. I spoke to Neville this morning while you were still asleep and he's like, crap!

He's, all, like, that Terry is totally unstable. I warned you. I trusted you. Neville never did.

Then she hits me with it. I spot it a mile off a millisecond before she delivers it. I know it's coming and I prepare for the shockwave that comes after the sucker punch.

I never get second chances.
I never have done.
I never get the harsh treatment and then a make-up shag.
They hit me I stay hit.
Women.
(Chloe)
I'm gutted and the feeling tightens my stomach like a gastric band. It's all I can do to stop myself vomiting: I nearly do an Exorcist impersonation all over Chloe's curtains.

So, we had a chat. I can't trust you. I'm sorry…

Chloe, listen…

…he's found someone else to drive me. I'm sorry. Jamal. He wants the car back, btw. Jamal will come around for it. Tonight. I'm working.

I don't get notice?

No. This is *so* not McDonalds.

(It's so not McDonalds. It's so not McDonalds It's so not McDonalds It's so not McDonalds It's so not McDonalds It's so not McDonalds. It's so not McDonalds. It's so not McDonalds. It's so not McDonalds. It's so not McDonalds. It's so not McDonalds. It's so not McDonalds. It's so not McDonalds. It's so not McDonalds.)

The rest of it, I tune out, though her rant goes on for another ten minutes. Tuning out is something I do. I can't bear bad news. I can't take rejection. Particularly from women. Mix it with injustice and I'm well-pissed off. If she were a bloke, I'd have already nutted him on the bridge of his nose, a Glasgow kiss. I hate most blokes, and beating them up is a natural extension of competitive processes and resource conflict that goes back a million years. Women? You can't touch them. You can't…in the nick, hitting a woman is one up from noncing…and I can't bear it, even though I…I…

My heart is like the wall of a badly built dam and the water to one side is hammering against it. It's going to break. Break into a million tiny pieces.

(It's over)

I want to beg. That's my main impulse, my primary compulsion. I want to beg forgiveness even though it isn't my fault. I've been shafted. I've been tickled under the chin and sent upstairs without any supper.

(Please don't sack me)

It circulates around my consciousness along with

(I love you, Chloe) a clear, technicolour, hi-definition image of my model maker's scalpel, slicing along my arm, the crimson emergence flowing like one long teardrop onto the laminate floor underneath my desk.

(love)

So I tune her out. I shut it all down.

All of it.

And I begin, for the first time, to formulate what I am going to do next. Mentally, I picture an old school radio, one of those my mum had on the windowsill of her kitchen. One with a dial and a manual orange marker, the size of a matchstick that travels horizontally from right to left. A Rediffusion radio, black, with a circular mesh speaker. I picture the volume control on the side of my radio and I mentally turn Chloe's speech right down to nothing and I wait for her to finish.

When I was married, to Isobel, when I was mid-twenties, this was a technique I learned to stop me killing her.

She was a bitch and a scold. She could spoil a party with one look and everything was always my fault.

Thatcher. The chemical spill at Bhopal. Chernobyl. The desalination of the seas. Overfishing. Black Friday in the financial markets and the failure of Andrew Ridgeley's solo career.

All my fault. I used to look at Isobel and think one of two things.

One, how would her head look amongst the turnips on my uncle Bill's allotment, and two, the radio technique. She eventually ditched me for not meeting her emotional needs and the last I heard, had married a pipe fitter from Loughborough.

This morning, the radio technique succeeds.

I look at Chloe and I expect her to be more distraught after all we've been through together, but she's pretty blank, certainly more deadpan than I would be, sacking a mate, someone I've shared time with, six months in the same motor, intimate time. She's wearing a rainbow coloured jumper and she's pale. I wonder whether she's been crying. Probably not. Her hair is hidden in a knobbly wooly bobble hat, more like a tea cosy, one I've not seen before.

She could be the kid I know her to be underneath it all and now she won't look at me, not a glance.

I ask if that's it and she says yes and I play it cool, shrug my shoulders, walk out the door with as much dignity as I can muster.

I get inside my house, go to the toilet, give in to the spinning in my head and vomit into the bowl.

(I've been shafted).

Then, I remove my clothes until I am naked and sit at my desk.

I place *The Verve* in the CD player

(Lucky Man...you are SUCH a Lucky Man)

Beset by pictures of Chloe

(you'll never see her again)

with the new driver

(the intimacy of the leather)

and

(its not like McDonalds)

(lesbian sex)

(jamal sex neville sex)

(Hope)

(I love you, Chloe. Love, love LOVE)

remove the modelmaker's knife from its pouch and without ceremony, make a precise incision from the pit of my elbow to the top of my wrist, about twelve inches long. The contact is clinical enough to break the skin with no undue pressure. It pinches and the slicing of the razor sharp edge impacts on my teeth, as if I am biting on tinfoil. With control that always comes in the cutting zone (and seldom in real life), I avoid the scars of previous eviscerations and carve an undeveloped pathway through the dermis. As the knife travels downward, my ears tingle. Sometimes, I cannot watch, but tonight, I cannot take my eyes away from the engraving of the pristine sharp.

As usual, I get a semi. Once, it would have been a boner to impress King Dong, but those days

(Chloe)

have long gone.

Long gone.

I wouldn't be able to satisfy anyone now with

(Please take me back, Chloe)

liquid the colour of claret and texture of syrup creates obscure patterns on the desk. Then, when the fascination is over, the bandage is on, I give in to the pain in my heart and begin to cry for the first time, probably since I was a kid, when dad left, and I don't stop crying until there isn't a single molecule of liquid remaining in my head.

Property of Jamal

Three things I have learned.

One. Finding a maggot in an apple is better than finding half a maggot.

Two. Men are full of anger. All of them, even the librarians and the accountants. Even the bloke you're married to, the lovely Ron, the affable Ashley, the mild mannered Russ, the even-tempered Henry. A cauldron of barely concealed ultraviolence. Watch the eyes. It's behind them, deep in their souls. It goes back a million years. It's in the genes. And that anger is expressed outward, in the form of rage, or inward in the form of depression and anxiety, (and my speciality, the scalpel's kiss). You can displace, sublimate or deny anger, (sex, sport, drugs, careers, power), but its there, always there, a permanent force, as old as time, an unconscious burning desire to destroy and kill anything that moves.

Three. Rugger buggers are a bunch of pricks.

There are six of them facing Pike and me on St James Street. We've been drinking in the Magic Spoons up there, a bad decision. It's full of gobby students who think they own Nottingham City. With their hi-vis vests and painted faces and adenoidal chants, and we've managed to upset that old academic sub-section, the **University Rugby Club**.

They're too square to dress up. They look like locals. Pike's been slapped by one of them, a throwback prop forward, a real dribbler, a real australopithecine fucker.

The scene outside the hairdressers, where locals get their hair trimmed for thirty seven quid, and where students like this shower of cretins can have their hair cut by a perfumed puff with pipe cleaner legs for fourteen, becomes a still life, a Mexican stand-off.

People are watching from the windows, others have stopped their journey to the Square to watch us. The revellers off to the Aussie bar up the road stop too.

Even the god-botherers in the Malt Cross have ceased their warbling for the Rapture and are forming an orderly queue to watch the massacre.

It's all gone slow motion.

There's a geezer with me in his sights who is the spitting image of Private Pile out of Full Metal Jacket, that same dull, salivating stare and as he approaches me lumbering and glassy eyed, I wonder idly how someone as evolutionary challenged as this gets to University. He probably gets a rugby scholarship plus a large donation from daddy before eventually joining the Police or the judiciary.

We don't need this. We cannot have this on our narratives. These rugby clubbers will be back to school tomorrow morning, eager beavers, lollipops for the professor and kisses for the Coach. We'll be eating sausage stew from tinfoil cartons in the nick at Central, looking for the face of Jesus in the piss stains on the walls then its back to North Sea Camp, no questions asked. For the next five years.

(One of Danny's lads. Young Forest. On a tag. Likes his Rap. Takes a risk. Goes into town with his mates. Sixteen, seventeen. Bit of blow, bit of music, bit of badman talk, compare the caps, you know the thing. Bumps into ten lads from Southwell, where I live. Rugby lads from Brackenhurst out in the big city. Danny's boy tries to walk away don't want no barney rubble but they end up fighting. Danny's boy hits back. Coppers come. Even though the posh boys caused all the mayhem, they nick Danny's boy. Now he's inside for a two. They let the Southwellians go on their way. Twas it ever thus).

At the same time, we can't have these giant posh kids making a show of us. It can't happen.

So we haven't run off, not that we ever would.

Notts don't run.

We've been on the pop and sweeties for three days now, since

Chloe dumped (sacked) me and this is not the first time we've attracted the attentions of the pissed. But this is the first time a blow has been landed. Not a good one, not a showpiece, not a Bruno on Tyson back in Vegas, or that one Pike landed on that mouthy Walsall at Woodall services ten years ago (I think he's still down). But it was enough to ruffle Pike's ego. Personally, I am so numb that I couldn't give a toss whether I get beat up or not, but Pike is a different kettle of fish. His ego is a monstrous thing. He isn't going to take that punch lightly. Neither of us are bothered about the odds – following Notts makes you immune to all kinds of pain – but its the other stuff...the judges, the cops, the screws. The other nutty prisoners. The psychos and the proper gangsters in the Camp who run the show.

We've been good boys for a year. And neither of us wants to go back.

The odds aren't good. Six versus two.

Army of Two

Pike grins at me.

Fuck it, he says, knowing full well the consequences of what he's about to say and the thought processes going through my head. Let's splatter the posh cunts...

...and then there's a flash of yellow from behind us and some local shouts cops, and the throwbacks, who see them first, revert to type, turn on their heels and sprint like naughty boys up the road and I can't help but feel disappointed that its ending. Emotionally, that is. The coppers ram us up against the wall, but I've been much, much worse on the ale than this.

After a while, being dumped, you can't get pissed.

Forty, fifty, sixty pints is no different from slush puppies and mineral water,

I remember that from Zoe's time, and it's happening again now.

We're good boys and when the six coppers have an exploratory natter with some of the onlooking locals, (none of whom having much time for student rugger buggers either, or students in general), they let us go.

Pike, who hates coppers more than anyone on planet earth, a potential Michael Ryan of coppers, even wishes them goodbye out of sheer relief. Not wanting to push it, we walk in the opposite direction to our assailants. Pike says I was looking forward to slapping that cunt who belted me. I put my arm round him and say oh well, we can have a proper Christmas dinner this year rather than one of them plastic trays of shit up at the Camp and he laughs. We go to the Dragon and in there I get a text message I do not expect. While Pike natters away, I think about the text and what it means, but I don't discuss it.

I think about the past three days.

Three days ago. Chloe dumped (sacked) me.

I've been getting confused. It doesn't feel like a sacking. Sometimes, being sacked is a relief, an excuse for a joke. I'd never feel like this if Danny Mannion told me there was no more work clearing the houses of dead people. Theoretically, that is.

This feels like a dumping. This feels like what Zoe did to me years ago.

It feels as if my heart is broken. *(She's Gone)*

The morning after I cut myself, I mopped up my blood (from the desk, chair and floor), added a second bandage, gauze and medicinal disinfectant and got ready for business. I didn't want to see Jamal and Chloe having fun through my window, (though the desire to stay clamped like a limpet to the glass was overwhelming, like some obsessive compulsion, the desire to dig into an open wound, or bend back a dying tooth). My subsconscious Imp wasn't helping: I dreamed that Jamal was ploughing Chloe all night in a goldfish bowl and I was forced to watch as she moaned and moaned.

At one point, she even looked at me, all Manga eyes and effusive lipstick, and said something, which I have either forgotten or didn't pick up in the first place. I like to think it was *I Love You*, but that would be a dangerous insanity on my behalf. I knew I had to get out of my flat, because it was in me to stalk and to observe and I was worth more than that, so I called Marge and asked to stay, but she told me that she was seeing someone she met at the Ocean on Saturday night, a nice bloke for once, and it wasn't convenient, so with a heavy heart and typical suppressed (hypocritical) self-pity, I wished her all the best and called Pike, who was pleased to put me up (though his long suffering missus wouldn't feel the same way).

Then, I took the three grand I had accumulated, from the bottom drawer of my bedside chest, and put it in my quilted coat. Packed a leather holdall I keep for weekends away, loaded up my phone and charger and as many prescription drugs as I could carry, and bailed out of Southwell. That was the first step. Still numb that morning, which meant I was capable of rational decision making but when the walls began to crumble, I understood it had ended with Chloe.

She'd gone

So I began to get miserable fast and by lunch, I was in despair. Only one course of action could help. This is where Pike came in handy. He was my Angel of Despair, my defensive wingman and he'd be there for me.

Once I told him what had happened and how it had made me feel, he called Danny Mannion and took a week off work, told his boss that Zeb would do the job, a flat clearance in Hucknall where some old bloke had cardiaced three months ago in the bath, leaving behind a cloth cap, a distressing smell upstairs and a mess on the tiles.

So we started to drink. A medicinal drink.

And that night, round at Crinkle's, we started on the Doom.

There, I slept with Rachel Melon on a filthy mattress in Crinkle's flat. A freebie from Crinkle, as we had bought wholesale quantities of confectionery. Well, I would have slept with her in the biblical sense had I not witnessed **PROPERTY OF CRINKLE** tattooed in ostentatious Celtic letters, floating in between her emaciated belly and her completely shaven soup plate. If only she hadn't have removed her **PERTH SURFERS RIDE IT LONGER** tee shirt. I might have enjoyed a restorative, medicinal shag. She was begging me to do her and even with Pike's donation of 100mg of Viagra, which ensured a decent effort downstairs, I couldn't do it.

It wasn't in me.

You don't own women.

This gangster shit made me angry and I wanted to kick the shit out of Crinkle for forcing the ink situation. The tattoo reminded me of Chloe. There was no difference, it seemed.

Melon, Chloe, Melon, Chloe.

It was all an ownership issue. It was all paperwork.

Then, as she started to get interested, I kept thinking of Chloe and how she was bound to be sleeping with Jamal, however lacking in evidence that proposition was, particularly bearing in mind the baffling issue of her confused sexuality.

(Or Neville. Or Ricardo. Or Beefy. Or Asif).

Or any of them down there at Tiffanys. It didn't occur to me she might find solace in a woman. You would think that's what I would think, if I thought anything at all.

I'd been surplused by another bloke.

The King Of The Pride.

And that hurt. That hurt bad.

Jamal.

I wanted to slice him up like roast beef on a Sunday afternoon.

As Rachel started licking my nipples with a cracked out tongue the consistency of sandpaper, I pictured **PROPERTY OF NEVILLE** tattooed on Rachel/Chloe's marble body, which I put down to the psychedelic impact of the Hand of Doom coursing through my body like a burning forest fire. In the end, I made Rachel go down on me because the V had inspired an artificial iron man down there, and she did, but it took an age for her to complete the job (and even then, I had to help), and she got angry afterwards, saying I didn't find her attractive and all that, which was true, but wildly beside the point. She stopped her bitching when I gave her a ton for her own sweeties (Base, Horse), and then said I was sorry.

She assured me I could fuck her any time, any place, whether Crinkle knew or not, and I said thanks, but knew that would never happen, not with that manky tattoo hovering above her polished tiling.

I wasn't very happy with Crinkle afterwards (in fact I started to feel some of that pathological anger I was telling you a bit about earlier), but I'm not stupid. I knew I was going to need a complete KFC family feast of Doom

(eight pieces, four fries, double pots of chicken gravy and a Tango's worth of Doom)

and he was the cheapest about, and for some reason, he liked us, so I overlooked the immorality of modern Nottingham street-level slavery on this occasion and we left at two in the morning into the darkness of a Radford night.

The next day, was a quiet one.

The second day after a dumping is the worst. The Dualities hit you like Interstellar Overdrive. You're in shock the first day, but it's worn off by the second. The morning goggle eyes welcome you to the cold light of day *(She's Gone),* the surreal visions hit you in HD, the emptiness invades your soul and you feel like death is your only friend.

Your whole life is a paradox, a recurring condition of bipolar extremes.

You want to call, you don't want to call.

You want to stalk, you don't want to stalk.

You want to sleep, you can't sleep.

You want to talk, you want silence.

You love her, you hate her.

You want to let her go, you want to imprison her in a box.

You want to live, you want to die.

You want people, you want solitude.

You want the light, you can't draw back the curtains.

It's carnage, a dumping. I wouldn't wish this on anyone.

Dumping doesn't seem to affect women like this.

Much more durable, women. Much more perspective on the matter. *"27 Dresses"* on DVD, a hundredweight of fruity chocolates, a family size box of tissues, and a party invitation to the BFFs. Before the weekend's out, she's met a new bloke at the Ocean and they're planning the engagement party. In essence, all men are interchangeable cocks. They may differ in size and engine capacity, but in the end, its all one multicellular throbber. I've never known a woman stress about the end of a relationship like men do, like I'm doing now (*and you've not even been dumped, you daft bas*) and I've never understood why. What the difference is. I'm always astounded to be dumped and women never seem to be.

Maybe we're incapable of perspective.

Maybe we never grow up.

Only one thing helps the duality and that's drink. Pike went out and bought forty eight cans of Thor's Hammer and we watched TV at his place while Lou, his missus, went out to work. We snorted Doom most of the day and that is pretty much all I recollect, except we watched the original Batman film, the one with the shark repellent spray, (*some days you just can't get rid of a bomb*) about twenty times, and completely annihilated the treasure trove of cans.

It worked. I didn't think about Chloe. From the first snort of Doom in the morning, to the last foamy dregs of the last tin of Hammer, I was completely munted and so was Pike. The cure stopped the duality dead. We were dribbling. Louise wasn't happy at all when she came home, but Pike simply pretended she wasn't there and she went upstairs to bed to play on Facebook.

And here we are, in The Dragon at the end of the third day.

We were supposed to go off to Crinkle's again for another Doom party. Only this time, I changed my mind. I needed something else. I called Marge in the toilet of the pub. She answered the phone and said she was in company and I said I desperately needed a chat, it was an absolute emergency, and she said come round, but Bart would be there

(Bart? What sort of name was that! Bartram? Bartholomew? Bartleby?),

and I said okay. I told Pike what I had done and that I would be back at his place in the morning and he called me everything from a pig to a dog, but I knew he didn't mean it and, by the looks of him, he was ready for an early night too and we rammed down two more pints of Agincourt for the road and I was off.

Uncle Leonard

Marge opens the door and she's fully dressed, jeans, tee shirt, but I'm looking beyond her and I see him, sitting on the sofa. Glasses. I don't think I've ever seen Marge go out with a bloke who wears glasses apart from me. He's got a shirt and tie on, as if he'd that minute finished work. He's a dweeb, a straight. 2.2 degree, a sister in Essex, a Vauxhall on the drive and a flat share on Mansfield Road. Not bad looking in a bland sort of way. No real imperfections. Like magnolia paint.

I can see Bart's future in a split second.

Account management, Forest on Saturday, pub football on Sunday mornings, two kids, sex twice a week, X-Factor with the missus and a fortnight in Cyprus every year.

That future doesn't involve Marge and I breathe a sigh of relief.

He's half her age for a start and I grin at her and she comes across as guilty. I feel cheeky daft. The flat, as usual, stinks of weed, but its cheap stuff, no Beelzebub, and I wish I'd bought an ounce of the Devil from Crinkle.

What do you want, Terry? Marge says as I sit next to Bart, offering my hand in friendship. I play up my answer.

It's the cops, Marge. They've been all over me like lice in a tramp's boxer shorts. I need to hide for a couple of days. Otherwise I'll be spending crimbo at the Camp. Sorry, lovebirds.

No way, Jose, she says.

Bart pipes up…its okay, Marge, totally. I don't mind. He can sleep on the sofa. Sure, yeah, it's cool.

(Cool?)

What do you do, Bart? I ask.

Contact Centre Supervisor, actually. Insurance, he says, with pride in his eyes. I look straight at him and I am looking for signs of fear and disrespect and any duplicity but he is completely innocent of the world in which I live. He's a civilian and maybe I'm wrong, maybe Marge has changed, maybe it's the end for me and her too, a double dumping, but then I know Marge and that's never going to be the case with a fella like Bart. She'd be his personal praying mantis for a start. She'd have him in the Magic Spoons crying into his lager in two months tops. I've seen it before, with some tough blokes too.

No pity, Marge. A proper hard un.

That's good, mate. Prospects?

Oh, absolutely, he says, with a smile on his face. He's so clean cut it's not true. I resist the urge to glass him in the face with the onyx ashtray and follow it up with a touch more tenderness. I let him know exactly who he pulled in the Ocean.

Marge likes it black, you know.

What?

Fuck off, she says from the armchair.

Black men. The bigger the better. She's been like that since school.

Has she? Bart says, looking uneasy.

Yep. She can't get enough black. I hope you've got a proper exocet in your boxers, mate. I couldn't satisfy her when we were together. She only went out with me for a bet.

Get out right now, Marge says, but she's stoned and it's all in the distance. I get the impression she should be angrier than she is and I look at her, look at the way she's behaving, and I know that Bart's another wannabe who has about five minutes left.

Did she? Bart says. I didn't know. She didn't say. She spoke quite highly of you, mate.

I don't care whether a bloke's white or black, she's saying, matter of fact. Colour makes no difference to me. I went out with you for ages, dint I? Don't be so bloody racist. Stop being an arse. Ignore 'im, Bart.

One of the West Indian gentleman who visits Marge on occasion for a chat and that is a proper nutter, I continue. He's a right psycho. They call him The Cutter.

The Cutter? Bart repeats.

Leonard the Cutter. Famous round St Ann's. Want someone carved up a treat? Call for Len. He'll do it for a bargain fifty sheets coz he enjoys it so much.

You are kidding? Fifty quid?

Especially white men. He hates us, Bart. Us white blokes. It's in his genes. He loves carving white men up, doesn't he, Marge.

She says nothing.

It's something to do with his Grandad Billy, the slave trade, or something. Every time he undertakes his morning constitutional around Stannz and sees white men going about their business, he's reminded of them slave ships and the suffering of his forefathers. And then, when the obsession gets too much for him to bear, when it all gets on top, out comes his magic chef knife.

Wow. You're joking?

Wish I was, chief. Straight as an arrow. Proper likes his white women too. Doesn't he, Marge? Got a well-stocked harem full of local young beauties and he's protective. That's another way he gets his revenge on the white man. Makes them call him Uncle Leonard when they're on the job. Marge had to, didn't you honey? *Ooooh, that feels nice and tight, Uncle Leonard. You fill me up good and proper, Uncle Leonard. You're the best, Uncle Len.*

Terry…she says, but I can see she thinks this is funny. Bart says nothing this time and I continue.

Marge dumped him a year ago, but he still comes round. He hates other men round here. He hates the thought of it. You go out with Uncle Leonard for a single gin and tonic in the Dog and Duck and you're one of his bitches for life. You can't ever leave. He only lets me stop over coz he thinks I'm her brother. Have you met him yet? Boxer looking bloke. Shiny head like the black ball on a snooker table. Slash across his left eye…

Serious? Bart says. He dated Marge?

Engaged to be married at one time, isn't that right, Marge?

You're a cunt. Ignore 'im, Bart.

Last bloke he caught round here he sliced up with a machete. That geezer from Capital One. Nice bloke. Forest fan…

Capital One? I work with them….Bart interrupts. We have regular meetings with their...

…look down there, I interrupt back, fearful of a long-winded Bart-centred vignette about his career.

He does so. On Marge's carpet, slightly in front of the kitchenette, there is a wine stain that she was too stoned to clean when it spilled and thus it became impossible to remove. Bart stares at it with a look of horror. I make a gesture along my cheek.

His face is a serious mess now, Bart. Frankenstein stitches. That was the end of his career at Capital One. He works at Boots on the line. Perfumes and Gift Boxes, I understand. Out the way in Department S where no one can see him.

OMG, he lost his career?

All gone. Up in smoke. Can't do business with a bloke face to face with Frankenstein scars like that. He frightened all the girls in the office. Had to go.

I can see that, yes, Bart replies, now obviously apprehensive.

I'm surprised Marge hasn't had Property of Uncle Leonard inked on her soup dish, Bart. He's a proper comedian.

Arsehole… she says, taking another deep drag on her spliff.

I think I'd better be off, Marge, Bart says. Work early in the morning. Er, a meeting with the Risk Assessors.

Bart, don't, she says, but it's not very convincing and when he puts on his half-length black office raincoat, she doesn't get out of her chair to see him off.

The door slams.

See you, Bart, I say.

You're fucking horrible, Terry, she says. Totally vile.

You could have asked him to leave beforehand.

Couldn't be arsed, she says.

I take it he won't be back.

He was a nice bloke. I should be angry.

I need you, Marge. *I need you.*

She pours me a wine and she comes to sit next to me and before you know it, we're snogging like teenagers, all gropes, moans, dribble, flecks of marijuana and the in and out of flickering tongues, and before much longer, we're in Marge's bed and she is at her very filthiest, a queen of shame, as she always is when stoned. It seemed that Chloe's dumping rejuvenated me, as if, like Zebedee arriving, by magic. She's a good looking woman, built for hard sex, takes it harder than a two grand whore, with just the right amount of flaws (a roll of belly fat, a little cellulite, some sex scars), to inspire a jaded palette. She's a magnificent shag too, always was, always will be, the right amount of aggression, the right amount of willingness and tender subservience. She banged her first lad at twelve, a newspaper delivery lad, in the bushes behind Redhill School after a school disco, and she had never stopped studying the sexual arts. Prepared, like a boy scout, I'd taken another Viagra in the toilets of the Dragon, which was something of a risk if Bart had proved a six foot five giant of the type Marge favours on occasion and this time, for some weird reason *(She's Gone)*, we go at it till six am in every position possible. In every hole, with every motion, observing every fashion, and she goes off time and time again, like a gyrating, bucking catherine wheel, all fountains and fireworks, all trembling bones and gyratory eyes, and she's swearing undying love to me and this time, I feel like reciprocating, because I do love her, deep inside, but I know there's unfinished business, because Chloe had texted me earlier and says she wants to see me at her house and she even left kisses.

Two, to be exact.

This is something I don't plan on mentioning to Marge because she's quite excited tonight.

This isn't about sex for her. Not at all.

And with all the shit I've taken in the past three days, I don't know what it is about for me either.

Chloe's Text

Hi Terry. I'm sorry. I'm so sorry. Can you come round? I know you are out because I have been looking for you. I will be in all day. Miss you xx

The text is still on my phone. I think I'll save it forever. It makes me feel like hot milk and biscuits before bedtime, which is a feeling I try and suppress as a rule.

Two kisses.

What does two kisses mean? One kiss? Three kisses? A strange barbed wire fence of kisses. What does an absence of kisses mean? Social media apocalypse, no doubt.

Marge is still asleep when I leave. I put her through the mill last night and I see no reason to wake her. I watched her walk to the toilet after I had finished and her legs collapsed underneath her and I picked her up and put her back to bed. She said she might piss herself and I kissed her and said good, I'd let you, as long as it was on me. She kissed me one more time and told me she loved me and then she fell asleep, a deep one.

It's midday.

It's raining outside and it will be probably be raining all day. I am looking forward to hearing Chloe's explanation of events.

I hope she makes a story of it because there's something about rain. All the best stories take place in the rain.

I kiss Marge on the shoulder and pull up the quilt. I know that I have to sort out my feelings and the way I am behaving. It's very confused and fragmented.

It's the sweeties. Hand of Doom Sherbet Strawberries.

JeSUS.

I can't feel any emotions. I struggle to feel the memory of emotions. I'm in Hell. I'm being led by my manhood and that's a bad position to be in.

At the root of it is Chloe.

Marge and I get on like a house on fire and we should get married and live happy ever after shedding happy tears down the aisle, but Chloe is in my head even deeper. I wish she wasn't, but she is. This pathological thing I have for Chloe is self-destructive *(but what if)*, self-defeating, paralysing *(she does),* and ultimately *(want you)* dangerous, so I have to sort it and I make the decision to deal with it.

I walk past the top of Hockley, the tram turning the corner like a huge metal grass snake, half full of blank, faceless shoppers on the way to the train station. I'll see her this once and come back and sort it with Marge. I call Pike too, because he is expecting me, hoping to give him the full SP. There's no answer, so I text him, tell him I'm going home to get some more gear and I'll see him tonight. He doesn't text back, at least by the time I get to the 100 bus stop outside the Viccy Centre Ladbrokes.

With fifteen minutes to wait for the bus, I pop in. It's a Sunday, half empty. A Somali machine player, an old boy waiting for his missus to finish her shopping at Marks. Another dirty old bloke in a cap and one of those country bodywarmers. I walk to the counter, take out fifty quid from my much diminished roll (once heaving, now flaccid), and write out a slip for Trap 3, the smash box. Blind.

The next race is at Hove. 515m. A stiff track with a minimal advantage for the three box, and as the black haired counter assistant takes the bet, I look at the price. 7/1, the outsider of six. *Shit.* Mentally, I give up the fifty quid but watch the race anyway. The old geezer next to me asks me if I have info and I ignore him. *It's got fucking no chance*, he says, a fit of pique and I suppress the momentary urge to nut him on the nose because he's a stinky old bastard close to death.

He's correct though. The dog falls out of the boxes, takes a snug position in last place and stays there for the whole next 500 metres. *Bloody greyhound racing.*

You were right, mate, I say magnanimously, and write out another slip for the next race at Belle Vue. Another trap three, blind, smash box, ping box. I pull off two hundred quid from my roll. The old bloke glowers at the money rather than me, ten purple notes, pristine (if slightly warped). The fat counter assistant takes the bet without even looking at me *(bitch)* and I turn to check the price.

7/2 third best and I feel better about this bet.

That's got a good chance, load of early, the old bloke chips in and I nod. A couple of other punters notice the size of the bet and stand and watch the race, a standard A8 from Belle Vue, a decrepit wasteground track north of Manchester city centre entirely appropriate for a wonderful but dying sport, in a world dominated by the bookie's obsession with fucking shit Premier League football.

Die you premier league fuckers. Die! Die! Die!

It's an exciting race.

Trap three breaks clear and surfs the first bend. The black jacket is in hot pursuit followed by the dutch striker. Smash box hurtles down the back stretch and the butcher's apron looms out wide as the black jacket fades. My dog is a length clear of the six, but I'm not confident – it's beaten.

The old boy next to me starts to shout on mine and even the dismissive counter assistant observes the sporting moment with something more than her usual apathetic sneer. Neck and neck, neck and neck, nip and tuck, the six and the three go at it hammer and tong down Belle Vue's long stretch and with a last desperate lunge, the two brave animals go past together, separated only by the width of a cigarette paper. I can't call it.

I check the time. My bus is due and I have no time for the photo so I completely ignore the old boy and start to walk out the door.

Don't you want to know who won? The old boy shouts.

I don't even look back. My bus is coming, I can sense it, and Chloe is waiting for me fourteen miles away and I simply don't want to miss her for a single second. I want her badly. I don't want the job back.

In fact, I'm thinking of asking her to stop.

Move in with me. Make an honest woman of her.

Thinking of Chloe gives me a hard on as I sit down on the bus. Unlike before, I am constantly hard and I suspect that Chloe and me are going to spend the rest of the afternoon in bed. Don't ask me how I know. Take it for granted. Then I will make my decision about Marge.

You might think I'm being optimistic about my prognosis for this afternoon. After all, where's the evidence?

But here's the rub: I'm not going to let Chloe say no, either, not for what she's done to me.

I'm not a nice guy.

I never have been.

I'm a category one bad boy.

It's all I ever wanted to be and I got the chance to live the life.

A real bad moth…

Some evidence, your honour, my curriculum vitae for your delectation,

(bone idle layabout benefit-claiming gangster never had a proper job beat people up scare people atheist don't pay tax don't give to charity robbed the few friends you've had wouldn't piss on a neighbour if on fire beaten up people I like slept with the WAGS of friends never been faithful to people that love me lie out of my back teeth done bad things at the football abandoned kids without a single look back and fucking murdered som)

assessment and perusal so if Chloe gets all arsy; all chastity belt, all prissy prissy and little girl lesbian lost, I'm going to show her exactly what a bad boy I *really* am.

Then, I come to my senses.
What am I thinking ????
It's the jelly babies.
(Got to stop)
(Got to)
(Stop)
(Stop)

I'd never do that to Chloe (*yes you would*) at all. I'll sit and talk, come to some arrangement, take my job back, forgive her, forget any of it ever happened (*but it did happen, she mugged you off*) and move on. The important thing is (*your sanity*) that Chloe's okay and that (*she probably had her lips around Ja*) she's safe and ready for me to look after again, which I will do.

That's the important thing.

Terry The Protector is back.
Terry The Protector is back.
Terry The Protector is back.
Terry The Protector is back.
Terry The Protector is back.
Terry The...
Terry....

Mentally, I shake my head and wash my mouth out for thinking those things.

I don't feel right at all.

Ride A White Swan

The journey home is a nightmare of bad traffic and it takes about an hour after an accident at the junction around Carlton Tesco. I could have done without it. My head is buzzing. I am keyed up to the max. I wonder whether it is because I am due to see Chloe. It could be anything. The bus is rammed solid, a single decker, and for the fiftieth time this year, I curse myself for not having my own motor. I have got used to driving the Audi, though I know I would not be able to drive today. I am tired, confused and frazzled.

Chloe's venetian blinds are closed. I cannot see through the frosted window panels on her door. She's not in and I'm not happy (*nothappynothappynothappy*) about this. Everything is supernaturally bright, almost white, as if the entire planet had been through a washing machine with illuminating Persil. The cars going past the Enclave sound like tanks. One of the neighbours is cooking curry and I salivate. The fact Chloe isn't in agitates me for some reason and I resist the impulse (a strong one) to kick her door in frustration. Instead, I rip a vine from the arboria behind me, smell the sap as if it were incense, and watch it fall, the soil crumbling onto the paving slabs like malt loaf crumbs onto an earthenware plate. I knock again. No answer. Then I text her, walk through her gate once again back to my place. I want to kick something, but there's nothing to kick. I notice a crow, which wasn't there before, sitting on the top rung of Chloe's partitioning fence. It's a brave crow, obviously *(a top lad crow)*. It watches me, silently, sentinel (*top lad, let's have it*). I pick up a pebble and throw it at the bird, but it misses. Still, it is close enough to scare the bird and still it doesn't move as if I hadn't thrown anything at all. It sits there on Chloe's fence. Silent and motionless, a crow template, a statue of a crow, a crow once removed, a painting, a still life in three dimensions. Portraits of birds have more energy. It's as tall as a Raven, though I had heard that they had been wiped out by the Welsh thirty years ago, in revenge for killing spring lambs

The Welsh. Killers of Ravens.
Raven genocide.
The Welsh. Raven genocidists.
Nazi Welsh Auschwitz Raven killers.
Wales. Welsh. Murder.
Arbeit macht Rabe frei.

don't know how true that is. Bird hunters and murderers I've never really considered the Welsh as genocodists of birds before but it seems obvious now, it seems a truism, self-evident, as if this is the most important of all history's facts, as if

I should have known this *forever.* The

(Soul Crew Raven Killers. Swansea Jacks, murderers of spring lambs. Wrexham Born Killers of Rarebits. Total Network Final Solution for Ravens and Spring Lambs and Rarebits).

crow transfixes me marble still with his leaden gaze. They used to call Lester Piggott the Man of Marble for his ability to sit still in the saddle, (Park Top, *Park Top*, **PARK TOP**) but this crow before me is even stiller. It pulls in my full focus.

There is only the crow. The vegetation behind it now merged with the fence in some bizarre optical parabola, like a fairground mirror. Yet, I know it is alive because every now and again it blinks, his black orvus eyes, unfeeling, dead, yet, paradoxically, resonant as if they are about to detonate into being. I am sick and spinning. I wonder whether it actually is a raven *(a survivor of the Welsh genocide).* Two feet tall, feathers sleek, like the paintwork on the Audi. Bony, skeletal claws, which grab the top rung without any effort, a mixture of fire orange and banana yellow. What colour feet do crows have? Could this be an escaped parrot, but I know that parrots aren't black and have never been black

(even in Wales, and unlike caterpillars and butterflies, crows don't metamorphosis into ravens, spring lambs or venezualan blue parrots)

then the crow squawks and the soundscape it creates fills the courtyard. It does so again and I'm deafened. I put my hands to my ear because the call echoes and crashes and pulsates around my skull. I want it to stop. Now. Stop. Stop. I sit against the wall underneath the window of my flat and bury my head. No neighbours are there to save me, no passers-by have business in the enclave, its me and the squawking crow thing and…

…oh no…oh no…it turns to look at me and calls once more, impossibly deep, a crunching, pounding, pulsating, oscillation. The window of the student couple opposite begins to shudder and I fear it is going to shatter under the frequency and the impact of the crow's relentless squawking.

Are you alright mate, a monster says above me, appearing from nowhere, and I shout and scream as I see this Gollum, this Basilisk, bending down over me, foul breath and with ears like wings, concrete faced and I stand up, force the apparition to look at the crow look look look is that a raven or a crow but the squawks have stopped and the bird takes flight with the wingspan of a glider, all swoops, all majestic sweeps of frigid air, and in my head the bird starts to laugh and the apparition is still there and he puts his hand on my shoulder and immediately before I notice that the monster is Gay Roger from

the house next door to Chloe, I've nutted him on the nose, connecting with a satisfying crunch (*Oldham, Peterborough, Town, Town, Town, Hull*), and he's crying and telling me to go away with blood streaming down his nose onto his work shirt and tie and I sa

y sorry and run, find my keys, and with luck that

(those Nicholls things yesterday afternoon; outsider pissed up, hot favourite unseen with Nelson's good eye and a long silver telescope)

sometimes escapes me, I let myself in the flat and collapse on the bed and curl up into a foetal ball, fully clothed, stinking of sex and violence, nasal blood dripping onto my quilt, experiencing the trip of *a (you never told me about* this, *Crinkle, you bastard)* lifetime.

I picture Chloe. Put her in different roles.

Chloe as waitress. Dancing girl. Lap dancer. Pole dancer. Hula dancer. Belly dancer. Flamenco dancer. Tango partner. Mother of three. Chief Executive. Secretary. Nun. Mother superior.

Carmelite. Barista Costa. Barista Starbuck. Barista Café Nero. Comfort woman. Comfort woman for a camp of officers and prisoners in a white dress. Jockey. Show jumper. Pony rider. High Priestess. With Boadicea on her chariot. Pagan witch. Sacrificial lamb. Druid's wife, sacrificing her soul for ultimate power. TV watching housewife. Nurse. Estate agent, in American tan tights and thick black framed glasses. Doctor. MP. Homeless in that wooly hat. Typing away at a YA novel full of romance and vampires. Naked before me, naked above me, naked on my face, her tender thighs balanced on each cheek, in my arms, crying, telling me she's sorry, laughing with her mate in the Tranquility, lying

(no)

in state on the mortuarian's slab *(no)* her face at peace, but no longer Chloe, a body in all but name, soulless, a statue, a plinth,

ashes, ashes

(no)

holding my hand in the park, telling me she loves me, and will love me forever, that there will never be another, that she is mine and I watch her float into the sky on the back of balloon swans with wings and she waves and waves and my stomach goes and I throw up on my pillow and lie in the puce, lumpy, foul smelling mess. This is how they all died, I thought, Hendrix, Joplin, Moon, in a pile of their own

my bowels empty, and then so do my balls,

at once, all control, and I know I am in trouble because I cannot move and Chloe has gone and there is the void, the darkness of perpetuity

and I curl up even tighter in the morass, the

swamp

of

my

own

destruction

and I know I will never

Chloe, Chloe, Marge, Francis, Notts, Chloe, Marge (*love you, love you*), Chloe (*love you, love you*), Notts (*love you, love you*) and *(I'm coming, Mum. I'm coming, Dad. I'm on my way)*

and before my stomach starts to cramp like someone has crushed it with a metal press, I smile, and I feel the warmth and the moisture of my piss dribble down my leg and I have returned to the womb and

and

and
and
and
and
and
and
and
and
and
and
and
and
and
and
and
an

TERRY! TERRY! OMG! TERRY!

head lifting from the sick encrusted pillow in tender hands and I am dragged off the bed, a new pillow placed underneath my head.

Terry, hon. Talk to me. It's me. Breathe, Terry. Breathe and don't move. I'll…get some water and stuff. Paracetamol. Don't move, hon.

Chloe's come back from heaven on. Ride a white swan. Chloe's come back from heaven on. Ride a white swan. Chloe's come back from heaven on. Ride a white swan. Chloe's come back from heaven on. Ride a white swan. Chloe's come back from heaven on. Ride a white swan. Chloe's come back from heaven on. Ride a white swan. Chloe's come back from heaven on. Ride a white swan. Chloe's come back from heaven on. Ride a white swan. Chloe's come back from heaven on. Ride a white swan. Chloe's come back from heaven on. Ride a white swan.

I breathe. I breathe.

My stomach hurts so badly I could cry but I cannot speak.

When Chloe returns I tap my drawer. She sees my tap, opens the drawer and sees a hot water bottle…recognising what she needs to do, she goes back to the kitchen again, leaves the cold glass of water on the bedside table. It's all gone insane in my head, but Chloe is here so I ride it out, the images, the sounds, the distortions and then she is back and she puts the bottle onto my belly and immediately, it starts to soothe the pain.

I spend the next few hours with my head over various bowls. Chloe cleans my linen in the washing machine at her house. I know this because as she keeps coming into my bathroom to see if I am okay, I can see the bundles of linen under her arm and I can hear the door go. Besides, I rely on the laundrette as my place is so small.

My head won't stop spinning and everything is the colour red, as if my eye balls bleed from the inside. I swear on my mother's grave that I will never touch this stuff again (*you've said this before, many many times*) and then I puke again.

Chloe has bought bed linen from her place and made my bed. She helps me take off my clothes and I get into the shower too wasted to be self-conscious. The hot jets pound me – I feel like a graffiti-spattered brick wall must feel in the face of a power blast – and I make sure it hits my aching and bursting stomach.

Chloe passes me shower gel and I spread it on my body without any enthusiasm. Incongruously, I think of Easton Ellis and *American Psycho*, the shower scene, which lasts three whole pages, a work of art, but I have no wish to make this like that as I need to lie down and showers have never been able to wash away my sins, so I get out.

Chloe says something I don't hear because I have water in my ears and she passes me my aquamarine bath sheet. I dry down, still beset by images no one should ever have to experience and I get into bed, naked, unconcerned at what Chloe thinks of my naked body and whether or not she notices the railway cuts on both my arms and along my sides. She probably does.

Marge knows. She licked my scars in bed last night.

(Wonder whether Chloe would).

The linen is cold and crisp and as I lie on it, it smells fresher than mine ever does, replete with perfume and mint and conditioner. All the stuff women pile in to the washing machine to make things nice, which men never do.

Chloe sits on the bed and passes me tea. I tell her that I want a jelly and she says jelly? and I point to the top drawer and she pulls out a strip. I need two and I take the tablets (talcum white, about the size of an old half pence piece) with a glass of water. I lay on my back, hot water bottle (newly boiled) on a towel resting on my belly.

Chloe is lying next to me, propped up on her elbow. I'll look after you. You scared me. Don't talk, listen. Like, don't say a word. Not a word, okay? Good. I'm here for you, old geezer. I'm here now. You've been so good to me. How could I have treated you like I did? I am so hating myself right now. I don't know what gets into me sometimes. I, like, get these things and stuff and they are so unawesome. That Conn told me some shit about you and I believed him. I feel so bad. So, so bad. You've always been there for me. I'll make it up to you. I really, really will. I've got something to tell you when you're better, but I don't want to tell you, like, now as you're totally sick. You smell of beer. It comes out of every pore hon. No more drink for you! Lots of TLC and hot chocolate. Did I tell you I wanted to be a nurse when I was a kid? Did I? Well I did and you can give me some practice. You never know, I might like it enough to go and do some training. I know, I know, the money's crap, but it's a lot safer than this lark. This is so dodgy, Mr Valentine, seriously is. Anyway, I shall tell you when you are better. So go to sleep and let's get rid of that poorly tummy. I have thrown all your dirty old linen away, by the way. I'll take you into town and buy you some more. I can't have my friend sleeping on those old ratty things. My treat! So that's, like, something for you to look forward to.

Chloe is crying.

She thinks I don't notice because my eyes are closed, but I do. I extend my right arm and lay my hand out flat and she takes it. We hold hands.

You looked after me, Terry. And I treated you like shit. I am so…

I squeeze her hand and shake my head ever so slightly. She notices. Then, she lays down next to me on the other pillow. She doesn't touch me but it is close to being intimate by the standards of friends, definitely by the standards of employer and employee. She squeezes my hand.

Her hand feels softer than I can possibly imagine. As space is infinitesimally black and eternally silent, so Chloe's hand is softer than a molecule of oxygen. There isn't a callus, a wrinkle, a pock, a divot, a scar on that palm, forged in Delphi and created by the master craftsmen of historical and evolutionary biology.

I have never, ever, experienced softer hands.

If I died now, if I were to pass over, holding Chloe's compliant hand, I would be happy, my sins, of which there are many, absolved and repented. My eyes remain closed. I hear Chloe's breathing. Sleep comes.

Doctor Strange

So while you've been out having fun…

Does this look like I've been having fun?

…I've been doing some thinking.

We're still on my bed, only its two days later. The jellies I took, according to Chloe, allied to the lack of sleep from the night with Marge, and my unfortunate Doom afterquake, wiped me out for nearly twenty four hours.

Then, after some soup, and a half of baguette she bought from the supermarket, I went back to sleep for another ten. Chloe had to go out – I assume on business – and when I woke I read *Jack's Return Home* to another conclusion, the second time I've read it recently, while listening to music. Sixties stuff. Beatles, mainly.

My stomach had improved to the level that I didn't need the hot water bottle and I had stopped imagining things, hearing sounds, seeing pictures in my head that I didn't want to be there. My cinemascope experience, in High Definition, is something that I never want to see again. I had been here before, when determined to give up drugs. The lamentations. The shaking of the head in both relief and defiance. The goggle eyes. The consideration of what might have been. The determination. The resolution, the fist on the palm. All this was familiar, a well-worn path, and I knew, as a man approaching his fifty first year that it was likely that I would forget all this angst and reach for the sherbet dib dabs whenever Francis wanted a night out. It's in me. It's always been in me.

Ever since the end of the football.

I don't crave. I don't steal. I don't inflict pain on others in order to enjoy drugs. After the football ended, I became drugs. I am drugs.

Subconsciously, despite my common sense, the good intentions, I saw this period in my sick bed as a break. The drugs are all we've got and a life without thrills is no life at all. You may as well be brown.

I don't plan to tell Chloe this.

Chloe comes back this morning with a shopping bag full of goodies and here she is, in my room, a vision. Its eight thirty, a time I don't generally have much to do with. I have to pinch myself. She's wearing denim shorts, which cut her in half, and gold sandals. Her nails (upper, lower) are bright pink and her hair flickers in the reflection of my bedside lamp. She's wearing a Betty Boop tee shirt (also pink) and she's been chirping away since she arrived. That doesn't bother me. I'm a good listener. If I hadn't have wanked my life up with this small-time thug shit, I could have become a counsellor. I'd have been a good one. I have the listening skills. Mind you, it helps that Chloe has the sexiest voice I've ever heard in my life. She could recite a report on North Sea Fishing Policy and I wouldn't interrupt once and I don't think she'd mind either. She's as quiet as a mouse on the way to work – considered, contemplative and shrewd – but in the day…boy, can Chloe natter!

She sits on my bed and I get both barrels. About her mates, her mum, the weather…but she is about to tell me about Tiffany's and it was something I wanted to hear.

She's made a tray of chamomile tea, for my stomach, in a royal blue earthenware pot I didn't know I had, which may have come from my mother's things after she died, and she's sitting next to me on the bed, with her legs pulled up and held to her chest by folded arms.

What have you been thinking about? I ask. Does it hurt?

She hits me with the pillow and it is lucky I don't have my mug in my hand. You're so cheeky, old geezer, she says.

Am I?

Yes you totally are. I've decided to, like, quit. Tiffanys.

Seriously? I say and then wait for her to continue.

Yeah. I feel guilty, though.

Why?

Well, she says, looking uncomfortable and I know what she is going to say, but still I let her say it. Like, you'll be out of a job and stuff. I won't…

…it's okay, love. It's okay.

What will you do?

Do I get a severance package? I ask, grinning.

She hits me again and tells me it's so not like McDonalds. We laugh for a time and she wells up a little bit. Not much, not tears, but her eyes glisten.

Are you sure you don't mind?

Course not. I'm glad. I'm buzzing. It's about time.

Is it? What about all the money?

It's not real money, love. It's fantasy money. It was never real. Now you can go and earn some of the real stuff.

She leans over and cuddles me and gives me a peck on the cheek. She's crying a little now and I feel a tear trickle down my cheek. I close my eyes and try and store away the memory of the sensation. She leans into me and whispers thank you and I say okay and smile and I never want this moment to end, this endless moment.

Then I recall something. Pass my phone, Chloe.

She does so.

I check my text messages. I'd not checked for two and a half days. There's nothing. I thought it would be full of messages from Marge, but there's nothing doing and I feel relief overwhelming the temporary feeling of guilt. Then I hand the phone back.

So how are you going to do this, I ask. Neville won't be pleased.

I told him last night.

How did he take it?

He was fine about it. I was surprised. That's where I went, last night to see him. I told him I was quitting there and then and I wouldn't be taking any more jobs. I don't want to see Jamal again either. Creepy!

I was wondering about him, I say, without going into any detail of my thoughts whatsoever. What is never voiced never materialises.

Horrible. He's not one of Neville's, by the way.

No? One of that lot in Gotham?

Yep. I told Neville I never wanted to see him again.

Did he try it on with you?

Oh no, absolutely not, thank God, but he was totally creepy. And it made me think about what I have been doing. What, I'm, like, actually doing.

Yes.

Especially without you. Jamal never said a word and he kept looking at me in the mirror. I wouldn't have minded and stuff if he actually said stuff, but he was, like, mute or something. Only, I know he wasn't. If he actually was mute, I'd have, like...well, you know. Been nicer. Jamal was being deliberately silent. Totally gross. There was last Tuesday too.

She unwraps a boiled sweet and puts it in her mouth. I try not to look. Last Tuesday, I think, Rachel Melon was giving me a complimentary blow job round at Crinkle's place. The thought makes me feel unnecessarily guilty.

What happened last Tuesday?

We had this job in Ravenshead, the wife of an American businessman. Spectacular house, lonely, exploring...well, I know you love listening to this...

I laughed. Yeah. Love it.

So, Jamal picked me up and, like, it's only down the road. He never says a word, but he keeps looking at me. I'm like, freaked out inside but I don't let him know it. I go in, do the job – awesome lady, in her fifties, proper lezzer, only it's way too late for her to ever come out and Jamal, when I got out, is staring at me even worse than in the car. He never stopped, mate. OMG, so I asked him what he was looking at and he totally grinned right back at me. Crap! What a freak! Freaked me out bigtime. Then the next night, Wednesday, he's waiting outside my house even though I've, like, *no jobs!*

Stalking?

Half an hour, mate. In his car. Just staring. I daren't go out to tell him, but I called Neville and told him I was freaked out. Next thing, Jamal drives off. Next night, we're down at Gotham...

...you went back there?

I know. Bad. I know. But I thought...well...you know what I thought.

Yeah, I say, not happy about it at all.

So, Jamal picks me up and he grins at me all the way down. Not saying anything, just, like, totally grinscape. OMFG! I was a nervous wreck by the time I got there. And do you know what?

What?

The next morning, Jamal had gone and guess who drove me home?

Who?

Conn. You know, the dishy one, she says, laughing.

I bet you enjoyed that, I say, seething inside.

She hits me with the pillow. I was kidding that time. You never did say whether you were jealous?

She grins at me coquettishly and like a sixteen year old on a mission. I change the subject quickly.

What happened to Jamal?

Dunno. Hope must have, like, pulled him off the case.

What?

Forget him. Can I tell you about that night with Hope? Have we reached this level yet?

No gooshy bits, Chloe.

You *wish* I'd tell you gooshy bits, dufus! K, I'll keep those to a minimum. There's Hope and me this time, so it's safe enough. So, we're in bed and we, like, do it, because that's what she's paid Tiffany's for, and I can handle that, it's the aftermath I totally cannot handle. Hope is so apologetic about Sunday, you know…the thing that made you and me argue…and, like, she promises me it will never happen again and she's like, I love you, and I'm like, OMFG, this has way got to stop, Hope, and she's like, but I can't Chloe, you know the way I feel and I'm like WTF, y'know, all the same stuff she gives me the first night. I told you about it.

You did, yes, I say, still resentful of that night and partly resentful about the way Chloe treated me in our own personal aftermath.

So, we have sex again…

…Chloe…

and then she's like, saying something totally weird.

What?

She's like, Chloe, you can learn to love me and one day, this would all be yours if you did, if you loved me, this would be ours.

Wayne Manor?

Totally. She's only proposing to me and I'm, like, OMFG. WTF, so I get out of bed and I tell her the truth.

What truth?

That she's, like, old enough to be my mum, that I love men and willies, and I want kids and a house in the country and all the usual stuff, whether I'm bisexual or not, and that I want to fall in love with someone and enjoy a family life, and I'm like, Hope, I will not be bought on this and do you know what she says?

No. What does she say, I reply, but I do know, it comes to me like second sight and I am right.

You will always be mine, Chloe. OMFG! I will always love you and I will make you mine one day. I will not give up on you, my love. I'm like fuck this and I get dressed and ask to leave. I'm like, Hope, tonight's sex was on me so, like, let's leave this as friends and I'm going home and she's like, okay, go, but we'll be together and no one else will ever have you, and I'm, like, whatever, dumbass crazy woman, but I don't say that.

People are weird, Chloe. Especially rich people.

So Conn takes me out to the car. Jamal's gone. He's like, I'll drive you home, Miss, in that cool English way of his and I'm totally relieved to be gone. Hope is crazy. Her eyes. She meant it all. No booze, no drugs. She freaking meant every word of it.

So on the way home, you decided to quit. And then you texted me?

Absolutely, mate. You nailed it. Conn was nice.

Was he?

She laughs. Oh, yeah. Dishy and suave. Mmmm.

Chloe…

Jealous? She's giggling.

He stiffed me bad, I say.

I know he did, dufus! I was kidding you. I didn't say a word to him on the way back, the asshole

And then you rang Neville?

Yeh, and I've got to go and pick some papers up from him this afto to, like, finish this. Tax stuff, a couple of signatures. He couldn't have been nicer.

You sure?

I know you and Neville don't see, like, eye to eye, but he's cool, y'know. I like him. Not as much as I like certain *other* people, but he's been good and he's totally been there for me. I'll still be his buddy and I told him I would do the odd special job for him for a Christmas bonus and stuff…but I probably won't. He was cool about that.

I say nothing. I know Neville and people like Neville. He is not going to be happy to let someone like Chloe basically walk away. A cash cow like her. He may be a businessman and he may have thirty or forty of them working for him, but Chloe is a show pony. No, she's a champion filly. In racing choicely bred mares are worth their weight in gold. Millions upon millions. The people that own those choicely bred mares aren't known for throwing money away and, generally, I suspect, they wouldn't be happy if one of them got up and walked out of the paddocks and into the sunset. But it would be pointless telling Chloe this.

I'll come with you later, I say.

Love it, Terry, but I'm meeting someone. Guess who called me yesterday? OMG, you will never guess?

Who?

Rebecca! Remember?

(Rebecca?)

I'm meeting her for a drink at 2pm. Pitcher and Piano. Isn't that wonderful!?

And coincidental, I think.

Yes it is.

I haven't seen her for a year! I am totally amped! Then after, I'm taking a cab to Neville's place and he's, like, getting one of his men to drive me back and stuff. Then, I thought…

…what?

If you were better, we could have a pint up at the Tranquility. About nine. I loved that night out. Did you? I hope so.

It was lovely. Superb night. And yes, I should be alright by tonight. Chloe?

I put my hand on hers and she cuddles me for no reason at all. I love it and I savour the moment.

Yes, old geezer, she says.

You be careful. Take your alarm. If anything cracks off, press the button and I'll be there like a shot.

Totally will, she replies. And then, tonight, we can talk about what I am going to do with my life, yeah?

I pull her closer to me, but its like father daughter precisely at this very moment and it feels right, it feels wholesome. I briefly wonder whether that's what I've felt all along…but then I know it isn't.

She holds me tight and says, you are so wonderful. I am so sorry for how I treated you. I am such an ass at times.

Hey, that's enough. It never happened.

She reaches up and kisses me on the cheek. Then she gets off the bed.

I'm going to cook dinner for you tomorrow night too.

What would that be?

Something green, mate. I've seen your pantry! OMG, I'm surprised you're still alive!

I'm not much of a cook, love.

Well, she says, pirouetting and then bowing, I am amazingly good. I'm off to get the ingredients. I shall see you later, alligator.

With that, she leaves me behind, a ball of thought.

I'm still weak and ill, and she comes back dressed up to the nines about midday. She is wonderful, all in black, with mauve lipstick and I only wish she was dressing for me instead of Rebecca, who she clearly has feelings for. She smells wonderful too. She tells me she's getting the 12.45 bus and that she wants to cook me soup. Nattering away like a good un.

I can't stop thinking about how convenient Rebecca's reappearance is, but what can I do about it?

I'm sick as a dog and I throw up as soon as I get out of bed. I can't persuade her not to go.

And then there's Neville.

But he's a businessman. He might try and persuade her to stay, but he's not going to hurt her. He's not a street corner pimp renting out crack victims for a tenner a blowie. Tiffany's

(Yes he is, arsehole)

is a business. He isn't stupid. I decided, on balance, that she was safe.

I won't sit on the bed. I'll ladder my stockings and like, get creases and stuff, she says, as I spoon asparagus soup into my mouth.

It's okay. You smell nice.

It's your favourite. I knew you'd like it.

First smelled it on the way to Stanton-On-The-Wolds.

The owner of the games company. Barbara. She had a funny minge.

Chloe, you know the rules.

It always makes me laugh. It was, like, such a weird shape. So gross.

Even I start to laugh at this and so does Chloe.

Well, Rebecca's a lucky girl, I say wistfully.

Is she, Terry? I am so looking forward to seeing her.

I know.

But do you want to know something else, mate?

Okay.

I am so looking forward to our pint tonight too. OMG, I cannot wait. About nine?

I'll be here.

Then she breaks her previous commitment, kneels on the bed and kisses me on the cheek. Her kiss lingers and the smell of her, perfumed, lustrous, opulent, regal, intense, explosive, envelops me like a shroud. There's a coldness about her presence. Not an indifferent chill, but a refreshing light summer cube of ice in a warm cola, something you want more of. I am completely in love with her, I know and she smiles at me and I know she knows it, what I feel and she isn't scared of it either.

Good, mate. Well, keep your phone on and I'll call you.

Laters, old geezer. Don't let the beg bugs bite!

I won't. See you, Chloe.

She blows me a kiss and she is gone. I hear the door shut.

Now, all there is to do is wait and pray for my love to come home....

…but she doesn't come home.
What a Cilla Black!
I knew it.
I fucking knew it.
Forty eight hours go by and there's no sign of her.
Not a peep, not a text.
I call her.
Phone dead.
They got her.
That slag Rebecca.
Neville.
And she was so looking forward to seeing her again.
I knew it.
I knew it.
Neville.
Conn.
Hope.
I knew it.

I couldn't even get out of bed without puking. The delirium in my head and fever in my body was so bad I couldn't even pick up my phone. And when I finally did, it had charged down and I was too weak to get up to recharge. My flat was a pit. Would have to remain that way for a while because I was going to get her back.

I knew what had happened to her. Conn had told me that weekend. She was in no danger, no physical danger. They might (*bastards*) rough her up, but they won't hurt her. That posh (*Messalina*) bitch was too into her. Too stubborn.

Two men could help me.
One man would have all the answers.
And one man would help me get Chloe back.

Barney Rubble

I'm weak and ill and I need some help. I try not to think about Chloe – I would melt. I figure she's safe….that's the only way I can prepare the job in hand. First stop is Neville's place. They'll know that's where I will go so he may have arranged some back up. Neville might even be arrogant enough to think he can take me and tonight, he probably could. I need help. I feel like shit and there's only person in the entire world I can turn to and I have to hope he hasn't been wiped out like me. He might even be worse.

He answers straight away. Francis. It's me.

Where you been, badman? You've got me anxious as to your whereabouts?

Forget that. I need a favour. And it's a proper one.

Without any hesitation, like the true friend he is, he says, go for it and I do. I tell him exactly what I need and its huge, its OTT, it's asking too much of a friend, especially a married friend, someone with kids (even though its something of a distant relationship, that one, after our time spent at Her Majesty's Pleasure), someone with a partner, and I expect him to tell me where to stick my favour and (to some extent) proposition, but he laughs, that slightly sick, slightly perverted, slightly maniacal laugh, like Muttley on mescaline. Says he's in, with no hesitation whatsoever. He makes a couple of suggestions and I go okay and he says he'll be round in three hours. I figure that's enough. I have an inkling where Chloe might be and I want to hit Neville when I have all the advantages. He's tasty. He boxes even now and he's built like a shithouse wall. One punch in my condition and I'm brown – literally, as the kids say now. Literally, brown.

I need to get positive. I need to start thinking I can win.

I turn on the CD player. Metal. I turn it on loud. Motorhead. I don't care about the neighbours.

Limb from Limb. From *Overkill*. Already I feel better. The music of bloody death.

(*Long legged lover…I'm going to tear you limb from limb*)

I shower for ages, it seems, and towel down. This could be it. I'm nearly sick in the bowl – a dry retch which might be nerves - and this time there would have been no Chloe to clean up after me. I go into the bedroom and start to dress. I need to be in top shape mentally so I raid the wardrobe proper, the stuff in protective bags, as I used to. Stuff I've not worn for a while, not since…not since before…

Proper gear. Vintage. Aquamarine Lacoste Chemise. Jeans, PH, the darkest blue. Fresh Ralph Lauren socks and boxers. Stone Island Artic (worn twice).

And for the piece de resistance, I pull out a blue shoe box. I open the lid. I bought these trainers online. Original. Never worn. Eighty quid in the box. I had my first pair when I went to Villa, the Holte End. I was a kid but I can picture everything about that day and I recall wearing those trainers that dad bought me for Christmas and thinking I was the dog's bollocks.

I've never forgotten them. Inside the blue box, enfolded and encircled in cream tissue wrapping that rustles and crackles as I touch it, I remove the trainers gently, as if they were made of alabaster two thousand years ago.

The blue itself is almost unique.

It isn't dark and it isn't light.

It isn't sea and it isn't sky.

I hold a trainer in my hand. I caress it. I tune out the music and focus. This trainer is a work of art. Every football lad worth the name had a pair.

Forget white trainers. Bollocks.

Forget them forever, as if they had never been invented, an anomaly in the space time continuum.

Cerulean blue kid leather.

Three white stripes on each side.

And in gold letters,

Gazelle.

The best pair of trainers ever made.

I put them on over my priest black socks and look at myself in the mirror. I don't wear a cap. You are either a hat man or not a hat man and I am definitely the latter. I have spiked my hair as high as it can go with wax as stiff as a bishop's cock on a missionary visit to a back street brothel. I splash on Givenchy aftershave. Lots of it. The very fact I am dressed like this makes me feel better able to take the challenge Neville has set me. I still feel like shit, but I feel less like shit than I did half an hour previously. I go to my desk and pull out my model making scalpel and place it in the inside pocket of my blouson. It has done enough damage to me in the past so what it will do to Neville is anyone's business and unless he tells me what's happened to Chloe in great detail, I'll cut railway tracks into his cheeks and remove an eye. I'll even chew it while he watches with the one he's got left.

I listen to music as loud and as heavy as I can get away with.

Thoughts of Chloe. The look on her face when I rescue her.

I think of Jamal and Conn and Neville and I clench my fist.

It's them or me. I know that. There is going to be death. Maybe a *lot* of death.

I wonder whether any of them have killed.

Conn must have.

I have.

Conn knows that. Neville told Chloe about me, he is bound to have told Hope, who would have told Conn, who would have informed all his Mr Troops. I'm not sure whether that puts me at a disadvantage or not. It may even give me an advantage.

The man who kills is a holy man in some cultures, the Aztec sacrificers, the Inca button men, the killer of souls, the man who sends the innocent to heaven and the guilty to hell, the killer, the high priest of death.

Brujeria.

The man of death meets the man of business.

Pike walks straight in without knocking. Surprise surprise, he's had the same idea as me, in a crimson Adidas tracksuit and gold striped Adidas Forest Hills. He's wearing his Hackett cap. He smells likes a tart's knickers but I don't place the brand. He's a good three stone overweight and he should have thought about that before considering the tracksuit combo, but he's a deceptively hard bastard and fast too – I've seen him in action. I feel like offering him a coat for modesty's sake. He's carrying a canvas holdall, which he plonks on my desk.

Turn that crappy headbanging music off and come look what Daddy's brought for Pass The Parcel, he says.

I do what he asks and get up and go over. He zips open the bag ostentatiously. Like Michael the Magnificent, he begins to remove the items from his holdall.

Voila, my trusty Kyocera. Anthracite FK. Double forged. Thirty five percent stronger than the ceramic version. Almost indestructible. You can't snap it and the edge stays sharp for fucking years. Atomic bomb hits the Market Square? The only fucking things left will be ants, rats, cockroaches and Kyocera knives and even then the blade will still cut through whatever you want it to. Fifty quid's worth of permanent scars. They tell me the kids are using these now, the young firms, but it's an automatic five years in Parva for a collar even if you're on your way to the Hilton for a shift in the kitchen.

He passes me the knife. It's ultra-light. The blade reflects weirdly, a shiny ebony light I don't expect. What possible excuse is there for carrying one? I acknowledge what I am shown and put it down on the table. He then picks up a Stanley knife – blood red, ironically.

The Scouse special. Probably the first hooligan weapon after the Doc Martin. That Bradford geezer when we were kids? Scousers cut railway tracks all down his back. Settle to Carlisle train trip without the refreshing English countryside and a stiff breeze to ease the pain. Front page news and the subject of sermons. Sparkly new blades have been added, badman; some plasterboarding I was doing last wik. Slip one out and slide it in.

STANLEY KNIFE.

If it is absolutely necessary to leave a mark on your enemy, to let them know who they've been dealing with, without causing any lasting damage to the vital organs, thus, reducing your potential gaol liability from ten to three years, you simply can't beat it.

Now, check this motherfucker out. Mau Mau jungle clearance a speciality. Forget them vintage Gazelles, Tezza: This is an original.1956. Straight from the steamy villages of Kenya. It were me Grandad's. Sliced the fuck out of one of them terrorists in the deep south. Chopped him to pieces. If you look closely, you can still see the bloodstains. He passes me over a dirty jungle machete, which is stained and heavy, the blade thin enough to cut skin and thick enough to break vine (or bone, in this case). I acknowledge the heirloom and put it down. Then he passes me a meat cleaver with no additional comment or back story, as if it's an afterthought. I run my fingertip along the edge. In comparison to my scalpel and the Stanley, it's blunt, but, like the machete, it will sever bone when used correctly. Plus the psychological damage inflicted by the sight of someone running at you with a meat cleaver (*Stoke, Birmingham, Millwall*), is enough to end most disagreements swiftly and without fuss. Cleavers always remind me of the old Ladybird book I read when I was a kid that got me into history. It goes something like this.

Saladin and Lionheart are in the desert having a pow wow. There is a tournament the knights of Europe against Saladin's elite. Lionheart is keen to demonstrate his broadsword's strength to his mortal enemy. He orders a metal bar to be placed between two brick columns. This is done. With one mighty blow, he severs the bar with his sword.

The wily Saladin acknowledges the feat of strength, calls for a servant, who deftly permits a silken bow to rise into the air. Before it can land, Saladin unsheathes his Scimitar and without fuss bisects it into two equal halves.

I ask the obvious question. Why so much stuff, Francis?

He shrugs his shoulders. Two reasons. One, choice. You choose. I can never make up my mind which is my favourite. I can never play First Person Shooters like Halo or COD, coz I want to shoot all the guns at once.

I suspect you're going to take the Kyocera.

I quite like the lump hammer, he replies. That causes some havoc. And the Stanleys are fast and light and geezers never see it coming. Remember Bolton?

You can't make up your mind, can you? I'll take this.

I pick up the machete and put it in the inside pocket of my

Stoney. And if you don't want the anthracite...

No. I'll take that, Tezza. And we can both take a Stanley. But I'm going into Nevs wi' lump hammer. He's a proper cunt. Rock hard. Ruthless. Sliced his best mate up in a fight over a slappy blonde outside Vic Centre KFC before he found God.

That's his best mate. Fists ain't going help here.

I know him, Francis. I know what he was like.

Man, course you do. I forgot. He battered your younger brother.

Yeh. I've never forgotten.

I wouldn't either if it were me.

Tilting the bag, I see he's thought of everything.

I bought these too, in case, he says, almost proudly, as if modestly discussing the achievements of his children on school sports day.

Nail gun.

Bolt cutters.

Yankee screwdriver (with sharpened point).

You've thought of everything, I say.

Second reason. Chloe isn't at Neville's, I can tell you that now.

I know.

He's a broker, a trader. He don't get his hands dirty, not unless…

…don't, Francis.

Fuck me, you've got her bad, mate! Not seen you like this, not since that Zoe tart fucked your swede up.

He's right. I say nothing, but the thought of Neville and…Jamal…and…makes my stomach go bad again and I get that humiliated, sick feeling.

We'll get her back, mate. Shall we get moving? My coat's in the motor. Where does Neville live?

Half way between Old Basford and Bulwell.

Ah! Bulwell. A salubrious destination for two gentlemen of sport on a fine evening like this. Oh, and I forgot…

He reaches into the pocket of his ill-fitting tracksuit trousers and pulls out a silver cigarette case. You've been feeling like shit, right? Well, me too. That last Doom tab was proper bad. Crinkle. Cunt. I popped round to ey a little word wi him to see what the craic was with that last fucking sherbert dib dab. He sez everyone went bug happy, but he were nice about it and I didn't whack him, and as compo, when I told him what we needed, he give us these little beasts for free.

He opens the cigarette case. Inside are four rocks, the size a tycoon's diamond engagement ring, off white, the colour of the pages of an old paperback book. Close up, they resembled snowflakes preserved in amber. I think I know what it is.

Augmented Base, mate. Fuck that yank crystal meth bollocks. This is Base. Special stuff. Mixed with some other stuff. Liveners.

Liveners?

Yeh. Steroid based gear. I told Crinkle what we needed and he came up with the goods. Hybrid.

Crinkle likes his hybrids.

Fresh off the boat from the Dam. Advantage of rock is that it oozes into your bloodstream and it takes about thirty minutes to hit the spot. Gis us time to get to Nevs. Then we'll fly, badman. We. Will. Fly. Know what they call this shit in the clubs?

No.
Nirvana. Fucking *Nirvana.*
I like it. Nirvana.
Drink?
I nod. Even though my belly isn't right, not by a long chalk, I pour two Glenfiddichs into my best crystal glasses (a present from mum a decade ago) and two separate glasses of water. He passes me my Nirvana.

Make that toast you make, he orders.
Which one?
You know. The one the barbarians make before they start raping and pillaging.
That one.
Yeh that one.
Right.
So make the toast. Do it.
I raise my glass. We clink together, invoking the spirits of good fortune. Being crystal, the brief connection resonates with a satisfying echo.

I make the toast.
Gird your loins.
Draw your sword.
Roll the dice.
Amen to that, cuntybollocks, he replies.
He places the rock on his tongue and washes it down with the malt. I follow his lead and take the water to reduce the heat in my mouth. Pike doesn't bother.
Now let's av it, Mr Valentine, he says.
I follow, turn off the lights and lock the door.

Nirvana

In order to get into Neville's flat complex Pike pretends to be a Pizza delivery boy. He contacts several flats through the intercom and pretends to be from Estonia or somewhere backward like that and eventually, someone is dumb enough to press the intercom buzzer anyway. I guess we could have called straight up, but its easier to kick down one door on the inside than attack from outside if, for some reason, he didn't choose to chat.

There's no CCTV feed and I'm surprised. I know where Neville lives because Chloe told me, she even gave me the number. 18, The Maltings, a converted tannery outside Basford. All glass, chrome, laminate, plastic plants and the smell of bleach and polish on the staircases, along with framed modern art prints mass produced in China for precisely this type of redevelopment. It's soulless, but I'd take it for the lack of damp – you'd get over a cold in a couple of days here. In my gaff, it takes a fortnight. Pike tells me to watch for security as we walk up the stairs, but no one's about.

We reach 18. Pike picks Old Lumpy out of his hold all and puts it in the inside pocket of his coat. I grip the machete, its shaft comforting and solid and do the same. I'm prepared to use it. I could slap the flat of the blade across his face, but I would go all the way because I hate him and I have nothing to lose. This is sub-judice. No coppers will come when the tears fall, no matter what we do to him or what he does to us.

It's about ten. I can hear TVs all over the show like static but nothing comes from Neville's place. Pike taps on the door. There's a shout. Who's that? It's not Neville and I know they are waiting for us. If they've got shooters, we're in bother. I put my eye to the viewer.

It's Terry Valentine. Chat needed. Tell Neville.

There is a shuffling inside. We stand either side of the door in case they shoot their way through, but the door opens quietly. Pike leaves the hold all under a giant plastic plant next door. I finger the machete inside my jacket. We go in. It's a sumptuous place. A palace. I'd expect nothing else. Neville is sitting watching TV on a crescent sofa made of virgin white leather. The TV is wall mounted, a home cinema system. He's barefoot, in a pink shirt and white trousers, more bling than Ratners. One leg is crossed over the other and he's sipping something clear from an ornate tumbler.

Drink, friends? He says without looking at us.

We both nod.

Hope you like rum. Top notch. The very, very best.

He gestures to one of two blokes standing staring at us. Real meatheads, one black, one white. Its difficult to differentiate on any other dimension. They're big. They're hard. And they're probably tooled up. If Neville doesn't come across, we're in shit.

The white one brings over two rums and distributes them. I'm not sure why he hasn't searched us. He knows I worked for Chloe without arms. Maybe that's why. Trouble is, there's Pike and he doesn't know him. He's a rogue element in Neville's calculations if that's the case. Maybe he's arrogant.

To what do I owe the pleasure? He asks. Again, he doesn't look over. He's watching football, Man Utd versus Arsenal. Plastic football. Viewed through a lens. Wellies on the beach. Sky TV. EPL. Wallpaper for wankers.

You know why I'm here, Neville. Chloe. She came to see you and she didn't come home.

And what's that got to do with me, dear heart.

She came here to hand her cards in.

Did she? Do you see cards round here, he gestured with a meaty arm.

She told you she was finishing. On the phone.

Never made it down here, chap. Never saw her. As far as I know, she still works for Tiffany's.

I'm sorry, Neville. I don't believe you.

He glares at me for the first time. I know he is lying. He knows he is lying. I stare back at him not moving.

You've got all your old County gear on, fella. You look very smart. Anyone would think you were ready for a punch up. Like the old days.

Neville, where is she?

The old days are over, sweetie. It's all this...he nods to the screen...HD football in the comfort of your own homes, glass of rum, central heating on full, a kip at half time, the missus rubbing your feet. Sexy teams, a superb occasion every week. Not to be missed. Fabulous Friday. Sexy Saturday. Super Sunday. Magic Monday. The same six teams the Pakis and the Yanks want to watch. United. Chelsea. City. Tottenham. Gooners. Scousers. No need to stand out there in the cold. No need to catch the flu. This is football. You can watch it in your pajamas with your mug of Horlicks and your missus can treat you to a wank while you're listening to the half time pundits.

Where is she, Neville?

One day, you'll have a footballer as Prime Minister. Not for a few years, but it will happen. Everyone loves football now they've put it on the TV where you don't need to sit next to some smelly geezer with a dirty hat, stinking of beer slops swearing, hating, abusing. Why, Terry? That coat you are wearing. Stone Island top of the range. Eight hundred guineas, if I am not mistaken. For the match? Good lord above! Look at me. I'm sitting here watching a great match of football with all the stars in the firmament and I'm in my pajama bottoms, lovely chaps.

I want to know where she is, Neville.

The escort game is like football, dear heart. When I first started supplying my customers with women, they'd accept any old boiler. Any hole's the goal. Any age, any height, any blemish. As long as they were breathing and could give a decent blow job, with or without their teeth in, they'd have contracts with me and make a good living. But then, it changed. My punters now desire a premium service. A little extra for a little extra. Like the people watching this match of football, they don't want to see Cardiff or Palace or Leicester – or, in a distant, parallel universe, little, tiny County. They want the star players every time. They cannot be doing with the ordinary any more. They want it now. IT. They want IT all now, the lot, a major occasion every time. So the cellulited housewives departed. Then the students with New Look knickers, the smokers with bad teeth, the obvious junkies, the stick thin crystal bitches I once sub-contracted from my bloods on the streets in times of high demand. The market changed, lovey. Tiffany's went premium. I went EPL. **The Escort Premier League**. And so when I met Chloe...well...like you felt your cock stand to attention – and we all know how you feel about her, don't we, dear heart – I, instead, felt my wallet expand. Exponential potential. Yes. *Exponentia*l, loves.

He was getting on my nerves. Pike hadn't moved except to sip his rum. The two blokes behind Neville were statues too. The Nirvana was starting to work...it took longer than I thought. It made me want movement and action. I didn't want to listen to a monologue. And he was taking the piss with every sentence. He continues, blithely. Where it leads...

We've made some money together, Chloe and me. She's been good for Tiffany's. She's given us respectability and along with a couple of other girls I have employed, she's created quite a niche for us with those business customers of a Sapphic persuasion. Those rather successful laminate munchers who run a great deal of Nottingham's business. Laminate munchers, hey! It used to be carpet munchers didn't it, before the, um, fashion changed. Hah!

The two men behind Neville laughed.

Yes, most ladies of my persuasion had a good Axminster sample on the pie dish at one time, keeping their juicy bits warm in winter, but nowadays, it's Norwegian Pine all the way.

Enough, Neville, I said, quietly. Get to the point.

I'll take as long as I want in my own gaff, he shouts, changing rapidly.

Tell me the story. All of it.

So, being honest. I was not best pleased with her planned career change. Especially with the little tickle I was offered last week. A very nice deal.

A deal? I ask, curious. Chloe had not mentioned this.

Your employer wasn't too happy, but I was. I couldn't believe what she was being offered.

She's there now, isn't she?

You have no idea how much money the Calder family have. And it seems that Hope Calder has it worse for Chloe than you do, old thing. It's a spectacular love job. The real deal. *Love Story. The Way We Were.*

On the screen, Rooney scores from ten yards and everyone but me focuses on the highlights. It goes quiet. I couldn't care less. Even Pike's watching.

Then it continues.

Hope Calder isn't stupid. She knows Chloe doesn't love her. Of course not.

But she thinks she might grow to love her if they spent enough time together, I say.

Indeed. Do you want to know how much Hope offered for Chloe's presence?

You're going to tell me anyway. How much?

Hope Calder, bombshell tycoon extraordinaire, offered little, gorgeous, sexy, Sapphic Chloe, your friend and mine, half of one million pounds for one year of her time.

I look at Pike. Half a million, I say, dumbstruck.

One half of one million pounds. In order to access such a sum, Chloe would have to move lock stock and barrel to Gotham. Leave it all behind. The Calder Trust of the Cayman Islands would pay me one hundred and twenty five thousand pounds four times per year. Chloe would get ninety thousand per quarter in an account that she couldn't touch and Tiffany's Escorts would get the rest. Hope would pay the remainder to Chloe as a bonus in exactly a year's time.

And me?

You were *sacked*. You didn't come into consideration, dear heart. You weren't even the inksplash on the contract.

Neville leans back on his sofa. Without looking at me, he tells me what I already know.

I couldn't have little Chloe leaving, Terry. Sorry. I couldn't have it. Not for a second, dear boy.

I say nothing.

All that money. *And Chloe said no.*

I know where she is. Pike knows where she is.

I have always known where she is.

I'm not even sure why I am here.

Yes, I am.

Thanks for the info, I say. I'll see you. Pike, come on.

We start to the door. Neville is having none of it.

I didn't expect him to.

I can't have you going round there spoiling things for me, sorry, he says.

Neville nods at his men of business who move towards us. They're both holding guns. Shit.

Be serious, Neville. Shooters?

You can have someone killed in our old manor for a pony you know that. Crackheads and kids. A paving slab on the head. A knock down. A single bullet from a wannabe. You two gentleman are worth nearly a hundred and forty grand. Think about it. It's what children call a no-brainer. There's nothing else to say about it, dear boy.

Well, if I'm fucking dead, I may as well have a giraffe, Pike says, pulling Old Lumpy out of his pocket launching it underarm at the black guard, while simultaneously, jumping to one side.

It goes off.

Party party.

The guards are slow and ponderous, probably scared and undertrained. They both fire, but we're speeding now, the Nirvana kicking in, the reaction times accelerating, our thought patterns acute, and when I hear Pike jump, I move instinctively too. The bullet with my name on it tears through my Stone Island, ruining it (bastard!), but misses my body. The black guard is down, the hammer hitting him on the nose, moaning, on the verge of unconsciousness. Pike is on the white guard and he's punching the lights out of him. I forgot how fast he is for such a fat bloke. Neville is coming at me and I stand, throw a right, but he ducks and floors me with one punch. I feel my nose forced to one side. Blood pours down my face. I bounce back but Neville hits me again. Then he hits me three times, mighty hammer blows and I'm down. (*this brings back memories*). I expect him to laugh, but he's cold eyed. He'll kill me with his bare hands. He picks me up by my coat and headbutts me and I shout...the pain is excruciating. My machete has fallen to the floor, but I still have my scalpel and I roll over, feign being dazed and reach into my top pocket. He kneels on my spine and punches me in the kidneys. My eyes water with the pain but I ignore it, even when he hits me again in the same place. I keep waiting for Pike to come over, but from what I can hear, he's fighting for his life too.

Neville likes the sound of his own voice and he's off on one.

You always were a loser, Terry. When I found out Chloe had employed you, I laughed. I laughed out loud. And I told her what you'd done. That you killed that man. Over football. Over *football*. She wasn't happy, I can tell you. She was *shocked.*

He hits me again and I can hardly breathe. Pike and the guard are going at it like Frazier and Ali and I feel guilty that I was whacked so easily. I'm losing my touch, but then, Pike was always stronger than me in a fight. And so was Neville the Nemesis.

But still I couldn't get her to disemploy you, as it were, he continues. No matter how I threatened her, she always stood by you. The silly girl. And to think I only offered her a job on the off chance in the club...

(What?)

Neville. Listen, I say, through smashed teeth and blood. Wait. What did you say?

You don't know? You don't know how I discovered Chloe? Ha! She told you nothing did she!?

What happened, Neville? Tell me, I say through bleeding lips and loose teeth.

I tried to fuck her, dear heart, but she wouldn't have it, not on the first night anyway. We canoodled for a while on my bed, but she wouldn't let the Panther anywhere near her. In the end, I had to content myself with her dirty pal, Rebecca. A total vixen with very few morals, the absolute, complete and total fuck of the year. Bathing in the afterglow, Rebecca told me about Chloe's mum. All I needed to know. The leverage.

(What?)

Chloe's mum? I say. Leverage?

Chloe slept in the spare room while I helped myself to Rebecca's slim little body. The information about Chloe's mum gave me an in on the deal when we met around the table for breakfast. Anti-cancer drugs.

Drugs? Chloe's mum is ill?

Did she not tell you? Neville says.

He laughs loudly and bangs my head on the laminate floor. Then he leans over me so I can sense his breath on my neck. I'm pinned down and he's twenty stone of muscle. I can scarcely breathe. He's loving this. I say nothing as he continues.

(Oh Chloe. Honey.)

What the NHS drug's czars will and won't supply for cancer! Who knows! It's a postcode lottery, dear heart. One street gets all the sweeties. Cancer-afflicted kiddies on the street next door waste away to nothing.

He's almost touching my ear. I detect rum, mouthwash and cheese and his breath his warm. I still say nothing.

Unfortunately, Chloe's mum is on the street next door. So, thanks to Rebecca, little me, little Neville, gave her an option which would help out. Chloe thought about it, said she'd like to fuck women, and voila, I signed up the hottest escort in Nottingham! Pity she wouldn't do men, but with a tycoon lebbo like Hope Calder around, it wasn't particularly necessary - though she could have made herself an absolute fortune with some of my many male clients, dear heart.

I know he is telling lies to wind me up, but there was one question, knowing Neville and his reputation, that I had always wanted to ask. Maybe it was the Nirvana or maybe I was stalling for time. They say you should never ask a question unless you know the answer already or can handle the answer you will get, even if it's bound to be bad, but I couldn't resist it. Even though he is lying out of his back teeth, I want to hear him say the words.

Did you fuck her, Neville?

Of course I did, old fruit, he replies without hesitation.

(Bastard. Oh Chloe. Oh Chloe)

I sample all the wares I offer my customers. It is a condition of the contract between my employees and me, and, if I may say so, it's a most delightful perk of the business. In fact, I fucked her and Rebecca together the very next night, dear heart. What a splendid night that was…after a sumptuous dinner at the Market Place Hotel. I can honestly say that I have never seen a show like it. My clients definitely get value for money. Here, actually. In front of the fire. All night long. Rebecca and me fucked her repeatedly and she begged for more. She could not get enough of Rebecca, and, if modesty permits, she was particularly partial to my growling Panther. Grrrrrr. Good lord, she paid him some attention. Indeed, she did, old boy.

You're a liar, I say, popping the sheath from the tip of my cutter.

Chloe's tongue, Terry. It's a one woman cock carnival in that mouth of hers.

He makes his mistake. As people who like the sound of their own voice are prone to doing. Bingo. The Nirvana kicks in fuelled by my indignance. My head goes. I feel my muscles expand. I spin round, throw him to one side. I slash at his arm with the silver scalpel and he yelps and I cut him again across the face, the climax of a long, sweeping wave of my hand. It connects exquisitely, a long slice bisecting his cheek.

He doesn't expect it. He tries to punch me, but he's in shock and he backs off, plasma spraying all over the carpet. I stand up. Rage has me. Now I couldn't give a shit. I'm going to kill and slash and burn and kill.

Neville stands too, punches my shoulder, a weak rabbit punch, and I step forward and hack at his face. The blade connects underneath his eye. He screeches, not my face, not my face, and as he bleats and cries, I skip the short distance between us, and with surgical skill, dig a trench along his left cheek with the diamond-sharp tip.

He's holding the skin of his cheeks together, the blood spilling onto his pink shirt, the combo, a swiss confection, like the inside of a raspberry ruffle chocolate. He goes into himself like a little baby, snivelling. I kick him in the face for good measure and it takes the stuffing out of him. I feel his teeth go, and I feel like I've settled a score.

Over the other side of the room, Pike is getting the worst of a bad argument. The meathead is pinning him down and punching him in the face. I pick up the machete and I walk over. He doesn't see me until its too late. Neville could warn him, but he's crying, holding in the two halves of his cheek which have been parted like the Red Sea. Free, taking my time, I take a swing and cleave him, Pike's Grandad's machete bisecting the middle of his skull. It wedges nicely in there, with a satisfying thud, and he falls forward, bleeding into Pike's face.

My friend is a mess but I haven't got time for tea and sympathy. I reach the lump hammer quicker than Neville can reach the pistol, pick it up and throw it overarm. It connects with the side of his chin with a dull thud which belies the pain the hammer inflicts. He goes down crying. I pick up the hammer again and slam it against his shin bone.

Now I know I've won.

He's not coming back from this. I've won. For me. My brother. For my school days. My degree. My wanked up life. All down to you, you evil bastard. I've won. I pick up the hammer and break his knee cap, purely for fun, for laughs, for giggles, for coffee and after-eight mints, for all his lies about Chloe.

And, of course, for slapping my brother on his head with a piece of four by two.

From behind.

I watch him weep.

Pike is up. Staggering, but up.

We stand over Neville, who is alternating between tears and laughter. A typical pain reaction. I've been there. I bend down next to him. All that was a lie, wasn't it. I say, quietly. About Chloe. A lie.

You fucking wish, he responds defiantly. You've not had the pleasure, have you!?

He laughs maniacally.

I don't respond.

Funny isn't it, he continues. You go up to Hope's place and rescue your fragrant love and you're condemning her mum to a slow death at the hands of the cancer. Isn't that funny, you talentless hooligan scum. Life is full of those little dilemmas, isn't it?

You're lying.

Think so? He responds tears pouring down his face. Go up and see.

Go up and see her reaction.

I shall do.

Neville calms down for a second and gives me the eye. I always hated you at school, he says. Always thought you were cleverer than anyone else. Always answering the teacher's questions. Always looking down at the rest of us. That was you, chap. I hated you for it. Every day I was at school I wanted to smash your face in.

You ended that, Neville. You ruined that for me.

He stares, defiantly, without saying anything, his face a bleeding mess, his leg twitching, tears welling up in his eyes, teeth bared. Then, he changes tack slightly.

Let her go. Please. Let her do her business. Life goes on…go home.

And what about you? I ask.

What about me? He responds.

If I leave her alone, what would you do to me? And my friend here. Would you leave us alone when you got better? When the face I most recently sliced had healed to a scar and you could walk again? What would you do? What would you say? You're connected, Nev. You *know people.* We wouldn't last a week. Now, would we?

He says nothing. There truly is nothing he can say.

Outside, a Police car drives past on the way to Bulwell. Siren.

There's no choice.

Go on then. Do it. Fucking do it, he says.

I remove a silky, opulent, pineapple-coloured cushion from the sofa and place it over his head. He struggles, but Pike hits him again on the already snapped knee with the lump hammer. That takes all his attention.

Were it not for the sumptuous padding (duck feathers?), his wailing would have woken the neighbours.

I pick up the dead henchman's gun, place the noisy end of the barrel at the cushion's epicentre and pull the trigger.

He stops instantly. Supernaturally.

There is a surprising, immediate stillness about the corpse once his leg stops twitching.

Bye, dear heart, Pike says.

The black guard behind us is starting to stir. We've no wish to kill him, so as he rises, Pike hits him on the back of the head with the flat of the machete. That pacifies him further.

Pike trousers his gun and I pocket mine, along with the cutter. Buzzing, we search the place for treasure. We find five wads of twenty pound notes in a metal CD case.

About five grand, I estimate. We take a chunk each plus some bling from his bedside table, sovs and chains. Pike stands on the giant double bed and pisses on it, swinging his cock about like a hose pipe on a hot summer's day in the garden. It's a good job the filth won't give a second thought about this. It's all gangster stuff. Not like real life. They'll be too busy hunting for football lads, council tax defaulters, politicos and shoplifters in the tourist ghetto.

Still.

To make sure, I leave two thick rolls of twenties and several sovereign rings on the bedside table as our contribution to the Police Christmas party.

We calm down and clean ourselves up in the bathroom. My nose is a mess, my front teeth are bleeding and loose, my kidneys and ribs are going to hurt bigtime tomorrow and one of my eyes is beginning to close, but the Nirvana is acting like an anaesthetic and I've had a lot worse than this. That kicking at Hartlepool, for example. Thought I was going to die up there. Those jocks coming back from Bruno. And in those toilets against Palace at Doncaster train station.

Pike cleans himself up in the bath. He's had worse too. One game, he got jumped by six Boro at Nottingham train station and no matter how hard they tried, they couldn't knock him down. Afterwards, his face was like John Merrick and he didn't go back to the refuse depot for six weeks, bless him

We are both laughing. Perhaps this is also due to the sweeties. Perhaps not. It is entirely possible that the moral implications of shooting Neville and cleaving the head of his hapless henchman will kick in tomorrow, so I shall leave it until then to worry about it

After we have stopped laughing, we shake hands. We sit on the magnificent, but now blood drenched, sofa and finish off another rum. The drugs inside us seem to mirror the external environment and we chill. This Nirvana is some gear. Intelligent drugs. Usually gear dominates, but I feel as if am in charge here and the drug is a willing servant. It kicks in when you need it to and it brakes when you don't. I feel wonderful, despite Neville's revelation about Chloe. It doesn't impact upon me because I don't believe it. No. I know he is lying. To wind me up. A last bullying moment. The glasses from which we drink the dark rum are substantial. Top of the range Austrian lead crystal. The diameter of the glass fills my hand. It makes the rum taste that much better. Manchester United have won 2-1 with a last minute goal and the Gooners are off their seats in the Library, not happy bunnies. Some are calling for Wenger's head. Nameless, faceless, pundits ejaculate over looped VT of Rooney scoring a simple goal from close range. You would think he had scored from thirty yards with an overhead kick. Neville's corpse, similarly faceless, lays still, blood congealing in pools under his shoulder and neck .It's quiet, a moment of calm and it stays that way for a few minutes. Pike breaks the silence.

How you feeling, mate?

Buzzing. You?

No, about what he said about…

It's all lies. I'm not worried. I know it's a pack of lies, I reply. Chloe told me the score in the rubadub one night. A friend of hers offered her a deal. It's business. Neville was winding me up. Bullying me again like he used to. There's nothing to worry about. I'll sort it with Chloe. She'll put the record straight after we get her out.

Okay, mate.

We'll sort it out up at Wayne Manor.

Gotham, youth?

That's what Chloe and me call it. Wayne Manor.

After where Batman lives.

Yeah. Chloe loves all that. She thinks it's hysterical that Nottingham has a Gotham.

Love Batman, Pike says.

You big kid.

There is a silence. Then, Pike ostentatiously empties the rum and throws the glass against the wall in the Russian style. It bounces, doesn't break and rolls a short distance along the carpet in front of us. We look at it quizzically. I throw mine harder. It doesn't break either.

Terry, mate, time to go.

Okay.

Part I's over. Good night, Neville.

Good night, Neville.

Yeah. It's been emotional.

Yeah, it has.

Now. Enough of this tomfoolery. Let's go and get your woman back.

Part IV: Army of Two

Home Comforts

We're driving in his Fiesta. Flying high on Nirvana, reaching that plateau, tapping our feet and moving to the beat, listening to seventies music, Pike's *"Seventies Forever"* CD, which seems to be permanently wedged in his player. We're listening to *Rubber Bullets* by 10cc but we're so wired into the world because of the rock kicking in, we could be listening to speed metal or total silence and it wouldn't make a blind bit of difference to anything.

Suddenly, I am gripped by another compulsion.

Francis, listen.

Go for it.

It could get bad up there, mate.

Do fucking tell, dear heart.

Please don't start talking like him.

You stop talking bollocks. I'll stop talking bollocks.

Okay. Just saying.

Then don't. It's fine.

I know. Mind you, I've murdered two more people, it can't get much worse.

Neville was a prick. Don't give him a second thought. He made your childhood a misery. What about that time at the Crich school trip?

Forgotten all about that. Thank you for bringing up a shit memory, Francis.

You're welcome. Neville deserved to die for that, ne'er mind for crowning your kid brother with a piece of four be two outside the scout hut.

Okay.

Right, enough regrets and all our yesterdays. Let's go through the options.

Let's do it.

It's dark now, and chilly, our path lit by amber streetlights and rapidly passing headlamps. We're heading out on Wilford Lane down towards Wayne Manor and we have about fifteen minutes to go at the chilled out pace Pike is driving. He's laid back, like he's in some form of Cadillac, driving with one hand on the wheel. I wish we had a better car for the purpose - the Audi, for example – because Pike's Fiesta wouldn't impress anyone. And it's pink too, though Pike will never have that, would never have it in a month of Sundays. He thinks its pale violet, which is as bad, bless him.

Number one, he says. Why don't we simply knock on the door and ask to see your bint? Pike says. Have a natter with her. A quiet chat.

That's not going to work and you know it, I reply. They don't want me anywhere about. They'll do anything to stop me seeing her. Remember what Conn said to me?

Yes.

I'm like the cold water in Chloe's face. Hope's strategy is clearly to keep her tucked up.

Boxing Chloe.

That's right. Forget that idea.

Next then, bollocks. Why don't you call Hope herself and discuss it? You've got Conn's number. Negotiate.

With what?

I dunno. An expose or something in the papers.

Pike's eyes are the size of flying saucers and he has a rictus grin on his face. I know that this is the worst situation either of us have ever been in. Pike is the bravest man I have ever come across but this is different gravy. This is promotion to a different league.

Same deal. There's no way he would pass the phone on…and you've forgot something.

What?

These people own the press. All the media at the party. We'd be missing before the weekend. And if he does answer the phone, we lose any element of surprise we might have.

What if she wants to stay? How would you know?

I admit that's a leap of faith. No way would she want to stay, Francis. Neville was lying. Trust me, she won't want to stay. She'd want me to go help her home. She's been held against her will. She would have called to explain yesterday otherwise. Neville has told us a pack of lies. Jackanory. Hope is going to keep her there. We're her only ray of light, trust me on this.

Her only Hope.

Are you taking the piss? I say, laughing.

Half a mil is a lot of money, Pike says. Personally, it would buy me an awful lot of get-me-the-fuck-out-of-Nottingham.

I know. If that bit is true, we could be in bother. But Chloe talked to me about getting a job. She's a decent chick. She's packed it in working on her back. It was all over for her. It's not real. It's fantasy and anyway, with Neville being brown bread, I wonder whether the deal's still on? I don't trust these people either. Do you genuinely think Hope is going to give Chloe half a mil?

Probably not. What about her mother? The cancer?

That's a lot of bollocks, I say and I believe it. Chloe would have said something. She had no reason to keep it from me. And anyway, I have an idea about how we can make some money AND get Chloe out of there in case it is. She doesn't need to do what she's been doing. We can make some money tonight.

Robbery!? Blackmail!? I like it, Pike says. You ought to be on a satellite gangster show. But what about Conn and the gang.

That lot?

They might have something to say about it.

At first I thought they were ex-military. But now I think they're bouncers and thugs. Football lads.

Like us?

Yeh. Thugs like us. And we've never been scared of other football lads.

You're right.

Following Notts was sado-masochism at one point.

You're not kidding.

We never ran. Hard to forget.

What about Conn?

He's a proper tool. Leave him to me.

Oooh, you sounded hard then, shagnasty. I was shit scared.

Did you like it?

Loved it.

We pull up to traffic lights heading out from Nottingham into the rural village network in which Gotham forms the centre. The compulsion hits me again. I feel as if I have to labour the point.

Pike, it could get proper tasty up there. You can drop me off and drive away.

Don't insult me, you cunt. As if I'm going to leave you up there, he says, sharply. I should have known better, but I carry on.

I mean it, Pike. Its…

Pike indicates left, looks over his shoulder and immediately pulls over to the side of the road. He turns off the engine, his brown eyes blazing.

Enough, Terry. I mean it. We're together on this.

But I'm single, Francis. I've got nothing. I die tonight and the world won't miss me for a second. You've got a wife and kids. They've got shooters.

He grabs hold of my shoulder. I mean it, cunt. Shut your trap. Enough now, don't neg me out. I'm on a fucking buzz here. Don't neg me, badman.

I'm just...

Pike glares and I know to shut up. He sits back in his seat and makes no attempt to start driving. I guess we have all the time in the world. For a minute or so he doesn't say anything. *Summer Breeze* by the Isley Brothers plays, and there are no other cars on the road. You could hear a pin drop, the beating of our Nirvana elevated hearts.

Since I've met you, you've killed three blokes and way I see it, it's my fault.

What?

The first bloke. I set upon em in the pub and you caught unlucky. He banged his head. I went to Camp too, but that was because I wouldn't talk to the Bill, not because I killed anyone.

Ancient history. We paid the price.

Neville's fraggle was battering me and you cleaved his skull into two equal sized bits. If you hadn't done that, he'd have beat the crap out of me and I would probably have been brown.

You would have done the same, I say, but Pike is off on one and I may as well have said nothing.

Neville's down to you, Tezza. He bullied you when we were kids. You went round there to settle a score, you didn't have to go there at all.

That one went back nearly forty years.

Still, two one to you. I owe you, mate.

No you don't.

Pike ignores me and shakes his head derisively.

Yes I do, let's not get fucking pantomime on this. I've been a bad influence on you all my life. You're a clever cunt – one of the cleverest blokes I have ever met, if not THE cleverest - but you like being a badman. You always have done, even when we were kids. Always wanted to be the outlaw not the sheriff and it got worse after Neville and the others battered you. You like the dirty girls and the easy money, the scrapping at the match. You want the fucking lot.

I say nothing, internally agree. I wish I still smoked. This seems like an appropriate time for a cigarette, but no-one smokes any more.

Can't say that I blame you, Tezza, but now, you've reached the end of the road. There's no coming back from what you've done in Basford, and what you are about to do up at the posh house. I should fuck off and leave you to it, there's no way the cops would know I was there at Neville's gaff unless you told them, which you won't.

I never would, no.

So, it's time to pay a few debts.

You don't owe me anything.

Yes I do, so enough.

What about Louise?

Pike laughs. The missus? Lou? You're having a giraffe. Know what she's doing now? Right this very minute? My beloved wife of twenty one years is most likely cybersexing some cunt from London. Some writer bloke. He writes…get this…get this one…

What?

…he writes **crime thrillers.**

That's funny. That's quality.

Makes me piss, badman. He would never have come up with this story in a month of Sundays.

No. Deffo not.

She likes his stuff and they got talking on Facebook. All the women are shagging writers now. Interactive fan mail, badman. It's not like sending letters to comics! I caught her at it on her birthday, one hand down her panties, one finger in her gob, chat box flashing like Christmas lights. I didn't even give her a kicking. Laughed at her. Seriously. Laughed. She looked a proper sight. She keeps saying they are finished, but she's all over him like zits. I ain't slept with Lou in a year. We hardly speak and to be honest, I couldn't give a shit whether she lives or dies. Marriage does that to you, mate. Twenty seven years of living with a woman and you don't even know her. You end up hating her. I loved Lou when we were young. You know that. You saw us. Couldn't do enough for her, you know, and now, I can't even bring myself to go down the Magic Spoons with her for a half of bitter and a packet of crisps. I can't even bring myself to ask how the kids are and do you know what? You know what? She hates me too. She can't even be bothered to acknowledge my fucking birthday. How does that happen, Terry? How do couples get like that? Motherfucker, the promises you make, the soft words of puppy love.

I know. I'm sorry mate.

Don't be. Happens.

What about the kids?

A memory to them now. They don't even text me and you know how kids text. Never were that close. They love their mum, a lot more than I do, and fair play. You know, if it wasn't for all this malarkey, I was going to leave after Crimbo.

Louise? Leave?

Yeh, but something stops me. I guess.

What?

Living in a damp infested shit hole like you do for a start.

I laugh and so does Pike.

I couldn't face that, mate, no offence. I've got my home comforts to consider, he continues.

Home comforts, I say, laughing. I know those home comforts.

You do?

Yeh.Those...

Stinky slippers, he says. *Those stinky slippers your kids bought you through their mother when they were six.*

Thermal house socks to keep the bills down, I add.

Hot water bottles.

Ratty old armchair.

Eighty Benson and Hedges and a leather strap ashtray on the arm.

Wall mounted Plasma screen

Eight cans of cider.

Family sized bags of crisps.

Pizza Home Delivery.

Naan kebab and double chicken and chips.

Pea mix, double battered sausage, batter bits.

Scratch your bollocks on the way to the bog.

Receding gums.

Thickening arteries and teeth that fall out into the soup.

Yellow dentures.

Colostomy bags.

Viagra Dependency.

Bowels leaking into your jeans.

Missus on the phone to her sister every night.
In a face pack.
Varicose vein comparisons
Catching the missus giving your mate a soapy tit wank.
X-Factor on a Sunday night.
Strictly Come Dancing on a Saturday.
Masterchef
Jamie fucking Oliver.
Gordon fucking Ramsay.
That clever cunt with the glasses and the Bunsen burner
That gang of gay chefs on Saturday morning
Including that fat cunt who used to do Soccer AM
With that fit blonde who dumped that four-eyed darter
The Real Housewives of Orange County
Shit music.
Shit films.
Premier League Football
Man United Cunts.
Man City Cunts.
Sky TV pundits.
Sky TV
Rugby
Golf.
Cricket exclusively on Satellite TV
The Derby on a Saturday.
Kids that don't like horse racing
And the dogs.
Kids that only bet on football coupons.
Wankers.
Football wankers.
No more heavy metal.
All the kids want to be a chanteuse.
Maxed out credit cards.
The ever present threat of redundancy.
Close circuit TV.
Police State.
The relentless rise of the British Middle Class.
The takeover of pop music by rich people
Mumford and Cunts

Public school bastards
Old people on cruises
Bleeding us taxpayers dry with their sumptuous and largely unaffordable final salary pensions
Tories.
Toby and Natalie at the BBC subsidised by starving lone parents in high rise flats.
Girls that don't even notice you when you're sitting next to them on the bus.
A missus who thinks about any fucker else on your one shag a week.
Cry yourself to sleep every night waiting to die.
Looking forward to the funerals of your family.
And the funerals of your friends.
Looking forward to your own funeral, motherfucker. You got it in one, sir.
Home comforts, Francis.
Home comforts indeed, Tezza.
I guess it's time for us to do something about all this shit. That's Pike's point. He starts the engine.
Life is a fucking suicide note in weekly parts and I, sir, have had more than enough. So don't worry about me.
You're right. I won't. Sorry.
On the Seventies Forever CD, the opening bars of Electric Light Orchestra's *Mr Blue Sky* play.
Remember this tune, I say.
I used to love this record, Pike says. Do you know the words?
Of course I do…you?
Ha. Come on, let's sing.
He pulls off into the empty road and we sing as loud as we can…

Sun is shining in the sky

There ain't a cloud in sight

It stopped rainin

Everybody's in a play

Hey there Mr Blue

(Sky) Hey there…Mr Blue…

Jack's Return Home

Pike has the bag over his shoulder. We park up about half a mile down the road and we walk across fields to get to the fenced off woods to the north of the Manor. We don't say much. We've taken the last of the Nirvana to keep us sweet and we're determined, buzzing. We're carrying pistols this time but we'll only use them in an emergency. Noise factors, rather than humanitarian ones. We go into the woods and take it quietly and slowly. We're gambling they won't expect us, though we expect them to be on some sort of alert. If I'm wrong about these blokes being ex-military, we're probably already dead and we don't know it yet. It's dark and nippy. It's likely that will be closer to the Manor. But halfway down in the woods, Pike bobs down.

Up ahead.

What?

Some dafto's smoking a fag. Two of them. Look.

I look ahead and towards the edge of the wood, I see sparks. A cigarette glow.

Daft.

Pike takes the lump hammer out of the bag. I have the machete. We slowly make our way down. We hear them rather than see them clearly and we have a decision to make. They are nattering away about nothing at all, two muscular blokes in wooly hats and thick black coats and gloves, clearly doing what they are told without taking much notice or expecting what is about to happen to them. Leaving the bag as close to the clearing as we can, we stalk forward. Pike is fast. They see us a split second before we hit them. Pike smashes a meathead in the face with the lump hammer. I slap the other around his face with the blade of the machete, both hands. They both go down, unconscious, slightly gormless looks on their face.

Pike's brought cable ties and we tie them up, then pull them into the scrub. The Manor is about a quarter of a mile down the hill and it is open ground, a grassy bank, very little cover. Some bushes, that's all. I nod toward the edge of the wooded clearing and we skirt around as we can't risk the direct approach. It adds ten minutes to the time, but soon we are down by the barn. I peek my head around the barn wall. There's two more of them sitting near a water trough. From down here, the moon above is acting the floodlights at Wembley. We can see everything, the two blokes, big fellas, like the sentries at the top. Carrying machine pistols loped over their shoulders like manbags.

See them? I say.

Pike takes a peek over my shoulder.

Wouldn't mind a go on one of them machine guns, he replies, a cheesy fat grin on his face. My insides are turning to ice water and he thinks all this is kushty, a walk in the park. What do we do?

We can't shoot them, I say, pointing at Pike's pistol. We need to be quiet.

Pity, Pike says.

The drugs are tickling his snake brain and I wonder if he's taken a larger dose than me, because I'm bricking it. I'm frozen to the wall and I'm not sure what to do. The guards are thirty yards away and in between the barn and the back kitchen door I planned to enter. There isn't a cloud in the sky and there seems little point in praying for one.

I got an idea, Pike says. I'll go back round the other side, round the front. I can do an owl hoot, you know that?

Is there no beginning to your talents, Francis?

I'll hoot like an owl. Then you attract their attention and I'll hit em from behind.

Okay, let's try it, I say and Pike nods, with a lightness of foot that always surprises me, he pads back around the way we came, circumnavigating round to the other side of the barn. I am even more nervous and I listen to the goons, smoking and laughing.

I wonder whether they expect this. I wonder why they are doing the job (*money, you dick*) and I wonder all sorts of things, mostly about Chloe in the Manor and then, I hear it, an owl hoot.

The guards hear it too. I pick up a pebble and throw it at the trough.

*Who the fuck...*I hear one of them say and I walk backwards. Before I do, I see them ready their machine pistols and walk towards my side of the barn. I have about ten seconds before they reach me and I ready the machete in one hand and the Stanley in the other. I wish the moonlight wasn't so bright because from where I am standing, there are no shadows in which to hide.

10.

9.

8.

7.

6.

I hear their footsteps. Boots crunch.

5.

4.

3.

I have no idea what I am doing here, none at all. I'm a bloody loser and this is…I am…I am…

2.

They turn the corner and they see me half way up the barn.

You. Get here nah, I hear one shout, pointing the gun at me.

Come and get some, I say and they scurry toward me, my weapons hidden.

It's that driver twat, I hear one of them say, a Leicester accent, plenty of London in it.

They are near and I'm grinning, ready to chop and slice and as they get close to me, I see Pike behind them (how is he so fast?) and he hammers one of them, sparko, straight down to the ground.

Gormless, lost, like the out of his depth bouncer he is, rather than shoot me, the other checks to see what's happened to his friend and it gives me the opportunity I need. I swing the machete with force and make inroads into his neck, his Leicester bouncer claret spraying over the grass next to the barn. I hack at him again from the other side and decapitate him completely, his life essence sprouting vertically in hot red springs. He stays vertical and his arms still move, as if he was waltzing with a ghost. His bald, trophy-handled head rolls from side to side like one of those plastic toy jumping beans, his expression awkward, regretful, surprised and the tiniest bit bewildered.

You'll be getting a reputation, Pike comments, looking down at the body.

Is yours brown?

He bends down. Checks.

Still breathing. He'll have a proper headache. And a lump like a Granny Smith growing from his bonce.

Then he puts down his lump hammer and picks up the machine pistol.

How easy are these things to shoot, Tezza?

No idea. None at all.

Best find out. Closer we get to your woman, hotter it's going to get.

(My woman. If only, Francis. If only).

(Happy ever after)

(Happy tears)

(Chloe will you take this...)

I crash it down. The Nirvana talking.

Yeh. You're right.

Let's ey a nobble with these little beauties, then.

Shiny pound we reach the bedroom before we're discovered.

Pike shakes my hand. One shiny pound says we start firing when we get inside the kitchen. We've had a charmed life so far, me owd mukka.

Let's hope not.

(Because I haven't the faintest what I'm doing).

Pike knows what I'm thinking.

Oh no...he says, clearly on a profound, ecstatic high one tiny step down from the one the thousand nubile virgins are waiting to give us in Muslim heaven, a mythological future he plans to access by converting to Islam immediately before he dies...I want to have chill out time with this baby motherfucker, he says, brandishing the machine pistol. We've got zero to lose. Especially after the naughty way you treated this gentleman here...

Whatever, I say. Joining in, I pick up the one most recently owned by the headless Leicester bouncer. It feels good, not too heavy, black, not metal as I expected, but a kind of heavy plastic. I check for extra ammo on the corpse's body, but there isn't any. We leave the bodies where they lay and stealthily creep to the kitchen. Through the window, I can see two blokes sitting round the table. Machine pistols and ammo laid out in front. They are playing cards. I suspect the others are in the billiard room and lining the corridors upstairs. The alternative would be to go through a window, but the French windows I saw lead to the lounge and the front door is (*watched by the evil eye of Sir John Calder*) out of the question. There must be a cellar, but I couldn't see it and I...I...can't picture the map I tried to memorise. In my head it was the kitchen, but shills...big fat shills put an end to that.

(What do we do? What? Shit...what?)

Psst.

What?

Look.

Behind us, we see three guards walking towards the prone bodies of the guards at the barn. One's using his radio.

We're hidden from the moonlight, but it's only a matter of time before they see us and the radio message will put everyone inside on alert. We have to act. I nod to Pike and he's already way ahead of me.

He gets into position on the other side of the door and gestures to me. I crouch down and knock, officially, three raps. I hear shuffling as the guards respond.

It all happens in a matter of seconds, the process unwinding, the tension releasing. I hear the lock go and one of the guards opens the door. He can't see us and that seals his doom. From a crouched, pivotal position, I chop at his leg above his knee cap with the machete, as if I was cutting my way through a particularly gnarled vine lattice. He squeals, like a little girl, surprised, falls back.

Pike, desperate to get started, swivels into view and grins at the other guard, black, with Rasta plaits, a stitch trench running down the full radius of his left cheek, who raises his machine pistol, but before he can fire, Pike's beaten him to the trigger, bullets (agitated, irritated, angry bullets) tearing into the Rasta's body sending him flying backwards. He bangs his head and he's out, dead or dying. Simultaneously, I stab my guard in the neck and throat a couple of times. This pacifies him nicely and he gives me a surprised glance. His whimpers and struggles are about to come to an end, along with his life, in a puddle of his own plasma, his eyes betraying the shockwave he experiences which tells him that his life is all over, that's it, that there will be no more bouncing and security for him, unless Satan is in the market for some brainless muscle, which he probably is.

Pike locks the door, picks up the ammo from the table, keeps one for himself and gives me the other, then gestures to the table; we ram it up against the door, a delaying gesture for the three goons heading our way from outside.

You owe me a shiny pound, Pike says.

Stewards Inquiry, I reply.

We hear footsteps in the corridor on the other side of the kitchen door, the access into the house. My balls are ice, I'm sweating like a horse and I feel like I'm going to cardiac any time soon, but Pike's got a grin on his face like some berserk Viking knee deep in the dead on some ancient beach, axe swinging, broad brush streaks of blood painting the skies, the unmistakable ecstasy of death and destruction in the wind. He gestures to me, same again, that he's about to open the internal door. I throw the machete to one side, the close quarter stealth stuff over. I crouch and ready the machine gun in case anyone comes through. I have no idea how to use it, but Pike does, and like photography, it's all point and click nowadays, I am positive.

As the door opens, I fire, a rapid fire burst, gentle on the trigger. Two goons outside and one goes down while the other lets off a volley in my direction.

I jump to one side out of the way, out of his line of fire, (*shit shit shit shit shit*), the bullets tearing into the oak sideboards, smashing into the Aga cooker and tearing down the utensils from the wall. He fires again, at nothing, several bags of onions the only casualties. The sound of the bullets like an ack ack ack, the smell of the onions soon rising into the atmosphere. Then, a louder blast

(shotgunshotgunshotgunboomboomboom)

opens the door of the wall mounted cupboards, smashing piles of plates like a Greek night out, the blast filling the air and now, I'm proper shitting bricks.

We're trapped.

Behind us, at the kitchen door, the three guards from outside are shooting through the window, the noise deafening. Pike, seeing the strategic error, points at me, then gestures to the window. I nod. I've got to get on the clock or else we are brown. Pike positions himself at the door jamb and fires the machine pistol into the corridor. I take advantage of the cover and fire at the window. I hear a shout as one of the guards outside goes down. Then they inform us loudly that we're about to die. Pike keeps firing, pinning down the guards in the house, (who are in no mood to die for the cause and stay happily in shelter). I crawl along the floor. I can see into the corridor. It's okay to be a clever sod, but one look down there tells me they have everything covered, the whole corridor a potential open ground graveyard for us.

There is no way we can move.

Inspiration hits me, an Archimedes bath moment.

Stay here, Francis, keep them pinned down, I shout.

As if I'm off to Fountain for a pint, he says, firing another short burst, which tears a painting off its mounting, coming down to earth with a crash. Taking advantage of the confusion outside, I make my way back the way we came by clinging tightly against cupboards out of the line of fire. Then, underneath the window, I take the scariest risk I've ever taken in my life. I see a saucepan, an old school milk boiler, a victim of the shotgun blast. I stretch and kick it towards the blocked door where it comes to a halt with a metallic rattle. The outside men fire at it from the window, then stop.

I jump up (surprise surprise) and fire everything I have straight at the window. My bullets tear through the remaining glass and smash straight into the startled face of a dark haired bloke who might be Timothy Dalton. His mate, an Asian looking bloke, throws down his gun and runs off towards the woods as fast as his little legs can carry him. With an effort that cracks a knee and makes me wish I had kept up the gym sessions I started up at North Camp, I jump onto the work tops and carefully, looking both ways, spring into the darkness. Pike is keeping the others pinned down. I can hear his clever, consistent, repeated bursts, but I know the ammo isn't going to last forever.

I know this is a gamble. Running, crouched low, I reach the front of the manor house. The moonlight, still illuminating like floodlights, tells me that the rest of them are inside. I hear gunfire and know Pike is under pressure. It's now or never. From the pocket of my Stoney, I take the ammo cartridge and insert it into the handle of the machine pistol.

I make my way to the front door. Pray silently to a God I don't believe in.

(I've had worse)

Then, with a scream, a berserker rage, I crash open the front door and start to fire.

The four of them gathered on the bottom steps of the staircase panic. I point at one and hit him on the chest and legs and he goes down silently. Another fires back and I go back behind the door. Pike, seeing this, increases his fire. A guard, in his zeal to get at me, ends up in Pike's eyeline and Pike catches him, sends him crashing to the ground. I fire back in, get fired on, fire back in, get fired on, a fusillade of bullets in the moonlight. I wish I had a grenade. I wish I had something like that, room clearance, but at least we now have a chance. I fire again from behind the door and hear a thud as someone goes down.

Pike shouts, you're clear. I watch the room closest to the kitchen, which I know as the billiards room and carefully I walk down there. The staircase mob are all corpsed or wounded and I take their positions, pick up a machine pistol. There is no sign of Conn, or Kipper, or Chloe or Hope. They must be upstairs, they must be waiting for us, safe. One of the guards pleads with me to help him, his face a gaping maw dug out by a hot bullet or three, but he's already halfway into the river Styx on his way to some alternative East Midlands football hell, sent there by a little Notts County fan (*who the fuck are Notts County???*) with a machine gun and I shove him away, let his life reach a natural end.

I don't grieve.
I don't feel regret.
I don't think about his family, his wife or his kids
I want him gone.

For some reason, I look behind me.

At the portrait of Sir John Calder above the door. Staring at me, accusing. Or congratulating. I wonder how many men Sir John sent to their deaths, how many corpses he had seen. Those eyes betray no conscience, the eyes of a hunter, the eyes of predator, a dictator of men. The screams of the fallen would have meant no more to him than the protests of starving vassals at the gates in times of famine.

It's quiet.

There are no conscious wounded around me. The mahogany floor is awash with the blood of the slain but there is silence.

I am exhilarated.
(Drugs)
I am high.
(Blood)
I am erect.
(Death)
I am life.
(Hellbound)

Looking at Sir John in the silence. Imperial. Narcissistic. Leaving some trace behind on the face of the earth. I hate him, have always hated him, his class, and all they represent but tonight, I realise, I have proven that there is no difference between the face in the portrait, the arrogant, Norman, triumphalist, murderous British Empire face and that of fat old Terry Valentine – hooligan, jailbird, gambler, cutter, junkie, cuckold, loser, bum, bailiff, waster

(killer)

and cleaner of the houses of the dead.

I nod to Sir John.
(See you in Hell, you Imperial old bastard)
and then get back on the clock.

Using the portrait-covered wall as a guide and a barrier, I make my way to the billiard room. I know it to be full of goons but they've gone quiet. I see Pike and he makes his way up, a pincer movement, a mirror, to the other side of the door. They're either in there or they've gone. We could go straight upstairs, but then, they could hit us from behind like earlier. We have to clean up down here first. Pointless knocking this time I think, and Pike, as if psychic, opens the door and quickly draws back.

Nothing. I roll down onto the floor and look inside. Its empty. We cover each other and enter the room. There's nothing – or nobody – in there. There are no other doors.

We walk all the way to the window and look outside into the darkness. The whole ground floor is silent, the billiard room; absent, cavernous, totally unoccupied.

I'm sure they were in here, Pike says.

Must be a secret passage or something. You know what these old places are like.

Leading upstairs.

Yeh.

Pike gestures upstairs. That's where the rest are. How are you doing for ammo?

I don't know, I say.

Let me check.

I pass him my machine pistol. He's taken to this game like a duck to water, certainly the logistics side of it. I don't think I did too badly on the military side. He passes the pistol back.

Half a cartridge left. I'm more or less out. You sorted it out in time.

We need to go back in the kitchen to find more before we go upstairs. How are you feeling?

Buzzing. You?

Totally. Haven't had this much fun since…

Coventry.

Nah…Oldham away?

Brentford in the town?

Posh…

We could go on with this forever. Eyes dilated, He stares, puts his hand on my shoulder, laughing quietly as if to himself. Overweight by two stone at least, maybe three or four. In his tracksuit, carrying a machine pistol, he is an unlikely soldier, the unlikeliest of killers.

Terry, my best friend says.

What

This has been intense. Unbelievable. What a ride. What a fucking ride.

You aren't kidding.

Intense.

You've lost your cap, I say, noticing for the first time. I hardly ever see Pike without his Hackett cap, his straw-textured thatch all over the place, hat hair, his face sweaty and bestial, like some rustic accidentally having discovered the wrong mushrooms in some distant wood.

Jesus. Why didn't you say!? Must be in the kitchen.

Along with the ammo.

He scratches his head and for the briefest of moments, he goes red, as if he had been caught with his trousers down. You're a hat man or not a hat man and Pike is definitely the former. Even when we were kids playing football on the park or walking to school, he would have the hood of his parka up or that blue wooly Benny hat. When the lads started wearing caps down the match, Pike was one of the first to get one and up till now it's been stitched to his head. No wonder he and Louise are splitting; he probably sleeps in it.

Along with the ammo, he replies, grinning.

You look strange without your cap, I say, perhaps unnecessarily, my tongue loosened by the drugs. Pike goes straight back.

Do I? Do I look strange, he replies, pulling a silly face.

Okay, okay, I'm sorry...I say, laughing. Let's go.

We walk back to the door of the billiard room. He walks ahead of me and then, as if troubled, he turns to me before we reach it.

Must be some comfort thing, you know.

What?

My cap...I feel naked without it usually. Can't reme...

and then, from nowhere

(*silence*)

(*footpad*)

(*ex-military*)

From over Pike's shoulder, I see Conn appear at the door.

(*shotgun*)

FRANCIS!!!!WATCH IT

He turns back to the door.

The Man of Business smiles.

Alwight, northern cants, he says, smart suit, slicked back hair, (dishy) supercilious, cockney grin, ebon pump action shotgun pointed straight at Pike.

My insides are icebergs.

I see it before it happens.

Conn

(shotgun)

(Dishy Conn)

(Oooh, he's handsome isn't he, Mr Valentine))

BANG!!!

blasts Francis Pike at point blank range, the impact causing his overweight frame wrapped in crimson tracksuit to fly backwards. Briefly airborne. Reeling into the centre of the room.

YOU…

I point my machine pistol at him. Conn arms the pump action at the same time.

(Kill…avenge…kill)

Put the Heckler down, County. Now, he says, his voice cold, commanding.

We stare at each other for what seems an age. The shotgun pointing at me. Point blank range. My machine pistol ready, full of angry, screaming, metallic gnats. They would tear him to pieces, but he would blow me to pieces too…like…

Francis…

Francis…

Oh God, mate, no, no, no

(Chloe)

(Francis, I'm sorry mate. I let you down. I love you, mate. I love you.)

I should shoot Conn and die too.

My machine gun is pointed at him. He's looking at me. My friend…

My best friend is in an awkward state in front of me

(Avenge)
(Chloe)
If I shoot. I'm dead. He's dead.
Everyone's dead.
(Chloe)
What a waste of time. What a senseless waste of everything.
(Chloe)
If I pull the trigger
(Chloe)
it will be pointless...have to
(Chloe)
gamble

(three fifteen at Chester 1990, New bird. Zoe. Moved in together. Housing benefit cheque. £300. Nothing else. Welshman. That was the horse's name. Welshman. Chester. Bottom weight. Stays the trip. Every chance. On the nose)

Conn scowls. Our eyes lock like tractor beams.

(Chloe)

One tiny, gentle squeeze of the trigger and

(Chloe)

(no each way, none of that bollocks. Each way is for cunts, Francis says, old ladies, babies, homosexuals on a hairdressers day out at the races, no each way for me. On it goes, on the nose, the bookie watched the race with me, Tote on Gregory Boulevard, now a Polish delicatessen and a Jamaican pineapple bar, would be a decent tickle, he says, over two grand, might have to send out for more money he says and I nod)

(Chloe)

Put the pistol down, County. Then we'll talk.

I say nothing. I think of her, wonder where she is.

I see Francis below me, shoulder shattered, a pool of blood, his face a bloody mess.

(Alive. Still breathing)

(Chloe)

(coming up to the final furlong Welshman is clear, Franny Norton, Franny Norton that's it, iron man Franny, two grand, iron man Franny, come on my son, come on my son, but there's something coming out the pack, and you're screaming, losing all control and you recollect what Barry Hills says about Chester being a stiff track and you wish you

hadn't because despite your screaming, despite your urgings)
(Chloe)

Go on, County. There's a good fella. We can talk. Put the machine pistol down.

(the other horse does you on the line, the story of your life, you've always been second, always been a loser, always lose, and the bookie gives you that look, that never mind mate look and you have to tell gorgeous, strawberry blonde Zoe that you can't pay the rent this month and after a few months of this kind of crap she dumps you faster than a curry made of dead cat but you can't stop gambling can't stop can't stop can't)

(Chloe)

Gambler.

Have to roll the dice.

I drop the gun and stand there like a plum.

Conn walks towards me...

You daft cunt, County. As if I'm going to talk to you, he says, grinning. You're a dead man.

Hope

Pike is bleeding, his shoulder destroyed.

Unconscious, mercifully, but in need of a hospital. Fast. He isn't going to get one.

And now I'm in trouble.

Conn is there with his pump action.

(You should have gone out in a blaze of glory)
(You always were a bad gambler)

It won't be long before he pulls the trigger. This is going to hurt. He has that supercilious look on his face typical of cockneys and if there's one thing I hate it's losing to a cockney: Even if he did hit us from behind, which doesn't count.

I've got my hands on my head and the barrel of his gun is more or less in my face.

It's over, the Army of Two destroyed.

(Bury my ashes at Meadow Lane)

We tried our best. That's all we can do.

(Chloe)
(Pike)
(Marge)
(Mum)
(Love)

Looks like this is it, County, Conn says. Not a hair out of place, wearing some dark blue combat jacket, a brand I don't recognize.

Looks like it.

Well, I want to say how impressed I am, County. You're a brave soul. I'm going to need some replacement security after all the fellas you and Fatboy here have wasted. I'd offer you both a job, but you know as well as I do it wouldn't work.

No.

It's not a good fit. Corporate wise, I mean.

Oh, definitely

For a start, there's all the resentment to consider. Smithy, for example. You shot his brother. In the corridor.

Sorry about that, Smithy.

You're a natural, Squire.

Thanks

They're twins. The Smith twins. Well, they *were* twins.

Okay, I respond.

Always was a hothead. His brother is inconsolable. He's crying like a little girl in the kitchen. You virtually sawed his twin in half with that Heckler. I don't think you'd survive the Induction because he's saying a lot of horrible things about you.

I'm sure the feeling would be mutual.

You and Fatboy killed ten of his mates too. You've made a right mess of Halford outside, by the barn. Twenty years he was with the Baby Squad. Fighting all over the country and you go and chop off his bonce. I've never seen so much claret.

Yeh.

What am I going to tell Sandra?

Who?

Halford's wife. I'm so sorry, Sandra, your husband won't be coming home from work tonight because he's been decapitated.

Sorry about that.

You pair of wallies! Why didn't you call? Save all this silliness. I didn't give you enough credit. That Neville said you were a right cant and not worth bothering over. He said you wouldn't have the bottle to come and get Miss.

Should never believe everything you hear.

Guess you finished him off too? He's not answering his blower.

He won't be getting in touch any time soon.

I should cocoa, Conn says.

He lifts the barrel of the gun.

Well, must dash, County. Time to go. Thanks for the memories and I'll see you in the afterlife.

Do it, West Ham, then shut the fuck up.

I bend down and put my hand on Pike's shoulder.

(live by the sword, die by the sword)

Chloe

(Sorry, honey. I let you down).

I stand and smile, confront my angel of death

(Cortez the Killer).

Conn shoves the barrel of his shotgun into my bleeding mouth. Gets ready to pull the trigger and then...

NO NO NO NO, like, WTF are you doing?

(Chloe)

Conn goes from being a rock hard executioner to a lemon in three seconds flat.

Miss, orders from...

Don't you DARE touch him, she says, and she's next to me now, holding me, tears down her face. She's wearing jeans and a sweatshirt, obviously Hope's, because they make her look a lot older than she is. No makeup. Conn backs off, unsure of himself, confused. I don't know fully how its happened, but I've suddenly gone from zero to hero with a last minute winner in injury time but I'm too cool to tell him. Conn knows it. He can't shoot me now.

Miss...

Put the GUN down, Conn. Like, right NOW, she says, and I'm impressed with her resolve.

Connor, a voice says, put the shotgun down. Do as you're told.

It's Hope, standing at the door.

Ma'am...I...

Right now, Connor, she says, pointing to the sofa. And while you're at it, call this number.

She hands him a piece of paper.

But, Ma'am, he says, looking confused and bewildered.

This man needs treatment immediately, she says, pointing at Pike. And you have seriously injured men to tend to outside. Call the Kingdom Private Hospital. Ask for James Thornberry. You met him. He'll deal with this situation. Quickly. This has gone on long enough.

Conn nods and reaches for his mobile phone. Hope gestures for him to go into the corridor to do the work and inside, I'm grinning, partly with relief, but also because Conn is being treated like the muppet he is by the top lad of the firm. He might be dishy and handsome and cool, according to the girl in my arms, but he's also a fraggle who answers to someone, which makes him a powerless fraggle too, in the end.

Chloe, love. Go outside. I wish to talk to Terry alone, Hope says.

Chloe kisses me on the cheek and it brings back memories of the three times she's done that before and each time I can sense deeply the afterimpression of her lips. This time is no different. Her lips seem to stay in contact with my cheek for infinity and I close my eyes.

I'll talk to you later, old geezer, Chloe says, smiling, tears in her eyes. It's easy to say, but I have never seen her looking so magnificent. Obediently, she stands, kisses Hope on the cheek too, something I didn't expect to see, something I didn't picture, something I didn't plan on. Hope touches her around the waist too and there is an intimacy about the way they relate to each other that wasn't apparent before.

I am as confused as Conn is, now.

The Kingdom's transport will be here in fifteen minutes and will take your friend. Hope says.

Well, that's him in the nick, then.

Hope smiles enigmatically. Not necessarily. Calder is the majority shareholder in that hospital. It was one of the first investments I made as a Chief Executive. As a local girl for much of the year, I need quality health care. Essentially, every member of staff there works for me. If anyone contacts the authorities, then they'll lose their jobs – and we pay well for good staff. They have an excellent time of it compared to the horrors of the NHS. Losing a job there would hurt. Your friend will be looked after. He will heal with the assistance we shall supply.

Thanks.

It all depends on you, Terry. This foolishness. This misery. This death. I must have this level of security. I am threatened a dozen times a year by bandits and kidnappers and this way, I can relax at home. I don't travel well. I'm a homebody, always have been. I do most of my business on videoconference. You ought to see the security when I visit my offices in Paris and Frankfurt.

Okay, I say, my stock response when I have nothing to say and I wonder why she's telling me this. She's an attractive woman but I was wrong about her before. She's as old as me. She's at least fifty and her face has been heavily worked on, maybe even her body too. Augmented in all the right places, a woman, like Valeria Messalina, who never wanted to get old. Her blonde, curly, freshly designed hair has not even the slightest streak of grey, which is a tell-tale sign.

Weirdly, when I notice how old she is up close, without make up, straight out of bed, I want to ask her whether she had always been a lesbian, or whether she was one of those women who got tired of blokes in her forties, that Mars and Venus thing, but I never would. That kind of tacky invasion I'll leave to the chat shows.

I love Chloe, you know, she says.

All this mess is down to your love for Chloe, isn't it. All this death.

That's a very harsh assessment,

It's also a very true assessment, Valeria.

Who?

Nothing, ancient history. Hope.

We walk out onto the conservatory and she addresses me quietly.

I have never felt the feelings I have for Chloe and they occurred instantly. Immediately. I was assailed by them. I felt sick, elated, despairing, energized, optimistic, alive, bouncing. The very first moment. Have you experienced that level of love? Have you?

I pretty much had it when I saw Chloe myself, but I keep the thought to myself.

It scared me. It still does, but with each day that passes, I love her more and more.

It's only been a fortnight, I say.

I know she doesn't feel the same way, but the more time we spend together here in the Manor, the more the barriers between us drop.

Did you offer her half a mil to stay?

For her mother. If Chloe were to stay with me, as my partner, that money would be scarcely relevant. I have even invited her mother and father to come and stay here. I authorized Conn to consult builders.

You're joking.

I am helplessly in love with Chloe. Helplessly. I have lived with women on three occasions and I know the difference between a crush and the real thing. I would lay down my life for Chloe. And her family will be my family.

You're not joking, then.

Terry, you've killed many men here at the Manor. You've probably killed Neville. You have been in prison for Manslaughter. I could have you arrested in ten minutes flat and you would spend the rest of your life in prison. I would make sure of that. I would also ensure that particularly dark accusations would appear on your charges too.

Dark accusations?

You know the type of accusations I mean. And I could make them stick.

I do know the type of accusations Hope is talking about.

I don't want those on my record.

My gaol time was more boring than anything else. No-one survives with the mark of the Beast.

I state the obvious.

You could have let Conn shoot me.

Yes, I could. That would have upset Chloe, wouldn't it, and I cannot have that.

Of course.

Personally, I like you, Terry.

Okay.

I admire brave men, men who do what you did and even though – she gestures around her, airily - you have made a complete mess of the Manor, and killed most of the help, I forgive you. I will forget too, all this. All this. I will forget it forever. If…

I don't need to answer. I know what she wants, but I ask Hope for the thing I want.

I want to speak to Chloe.

Yes, of course you do. You've come all this way…Hope says, dreamily, her cut glass accent. She stares into the darkness outside, arms folded. Then she turns round. Of course you may.

She's in the drawing room. First on the left, next door. You have five minutes.

Without acknowledging her, I walk back into the living room. I check Pike. He is still unconscious, but breathing. There is no one about, only the bullet riddled corpses scattered in the corridor.

I find the drawing room.
Chloe's there. She runs to me.
(Crying)
We embrace.

Love you, old geezer.
Love you, Chloe.

I'm so sorry, she says, hugging me, cuddling me and her body is warm and tender and I embrace her, stroke that hair of hers.

You look like a bag of shit, I say, grinning.

And you look like an old geezer, she says, snivelling and sniffing.

We hold each other for a minute. I haven't got long and I know it. Chloe knows it. There seems little point talking, no point persuading, because she's holding me so tightly I know she's made her mind up. I think I've always known. For the first time since I was a kid, since I was about seven, I feel it welling up and I start to cry.

Chloe breaks the silence and it's a good job, stops us sobbing like mental cases.

I'm sorry for lying to you, Terry.

About what?

Mum. I just…just…

It's okay, Chloe. It is. You don't have to explain.

It was family business. I'm a totally private person. The story I told you was…easier. I would have told you. I was going to tell you that night, before Neville and Rebecca brought me here.

Honest. Totally going to tell you.

She looks at me with those Manga eyes, like sparkling, rippling pools seen in sunlight. The iris in each of her Manga eyes is dilated and it only makes the chestnut brown resonate further. A residue of mournful, solemn tears spatter the meniscus adding a fourth dimension (emotion, time, space, regret). Those eyes are the orbs of truth. I believe her. And even if I don't believe her, I choose to do so. What other choice is there? I have to ask one thing though and I do, even though the answer could finish my peace of mind.

There is one thing I want to know, though.

What?

Neville said you and he...

Chloe looks at me astonished, then pushes me away. NO WAY!!! That is so totally GROSS. I never went anywhere near Neville. He's, like, *way* older than you.

Thanks.

I so didn't mean it like that, she says, looking guilty at the blurt-out.

I know. He said you had a choc ice with him and Rebecca.

Chloe is shocked. A choc ice? Ha! It so never happened, Mr Valentine. Did you believe him?

She glares at me accusingly, like that time when Jaden got the bullet for not believing her ghost story. I'm far too long in the tooth to fall for this one.

Of course not. You've got loads better taste.

I've got *awesome* taste, old geezer. How is Neville by the way?

Relaxing.

I've not heard from him.

Don't hold your breath. So you're staying, then?

Chloe buries her head in my chest and she holds me tightly. I sense her nod her head in an affirmative gesture.

Will you ever forgive me, Mr Valentine?

One day. I have to go now, Chloe. It's got to be for good too. You know that.

I know. I know, she sobs. I'll miss you. I'll miss you every day.

Don't miss me, Chloe. Life's too short for that. You're going to be a Lady of the Manor now. You've come a long way from Rochdale.

Darwen, originally.

I hear footsteps outside the door and I know my five minutes are up.

I have to go. Hope's here.

Chloe kisses me, with fire and tongues and desperation and she strokes my cheek. When our first and last kiss is over, she stares at me with those Manga eyes, inflamed, reddened, despairing, eyes that have witnessed the death of love.

I break away from her.

Subtle bow.

Do me a favour, old geezer.

What?

Don't say goodbye.

Okay,
Just don't…

I affirm my agreement.
But I think it.
I'll never stop thinking it.
Goodbye, Chloe. I love you.

I turn and walk to the door into the corridor. The ambulance has arrived and the first man they have picked up is Pike. The footsteps I could hear. I follow. Before they deposit him in the maw of their vehicle, I bend down and remove his car keys from his tracky pockets.

Hope calls me back one last time.

She says what she has to say and I listen and I agree, a man of my word.

I actually wish her well.

I almost mean it.

At the front of the Manor, Conn is supervising the removal of the injured into the other ambulances. He gazes my way, blankly, as if he is looking at an uninteresting painting in some museum. There are no Police. This clean-up, a function of the mad, desperate love of three desperate people, is all sub-judice. Neville's body – and the bodies of his two Men of Business (*one slain, one about to die, for everyone's sake*) – will disappear. I know that. Burned in some fiery furnace, or aggregated in a cement works somewhere, maybe even buried quietly in one of Hope Calder's many worldwide mines.

That's what the rich do.

They sweep.

They clean.

They burn.

Money is above the law. So is power and history. I saw in Hope's eyes back then that she was a daughter of the Norman Conquest and I knew even then that, even if I wanted Chloe, even if I finished the job off with fire and sword, even if I died a warriors death, I would never win.

England is the country of the rich.

It always was and it always will be.

I could never win.

No-one could ever win.

Somewhere behind me, Chloe, the love of my life, cries and Hope's obsession is left to fill the gap. I'm not sure it ever will. They say money can't buy you love, but it can try its hardest. It may succeed. I saw Chloe kiss Hope earlier. It could work and do you know what? I would pray it does, if I believed in God, that is.

Which I don't.

The moonlight is not as strong as earlier as the moon sinks toward the horizon. It's near dawn. In an hour the sun will rise on a new late autumn day. It's been unseasonably warm, but that won't last forever. I feel the early morning wind on my cheeks, along with the memory of Chloe's tender kiss. I know I will never see her again, but I know I was loved. Even if it was a mad love, a strange love, a love built on bleak foundations, a love forged in blood, death and sin, founded on untruths and denial, it was love nonetheless

I take out my mobile phone.

Text Marge.

Pick up the holdall and start my walk back to Pike's dirty pink Fiesta.

The Work of Mark Barry

In order of publication:
Ultra Violence
Hollywood Shakedown
Carla
Violent Disorder
The Night Porter
Once Upon A Time In The City Of Criminals

Currently deleted and/or in reconstruction:
Kid Atomic
The Ritual
The Illustrated Woman (banned in the UK)

Short stories:
Reality Bites
Pieces of Eight
LA Punk Rocker (to be published)

Blogs:
Greenwizardpublishing
The Wizard's Cauldron

Book Trailers:
You must be having a giraffe :-D

Printed in Great Britain
by Amazon.co.uk, Ltd.,
Marston Gate.